BUFFY AND THE ART OF STORY SEASON TWO PART 1

THREATS, LIES, AND SURPRISES IN EPISODES 1-11

L. M. LILLY

INTRODUCTION

My love of **Buffy the Vampire Slayer** started when the show began. I did my best to watch every episode even though the Chicago TV station that carried **Buffy** kept preempting it for Cubs games. (Seriously, WGN, priorities!)

Later, when DVDs became available, I marveled at how well-crafted each season was as a whole. As a writer I loved the clever dialogue and compelling plots, plus the way the writers created characters who grew and changed over the course of seven years. As a viewer, **Buffy** broke my heart and drew me back every episode for more. The show helped me cope with loss, appreciate the people around me, and sort out conflicts in my own life.

Buffy spoke to me on a very personal level, as it probably did to you. As if the writers had looked into our hearts.

So when I started thinking about starting a podcast, **Buffy** seemed like the obvious choice. And being a novelist who loves to take apart how the stories I love work, I decided to approach each episode that way.

Who Am I?

As Lisa M. Lilly, I'm the author of the bestselling four-book Awakening supernatural thriller series. The Awakening books have been downloaded over 90,000 times in over 35 countries. And the first book in my current series, the Q.C. Davis Mysteries, debuted as the No. 1 female private eye novel on Amazon in Canada. The second Q.C. Davis Mystery is a 2019 Finalist in The Wishing Shelf Book Awards. As I write this introduction, I'm putting the finishing touches on the fourth book in the series and am planning the fifth.

I also write non-fiction, mostly aimed at other writers, under L. M. Lilly, and work as an attorney and adjunct professor of law. A few years back, I founded WritingAs-ASecondCareer.com to share information with people juggling writing novels with working at other jobs or careers. Not that I know anything about that...

Is This Book For You?

As I say at the start of each podcast episode, if you love **Buffy the Vampire Slayer** and you love writing stories – or just taking them apart to see how they work – you're in the right place. In these pages, you'll find a breakdown of Episodes 1-11 of Season Two of **Buffy the Vampire Slayer**.

Much of this content is in the podcast. But here it's edited for better flow and organization. For those who write fiction themselves, I've included questions to consider about your own writing based on each episode.

How This Book Handles Spoilers

The main part of each chapter, like each podcast episode, is spoiler-free. After a spoiler heading, though, I discuss fore-shadowing, which requires talking about future **Buffy** episodes. While I try not to spoil anything major that's more than a season out, occasionally it's relevant. So if you haven't watched the whole series, proceed with caution.

Getting The Most From This Book

If you're looking forward to revisiting the first half of **Buffy** Season Two, I recommend simply reading straight through. That way, you'll experience the episodes in order. If you like, you can watch each episode before reading the chapter about it. But I do break down each episode, so you don't need to do that to enjoy the book.

Another way to read this book, particularly if you're looking to learn more about fiction writing from **Buffy the Vampire Slayer**, is to look over the bullet points at the beginning of each chapter and the questions at the end. Between those two sections you'll get a pretty good idea which aspects of storytelling each chapter covers. Then you can flip to the sections that particularly interest you.

Whichever way you read I hope that, like me, you'll enjoy reliving each episode. And, if you're a writer, that it will help you further hone your own writing skills.

Finally, if you think you'd find a more in depth discussion of story elements, novel writing, or character development useful, check out the Also By section at the back of this book. There you'll find a list of my books on writing.

Okay, ready? Let's dive into the Hellmouth.

CHAPTER 1

WHEN SHE WAS BAD (S2 E1)

THIS CHAPTER TALKS about **When She Was Bad**, Season Two Episode One, written and directed by Joss Whedon.

In particular, we'll look at:

- **How the key plot points here, despite all the action, are emotional ones for Buffy**
- **Why Giles can hang out with a group of students all the time and not have it be disturbing**
- **Showing a character's fears through indirect dialogue and behavior**
- **The way this episode foreshadows the whole of Season Two and aspects of the rest of the series.**

Okay, let's dive into the Hellmouth.

OPENING CONFLICT

The initial conflict in a book or TV show or movie ideally appears on the very first page or in the first scene. It might or might not be related to the main plot. The key is to draw the viewer or reader in right away.

Here, we start in the graveyard, but not with Buffy. Xander and Willow are walking. They're playing a movie game, where one says a line from a movie, and the other tries to guess what it's from.

Willow uses a line from my favorite movie of all time, **The Terminator**: "In that short time we had, we loved a lifetime's worth." Xander guesses it fairly quickly, and after that the lines get easier and easier and we can tell they're bored. They've played this game a lot.

Xander in particular is talking about how the summer is dull. Willow teases him about why he's so eager for school to start – because Buffy will be back.

When they can't think of more movie lines Xander, who is holding a vanilla ice cream cone, dabs ice cream on Willow's nose. He says a line from the movie **Witness**. Willow laughs, and the two have a moment where they almost kiss.

I found this very believable even though before this we didn't get any sense that Xander reciprocated Willow's feelings for him. It's just this really nice moment with the two of them.

The opening conflict here is subtle, and it's implied. Xander can't wait for Buffy to come back. Willow, while she misses Buffy, is happy to have this time with Xander.

Then we get the plot-based opening conflict.

We see a vampire behind Xander and Willow as their

lips almost touch. It's 3 minutes 39 seconds into the episode. Buffy appears, slays the vampire, and we cut to credits.

Story Spark for When She Was Bad

I had to think about what the Story Spark or Inciting Incident is for this episode. Usually that spark comes right around 10% through a book or movie or television episode, and it sets our main conflict in motion.

There are a number of things that happen right around that time.

It could be Buffy slaying that vampire. But that isn't out of the ordinary for Buffy. That could set off any episode, so I don't think that's it.

She and Xander and Willow walk in the cemetery. It is very symbolic, as Buffy is walking between the two of them. She asks if they had any fun without her. Xander says no, and Willow says yes. It is a little bit heartbreaking for Willow because we can already see where this is going to go in terms of her and Xander, though she is clearly happy to have Buffy back.

At about 5 minutes in, they tell Buffy that there've been no monsters all summer. Which explains for me why they were just casually walking in the graveyard. They were less worried. Everything seemed fine. Since the death of the Master, the first vampire they saw was just now.

Buffy: It's like they knew I was coming back.

I see this moment as the Inciting Incident or Story Spark. Because the entire episode will track Buffy's reaction to having killed the Master and having died herself. And to her fear that evil continues and the Master will return.

You could also see the Spark as the moment when Willow and Xander tell Buffy they buried the Master near the trees while she was gone, and she looks extremely disturbed about this idea. That, too, could drive her behavior.

Willow and Xander ask if Buffy has seen Giles. She says no, why would she do that? She'll see him at school. And this really gives us our sense that something is not quite right with Buffy.

We switch to Buffy's parents, Joyce and Hank. Buffy spent the summer with her father. He is helping unpack her suitcases, which are full of new clothes and shoes. Joyce and Hank bicker.

Hank says Buffy didn't act out over the summer. But she was distant, and there was no connection. At least when she was burning things down, he knew what to say. About that lack of connection, Joyce says, "Thus the shoes." And he says he might've overcompensated a bit.

When Hank tells her it was as if Buffy was there but not really there, Joyce says, "Welcome to my world." Also she tells him she just hopes Buffy makes it through the school year.

I liked these moments with Joyce and Hank. It gives us a sense of what happened since the divorce. What their relationship is like. You definitely have that tension there. But you also have that joint concern for their daughter.

Themes And Character Back Stories

Back at school, we get our first glimpse of Cordelia. She's with her friends saying it was a nightmare. We think maybe she is talking about the Master and the vampires. But no. She is talking about her terrible summer.

Her parents promised to take her to Tuscany and instead took her to St. Croix.

I like the humor of Cordelia's idea of a nightmare, which is so very different from Buffy's. Her words also highlight the socioeconomic differences here. Xander and Willow are struggling to find something to do, making up games and playing Rock, Paper, Scissors as they walk through the cemetery. And Cordelia is being taken all over the globe for lovely vacations and complaining about it not being quite to her liking.

Also, I love this quote we get from Cordelia: "I think that kind of adversity builds character. And then I thought I already have a lot of character. Is it possible to have too much character?" I

It encompasses the theme of the entire show. Cordelia is talking about a very minor inconvenience. But it is a very real question that most of us feel even if we don't articulate it when we are facing loss and trauma.

Certainly, it's something that could apply directly to Buffy in this episode.

The Words Characters Use Set The Tone

We then get Principal Snyder talking to Giles. Snyder is saying basically how wonderful the campus was the day before when it was empty. But now students are swarming everywhere like locusts bent on feeding and mating. Giles suggests perhaps Snyder is in the wrong career, given his abhorrence of children. This contrast between the two is so much fun.

Giles refers to the high school students as children. It's the first of a couple times they will have this conversation talking about kids and children.

And I feel like this is a lot of why we can have Giles hanging out so much in the library with three high school students. (At this point I think they're in their junior year, but when the show started, it was Buffy's sophomore year.)

In other circumstances that would be worrisome. It's not for us as the audience because we know the context. But the reason I feel like it works so well without there being anything uncomfortable is that Giles always views these young people as children, as students.

And I never have a sense even as they age that Giles ever even considers crossing any sort of line with any of them. A large part of why I believe that is the language of the show (and how the actors play it). We repeatedly have Giles seeing them as and talking about them as students. As children.

Snyder is commenting about how every time a pretty girl walks by, every boy turns into gibbering fool. And we see Miss Calendar walk up, and Giles stumbles and stutters over his words. They agree to go together to the teachers' lounge, leaving Snyder, who hasn't realized that Giles fell behind him, going on about how terrible this is and that he might as well be talking to himself.

In the hallway, Jenny is telling Giles about Burning Man and how great her summer was and he should've been there, he would have…. And then she says, "Hated it." They joke around about books and flirt a little bit.

Buffy's Actions And Words

We then see Willow, Buffy and Xander. They encounter Giles and comment about being surprised at all the vampires still around. Giles says the Hellmouth still has mystical energy even though it closed.

Buffy says she's ready to start training. And we see this training montage. It is so intense. Buffy is training hard, hitting fast and flashing on to the Master's face. She finally knocks over the training equipment.

Buffy: I'm ready. Whatever they got coming next I'm ready.

Giles is clearly worried about her.

Approaching The One-Quarter Plot Turn

About 11 minutes in we get the first scene with vampires. They seem to have a new leader. I just have him in my notes as Scary Vamp Leader because he's so intense. He is speaking almost in rhymes, in a very rhythmic, sort of poetic cadence that sounds like prophecies or scriptures. He says something about "but despair is for the living." And that in 3 days a new hope will arise, and he will show them the way.

This could be the One-Quarter Twist of the episode. That plot turn usually comes from outside the protagonist at 25% to 33% through a story. It spins the plot in a new direction and also raises the stakes.

Here, now as the audience we know something new is happening. But I don't think that this is the one-quarter turn, because this already has been going on in the background. It's not a new development.

In the next scene, Buffy sits in this nice little seating area (by the way, my high school had nothing like this, all this just sitting on couches and hanging out), and Xander and Willow are with her.

They're talking about dreams. Willow starts to tell a dream she had about Xander and quickly backpedals. Giles comes up and says he knows what's happening.

He seems very concerned.

Buffy: Trust me. You know we'll handle it.

The One-Quarter Twist

At 13 minutes – so very close, maybe just a little past quarter way through this episode – Giles' words change the entire scene.

Giles: I killed you once, it shouldn't be too difficult to do it again.

And here is where it hits me as a viewer that this is Buffy's dream. Xander and Willow are looking on as Giles attacks Buffy. They don't try to help. They don't even look upset. Buffy pulls off Giles' face and underneath is the Master.

I see this as the first major plot turn in the story, the one that spins it in a new direction. Because this is what really drives Buffy from this moment to the Midpoint. This feeling that the Master still poses a threat, which is somehow tied up with Giles. And we'll see later how angry she is because she feels Giles didn't tell her what she needed to know.

Conflict With Angel

When Buffy wakes up, Angel is sitting in her bedroom window, which is open. She acts like she doesn't care that he's there. And she's very sarcastic with him, asking if it's a social call. He says no, and she says I guess that means grave danger.

Buffy makes a joke about how some of his relatives are in town and for barbecue and Buffy and her friends are all on the menu.

Angel tells her the Anointed One (the child vampire who was by the Master's side in Season One) is gathering forces. He doesn't know why, but he warns her not to underestimate him because he's a child.

Buffy acts like she will handle it. It's no big deal. She doesn't care that Angel's there, and she wants to go back to sleep. He says he missed her. She turns and says she missed him, but he's already gone.

Joyce Worries And Buffy's Mean

In the morning, Joyce drives Buffy to school, asks her about her classes. She can tell something is wrong.

Joyce: Is there the slightest chance that if I asked you what was wrong you would tell me? Of course not. It would take the fun out of guessing.

At school, Willow, Xander, and Buffy are talking near their lockers. Cordelia comes up.

Cordelia: Oh, look, it's the Three Musketeers.

Willow explains to Cordelia that that's really not an insult, that the Three Musketeers were cool. Cordelia says she sees their point. Then she excitedly asks if they fought any demons. They try to cover and explain to her that they have to keep it quiet that Buffy's the Slayer and all the things that go with that.

Buffy insults Cordelia and sort of insults Willow and Xander. Or at least looks very irritated with them. It ends with Cordelia saying she will keep Buffy's secret. And Buffy says something like, you know, that's great — Cordelia won't tell anyone that Buffy's the Slayer and Buffy won't tell anyone that Cordelia's a moron.

Willow and Xander are a bit surprised at this outburst.

Willow Sees And Xander Doesn't

At the Bronze, the two of them are talking, and Willow says there's something wrong with Buffy. She's different. Xander says Buffy's always been different.

Willow: She's never been mean.

I like that Willow picks up on this difference. I also like that while we have seen (or been told through dialogue at least) that Buffy used to be more like Cordelia —the popular girl, the prom queen — we get a sense that Buffy probably never was mean. Even before she became the Slayer and became so isolated herself.

Xander isn't really paying much attention to Willow.

She puts a little bit of ice cream on her nose, clearly hoping to remind him of that moment when they almost kissed. He doesn't pick up on it at all. He glances at her.

Xander: Oh, you got something on your nose.

I felt so sad for Willow in that moment.

We switch to the graveyard where the vampires are digging up a grave. And the leader is pushing them to dig more, telling them to dig with their hands if they have no shovel. That burns the vampires' hands because it is conse-crated ground.

Back at the Bronze, we have live music. This is part of what gives the Bronze so much energy. That there is a different band every week. The Bronze would be a great place (other than the high death rate) to have in any town. And I love that the high school students can hang out there, so long as they aren't drinking.

Buffy Ignores Angel And Willow, Comes On To Xander

Buffy walks into the Bronze. We see her shoes first, a nice little call back to Hank unpacking that suitcase with all the brand-new shoes. And then the camera goes up to her legs. We see that she is wearing this very sexy dress.

Angel sees her. He says he thinks he made her angry and it bothers him.

She says she's not angry. She doesn't know where that's coming from. And she tells him to get over himself, she didn't moon over him all summer, she moved on — to the living.

Cordelia watches this interaction. Buffy goes over to Xander and asks him to dance. He says okay, seeming very hesitant. Buffy then dances with him. We have seen her dance with her friends before, and we will later in the series. It's always in fun, and we don't see her dance with Xander any differently than when she and Willow are dancing or when the three of them are dancing together.

This is different.

Buffy's Midpoint Commitment

Buffy's very close to Xander. She's swaying, she's pressing against him. We close up on Willow looking on, seeming very hurt. And right around 23 minutes in Buffy whispers to Xander, asking if she ever thanked him for saving her life. And doesn't he wish she would?

Buffy then walks away, grabs her purse from the table, which is right in front of Willow, and walks off without saying anything to Willow. Or to Angel. And she goes outside.

I see this all as Buffy throwing caution to wind at the Midpoint of the episode. She is going All In on a quest. Not to defeat the Master, but on almost an emotional quest of denial. To simply not deal with her feelings about having died when she faced the Master and her fears on a deeper level about being the Slayer and what that means for her life.

It's throwing caution to the wind because she is alienating her friends. She already feels isolated. And now she is pushing away everybody who is close to her, who offers her support.

Cordelia's Character Growth

We then get a scene where I start to love Cordelia. In this episode, she follows Buffy out to offer advice.

Cordelia: You're really campaigning for bitch of the year, aren't you?

Buffy: As defending champion, you nervous?

Cordelia: I can hold my own.

But she goes on to say she and Buffy aren't really friends, but since Buffy has saved the world on occasion, she'll give her some advice. Which is to get over it, deal with whatever her issues are, and move on because pretty soon Buffy won't even have the loser friends she has.

In typical Cordelia fashion, we get a little bit of an insult wrapped into the advice. But it is really good advice. And I also love her response when Buffy says it's time for Cordelia to mind her own business. Cordelia doesn't get offended. She just says, "It's long past."

Cordelia said what she had to say. She turns back toward the Bronze. But she can't resist one last little dig – maybe she'll see if Angel feels like dancing. And this is fun because not only is she getting in a dig, I believe Cordelia's plan is to do just that.

If you remember in Season One, when she first saw

Angel, she had no idea he was connected to Buffy. And she was going to go up and talk to him because she found him so attractive.

However, Cordelia never makes it into the Bronze. Because someone grabs her from behind. Buffy doesn't see it. She's already heading out.

We follow Cordelia. She is thrown into a dark basement. Someone else is lying there on the floor knocked out. It's Miss Calendar.

In the meantime, Buffy is walking through the graveyard, and she sees that the Master's grave is empty.

Buffy Shuts Xander And Willow Out

We switch to school the next day. Willow is saying to Giles that Buffy's possessed. Xander says aren't they over-looking that she may be attracted to him? And they all agree no, she's possessed. Or there's something wrong with her.

Giles points out that she might not be possessed. The answer might be more ordinary. She may have, "What you Americans refer to as issues." He says that technically Buffy died, and that she had convinced herself that she was invulnerable. Now she knows that she's not.

He doesn't realize that Buffy is walking up behind them. Xander tries to cover by saying they're talking about trout.

Buffy is angry that there is a vacancy in the graveyard where the Master was buried. Giles says something about he doesn't know of any revivification ritual that was successful. And Buffy says, "But you've heard of them?" It's something he didn't mention to her.

She's rude to Xander and Willow when they try to chime in and talk about how they buried the Master and went through a ritual. She says this is Slayer work, it's not for them.

This, too, is different for Buffy. Yes, in the very first episode, our pilot, she pushed back against the idea that they could help, saying it was her job, not theirs. But since then she has mostly appreciated having their support and has turned to them on many occasions. So now she is pushing back and trying to shut them out.

Principal Snyder interrupts, and they go back to class. Snyder tells Giles that he smells trouble, and it's Buffy. He smells trouble, expulsion, and the faintest aroma of jail. He also finds it weird that Giles has faith in these kids. So we have another reference to them as kids or children. And he shakes his head at what he sees as Giles' naïveté.

The Trap In When She Was Bad

In the library, Giles tells our friends about the revivification ritual. The vampires need the Master's bones and the blood of someone close to or connected to the Master. Buffy says it's her. She killed him. You can't get more connected or closer than that.

About 29 minutes in, a rock comes crashing through the window. Cordelia's watch is wrapped around it. There's a note telling Buffy to come to the Bronze.

Willow and Xander argue with Buffy. They say she can't just head off to the Bronze in response to the note. Willow says what about the rest of the note where it says it's a trap? Of course, that's not written there, but it might as well be, as Willow points out.

Buffy says she can handle it.

Buffy: This is my fight.

Buffy Calls Out Angel's Stalking

In our next scene, Buffy is heading for the Bronze and Angel appears. He takes her by surprise.

Buffy: You know being stalked isn't really a big turn on for girls.

But Angel says she needs help, and Buffy says she doesn't trust him. He's a vampire. She is again very sarcastic about it.

Buffy's sarcastic tone throughout the episode tells us so much about how afraid she is. Because while Buffy has always engaged in word play— she jokes, she quips, she has a sort of dry sense of humor — she isn't usually sarcastic with anyone. In fact, there was that wonderful quote where she told Giles he was abusing sarcasm. So we see that Buffy is using sarcasm to try to keep everyone at a distance. To keep her own feelings at a distance.

Angel tells her she has to trust someone. And she says, "I trust me." He says she's not as strong as she thinks. And she's saying, hey, come on, let's fight. "You must've thought about it. You're a vampire, I'm the Slayer. What would happen if we fought?"

But he refuses and reminds her that she has somewhere else to be.

The Three-Quarter Turn In When She Was Bad

We then get to the third major plot point. Which generally is around three-quarters into the episode and spins it yet again in a new direction. Here, as it should, it arises from Buffy's actions at the Midpoint.

I say that because it's from Buffy's emotional Midpoint. Where she threw caution to the wind and really embraced her fear and her denial of what was happening by that dance with Xander and coming on to him. Despite that she knew how much that would hurt Willow's feelings, and that she knew it would ultimately hurt Xander.

But she is so afraid and in so much pain and turmoil that she did it. That has driven her forward to this point.

Now she has headed off to the Bronze. Without her friends, leaving them unprotected. Which sets the stage for this plot turn.

In the library, Giles finishes the translation and figures

out that closest to the Master means physically close. It's the nearest of those who were with the Master when he died.

Giles: It's a trap. It just isn't for her.

That line comes at 32 minutes 55 seconds in, so right around that three-quarter mark through the story.

Xander Threatens Buffy

In the Bronze, Buffy finds a vampire who looks like Cordelia. But Buffy realizes very quickly it's not. No one else is there. And Buffy figures out that they did set this up not to trap her but to leave her friends vulnerable. She leaves Angel with the vampire, telling him not to kill her unless he has to.

Buffy runs back to the library, and finds things just a mess. Everything knocked over. Xander is still there. He's injured. Giles and Willow have been taken.

And Xander tells her he doesn't know what her problem is, and he doesn't care. If she had worked with them for five seconds, she could have stopped this.

Xander: If they hurt Willow I'll kill you.

And he explains to her that the vampires need whoever was near the Master when he died.

This explanation made me think of the Season One finale when Angel and Xander were posted outside the library. They were supposed to keep watch and stand guard. And now I think, okay, the writers did that because they wanted to set up that it was Giles, Willow, Jenny Calendar, and Cordelia who would be at risk in this episode.

Back at the Bronze, Buffy tortures the vampire, trying to get her to talk. The vampire says what will you do, kill me? And Buffy says yes, but the question is what they do until then.

And she's putting the cross, her cross that Angel gave her, into the vampire's mouth and it's smoking. Finally, the vampire tells her where everyone is.

The Climax Of When She Was Bad

We switch to this old warehouse. The Anointed One is there. He gives a small box to the vampire leader. We see that Cordelia, Jenny, Giles, and Willow have been hung upside down by their feet. They are reeled out on a pulley system to hang over the Master's bones, which are on a table.

The leader is reciting more poems or prayers of resurrection. Xander, Buffy, and Angel sneak in. She tells them to get the others out. Angel says she needs to distract the vampires.

Buffy: I'm going to kill them all. That ought to distract them.

We see from behind them the vampires performing the ritual. One of them is dusted as he answers the Leader's chant, and we see Buffy there behind him. There is a huge fight. The Anointed One climbs up and out of the way. He watches Angel and Xander wheel our four friends on the pulleys away from the fight and get them down.

Buffy kills multiple vampires. Angel fights another vampire. Jenny and Giles wake up. Giles asks where Buffy is? Xander says she's working out her issues.

The Leader confronts Buffy. He's giving this monologue about how he'll grind her into a sticky paste and hear her beg. He lunges at her with a mallet. She grabs this torch – who knows why vampires have torches around, but I feel like that is the show's call out or shout out to vampire lore. She takes his torch and turns it sideways.

With one end she stakes one vampire heading toward her. With the other she sets the leader on fire. His mallet drops and he's gone.

Willow, who has been watching, says it's over. And Xander says it's not. Buffy picks up the mallet and smashes the Master's bones with it.

One after the other, over and over.

This is the catharsis that Buffy needed. I don't think that it was the fight itself. It was getting rid of that Leader and all the vampires. But more important, smashing the Master's bones.

And I always tear up when she does that. I think it's the symbolism of her trying to smash death, trying to kill her vulnerability. And then with her hands over her face she cries.

Falling Action And Bookends

Now we are at the Falling Action. 41 minutes 30 seconds in. This is where we tie up the loose ends of the episode.

Angel stands behind Buffy, holds her, and tells her very quietly, "It's okay. It's okay."

The others look on as Buffy cries.

Now we switch to a sunny day. Cordelia and Jenny are walking across the lawn. And Cordelia says what an ordeal that was. And the worst part is it stays with you forever — none of that blood and rust ever comes out of your clothes no matter what they tell you.

This is such a nice bookend to Cordelia's comment at the beginning about a nightmare that turns out to be about vacation. And now she's talking about an ordeal that turns out to be the lasting trauma to her clothes, and the drycleaner not being able to fix it.

And Jenny says, yes, of course that is the worst part.

I've always thought of these types of lines from Cordelia being there for humor. But I also think this is why Cordelia can cope with things. The fact that she frames the experience this way leaves her with less trauma than probably Jenny suffers, or Willow or Giles.

Obviously, this is not a realistic show when it comes to how people deal with trauma. If someone went through that kind of experience it would have such a lasting effect. And yet we have our main characters going through these things all the time in the world of the show. Where these types of experiences, rather than being once-in-a-lifetime, just happen on an ongoing basis.

In that context, I see Cordelia being able to almost trivialize it being a strength.

Buffy Fears Facing Her Friends

We then see Buffy and Giles. And she is saying she doesn't know how she can face her friends. She really feels the weight of having run off and left them vulnerable because she wasn't dealing with her emotions.

She says what is she going to say to them? "Sorry I almost got your throat slit and got you killed on the first day of school?"

Giles tries to comfort her. But maybe doesn't do such a great job because he says it's hardly the worst mistake she'll ever make. And then he says oh, that wasn't as comforting as he meant it to be.

I love that interchange because it is a very real thing. Anyone who is not just young but new at whatever their profession is (or any other pursuit) is going to make mistakes. And sometimes that is exactly true. It feels horrible and it's not the worst mistake she'll ever make.

So there is comfort in that. And then there's not.

But I feel like Giles is pointing out, yeah, you can make mistakes and your friends are going to understand. Buffy isn't convinced. She goes to class. We see her hesitating in the doorway.

There's an empty seat next to Xander and Willow, who are joking around. They look up, and I think it's Willow who says, "We saved you a seat."

Buffy sits down. Her body language still tells us she's a little hesitant. She's holding back a bit, waiting to see what her friends will say. Xander and Willow make a joke about the teacher. They talk about what they'll do tonight. And then –

Xander: Well we could grind our enemies into talcum powder with a sledgehammer, but gosh we did that last night.

Willow gives Buffy just the best smile, kind of a little wicked grin, telling Buffy it is okay. Buffy smiles back, and they all start to talk. And this part always makes me tear up as well because these friends are just so amazing for Buffy.

We would think that is the end of the Falling Action. We have seen all of Buffy's part of the story wind up.

Just One More Thing – A Hook

But we are back to the warehouse. The first time I watched I forgot that the Anointed One had gotten away from the fight, so he was not one of the ones who was killed.

We see him standing in the warehouse, some fragments of the Master's bones around him. And he says, "I hate that girl." And we close the episode.

Such a nice way to end. Because while we wrap up the story, we also add that little hook. That little question I love. Yes, the Anointed One is still here, and what is he going to do next?

That covers the episode itself. There is a ton of foreshadowing in it for the rest of the season, so I hope you'll read on for that.

Spoilers And Foreshadowing

Buffy, Angel, and The Terminator

We get foreshadowing from the very start of the episode with Willow quoting that line from **The Termi-**

nator. "In the short time we had, we loved a lifetime's worth."

If somehow you have not seen **Terminator**, I'm about to spoil part of it. So skip to the next heading if you don't want to read it, but I hope you will.

In that movie Kyle Reese comes back in time to protect our protagonist, who becomes quite fierce herself, Sarah Connor. The two of them fall for each other in the midst of all of this action going on. And they have one night together, and that is it forever. So that is Willow's quote. It so foreshadows not just this season, but the entire Buffy and Angel romance and relationship.

Because this season, they will have that one night together and then everything goes horribly wrong. Angel turns on her, turns into Angelus and becomes the villain of the season. And while later down the road he does become Angel again, they never are able to make that relationship work.

So it is such a great line to put in the beginning of the Season Two pilot. Where our main arc is what happens with Buffy and Angel and her having to fight him.

The School Year's End

Then there's the moment where Joyce says "welcome to my world," and she just hopes Buffy makes it through the school year. I never noticed this before, and it struck me now how the episode starts getting the audience ready for the end of the season where Buffy is kicked out of school.

Snyder also foreshadows this when he says he smells trouble, expulsion, and the faintest aroma of jail. All these things are coming. Not literally jail. But Buffy does get expelled. And after Kendra is killed, Buffy is the main suspect for some time. Snyder knows that she didn't do it. He tells her that the police will not care. They will come after her.

We get a great quote from him in that episode, and I think it is the finale. It might be the episode right before that. But Buffy is saying, the police will figure it out. And he says something like the police in Sunnydale are deeply stupid.

So we get all of this foreshadowed in this one line from Snyder. And his reference to jail and law enforcement also foreshadows that we will see the police in this season of Buffy. We will get a greater sense of who the police are. Maybe what role they play in Sunnydale.

And actually more than once in the series the police will be a main part of the story when it looks like Buffy has committed murder.

More Buffy And Angel Arc Foreshadowing

We also have major foreshadowing of the Buffy and Angel arc in the interplay between the two of them. This struck me when I re-watched the whole series for the first time on the DVDs. That's when I noticed how when Buffy and Angel are talking on her way to the Bronze, she says he must've thought of it. "You're a vampire, I'm a Slayer. What would happen if we fought? Who would win?"

And I thought oh, right there in the first episode is what is going to happen in the last episode. Buffy fighting Angel and having to fight to the death.

So we are putting that right out front, but in a way it doesn't tell the audience that, in fact, this will happen. Because right now we have no reason to believe that Angel would be trying to kill Buffy.

Also, the reason that the scene doesn't give that away is because there is such a good reason for Buffy to say it. Through the whole episode, she is grappling with her role as a

Slayer and the fact that a powerful vampire killed her. And remember, it wasn't Angel who was able to bring her back to life. It was Xander, a human being. She has every reason on an emotional level to equate her fear of death, her fear of the Master, her feelings about being the Slayer, with Angel, who is a vampire. So we think we know that it is coming from there.

But this masks that it is a well-founded fear.

She has every reason, it turns out, totally aside from the emotional issues she's dealing with, to have this concern. What would happen if she and Angel had to fight each other?

Buffy's Strength

We also get a little more foreshadowing there of a key moment in the season finale. And this I didn't pick up on until I watched it this time for the podcast. When he is telling her you have to trust someone, and she says, "I trust me."

This foreshadows that moment in the finale when they're fighting and he's got the sword almost at her throat. And Angelus says to her that everything's stripped away, no friends, no family, what's left? And we think he is going to kill her and she says, "Me." And claps her hands around that sword he's thrusting and stops it.

And this strength that Buffy has inside herself is key to that season finale. And also so heartbreaking.

I love the way the Season Two pilot episode foreshadows all of that. And it encapsulates a conflict that will continue not just for the season, but for the series. The conflict between Buffy as the Slayer — of her role as the only one in all the world, so isolated — and yet her breaking with tradition. Having close family ties, caring about her mother, valuing these close friends who do get into the fight with her. And that struggle that she has with whether it's harder to protect them — could she fight better all on her own — or can they help her?

Friends, Sidekicks, Both?

In addition, Buffy's friends will struggle with their roles. Are they merely sidekicks? Willow in particular will struggle with that.

And their feelings about wanting to be part of the fight, needing to be part of it, and also feeling that they do make very real contributions that sometimes Buffy overlooks. Some of that leads to that great line in Season Four where Buffy says, "I guess that's why there's no prophecy about the Slayer and her friends."

We will see this conflict come up again and again, with a different angle each time.

Does it work to have the Slayer and her friends? Ultimately I think the show says yes, but it's a difficult balance, which makes for great conflict throughout the series. That balance between (a) Buffy has to have all the strength in herself and (b) she also has strength because she has these close relationships.

All these hints, all these ways of opening conflict we don't even grasp is so key, are a big part of why **When She Was Bad** is one of my favorite episodes. And it is my favorite season opener of all the **Buffy** seasons.

Questions For Your Writing

- **Do your story's major plot turns affect your protagonist emotionally?**
- **If not, can you revise them to make your story stronger?**
- **What words do your characters use that**

reflect the nature of their relationships
or set a tone (like Giles' use of words
like child or students)
- **What are some actions your characters
can take to show how they feel in key
scenes?**
- **Does the beginning of your story hint
at the ending or at major
developments?**

Next: Some Assembly Required

NEXT WE'LL TALK ABOUT **SOME ASSEMBLY REQUIRED**.
It's a self-contained episode and something of a tribute to
Frankenstein. We'll look at how unclear plot turns and
multiple antagonists affect the story.

CHAPTER 2

SOME ASSEMBLY REQUIRED
(S2 E2)

THIS CHAPTER TALKS about **Some Assembly Required**, Season Two Episode Two, written by Ty King and directed by Bruce Seth Green.

In particular, we'll cover:

- **Unclear plot turns that make the story flag**
- **The trouble with a jumble of antagonists**
- **Why you want the audience to care about your antagonist**
- **The power of stating feelings indirectly**

Okay, let's dive into the Hellmouth.

Opening Conflict In Some Assembly Required

Here, we get two Opening Conflicts.

The first one is Buffy in the graveyard. She's waiting for a vampire to rise. It's not happening, and she says something like, "Rise and shine – some of us have trig homework."

This is a great way to very quickly summarize the core conflict in Buffy's life: dealing with being the Slayer and having a life as a teenage girl.

Angel appears, bringing in our second initial conflict. He asks her if she's alone. And there's some really nice dialogue after she says yes, she's alone.

Angel: I thought you might be with someone. Xander or someone.

Buffy: Xander?

Angel: Or someone.

And then Angel denies that he's jealous, though when she says all she did was have one little dance with Xander, he calls it more like a mating ritual.

They're arguing. Buffy says she didn't come here to fight. And in a nice moment of comedy we get her saying, "Oh yes, I did," when the vampire finally does rise.

Buffy and the vampire fight. Then she and Angel pick up their argument immediately after she dusts the vamp. Angel tries to walk away. She follows him and falls into an open grave. And it's not just an open grave. The coffin inside it is open as well, and we cut to the credits.

Opening Conflict In Some Assembly Required

This falling into the open grave happens about 3 minutes 15 seconds in. Typically, at 10% into any story we see the Inciting Incident or what I think of as the Story Spark. It gets the main plot moving.

The episode here is about 42-43 minutes. While this moment is a little before 10%, I do think this is it. Because this open coffin in the open grave is what sets Buffy investigating and makes her aware of what is going on.

After the credits we come to one of my favorite scenes in **Buffy** that involves Giles.

Evolving Giles' Character Through Vulnerability

Giles is in the library. His back is to the door and he is awkwardly practicing asking someone out. He can't get it right. He calls himself an idiot. At the end, and of course because it would be the most embarrassing thing for him, Xander and Buffy walk in and catch part of this. They immediately start giving him advice. And making fun of him.

Buffy tells him to avoid words like "amenable" and "indecorous."

Buffy: Speak English or whatever they speak in –

Giles: England

She tells him to say something more like "I have a thing, maybe you have a thing, how do you feel about Mexican?" And Giles is just not really getting it.

They keep teasing him. He shuts it down and asks if Mr. Kolchak showed up on schedule. He was the vampire that Buffy was waiting for.

(I couldn't help wondering if this was a reference to the show The Night Stalker. It was on when I was a kid, and I thought it was so scary. This guy Kolchak goes out stalking vampires and other supernatural creatures. It was an inspiration for the X-Files. The writers of that even did a tribute episode to it. I've got to think the **Buffy** writers also may have been Night Stalker fans.)

Buffy tells Giles about the open grave. He mentions there could be a grave robber.

Antagonists Introduced

We switch to the Science Fair. A boy named Eric is taking photos of all the girls, including Willow. Later he'll photograph both Buffy and Cordelia. He is friends with Chris, and Chris and Willow know each other. They've been competing in the Science Fair. Chris always takes first place. But he gives Willow the tip that if you design something that the teacher who is judging it doesn't understand, he will give it more points.

After taking Cordelia's picture, Eric tells Chris that Cordelia would be perfect.

Chris: Don't be an idiot, she's alive.

Back in the library Cordelia comes in to ask for help from Willow. I wish I'd written down all the exact words, but she says something like, "I hate to interrupt your little undead playgroup." And she's talking about the Science Fair. Cordelia makes these references to her pain and how sad it was – something about Chris.

But everyone ignores her because they are focused on the empty grave and sorting out what happened. The grave belonged to one of three girls who were killed in an automobile accident on the way to a game.

Our friends decide that what they need to do is go and check out the graveyard and see if the other two girls' graves are empty.

In terms of what could've done this, Giles says there could be demons who eat the dead, voodoo, and zombies. Someone asks Buffy if they should call Angel to go with to the graveyard. She says no and starts to explain about their argument, but then just says, "As far as he's concerned, I'm taking the night off."

When they ask Cordelia if she would like to go, she says she has plans.

Cordelia: Boy, I wish I knew you were going to be digging up dead people sooner. I would've canceled.

Grave Digging

At about 10 minutes 30 seconds in we have Xander and Giles grave digging. Buffy and Willow are sitting to the side talking about Angel being jealous. And Buffy says she's never going to live down that dance, but that Angel really over-reacted.

Willow: Love makes you do the wacky.

This line comes back later, though I don't think it works quite as well when Buffy repeats it at the end.

Giles and Xander point out that the digging would go faster if Buffy would help.

Buffy: Sorry, but I'm an old-fashioned gal. I was raised to believe men dig up the corpses and women have the babies.

Buffy asks Willow what Cordelia was talking about, and Willow tells her that Chris' older brother Darrell was a very well-known football player at Sunnydale High. He was a running back, and he died rock climbing. Cordelia dated him, but he rejected her. Willow says that Chris has been in his own world ever since his brother died.

About 12 minutes in Buffy jumps down into the grave. We don't see what she finds.

The One-Quarter Twist That Might Have Been

We're a little bit past the one-quarter point of the episode. Often at that point we see a twist or turn that spins the story in a new direction and propels it toward the Midpoint. Buffy jumping into the grave could be it. Because whatever she finds out will change the direction of the story.

However, here I think that that first major plot point comes a little bit later.

First, we get Cordelia. She's in a dark parking lot – because everything in Sunnydale is dark – walking to her car. We get what I feel is something of a cheap scare. Or at least a not quite believable encounter between her and Angel. She's going to the car, seeming nervous. I think she senses someone behind her. She drops her keys. When she bends down to get them she looks underneath the car and sees feet.

Cheap Pop Scare

We don't know whose feet they are. She runs and she hides in a dumpster. She waits, and when she opens up the top, Angel is there. He startles her.

The reason I say it's a bit of a cheap scare is it's unlikely Angel wouldn't have said who he was or called out to Cordelia. He doesn't seem like the type who wants to just scare people for no particular reason. He claims that he wasn't sure it was her.

That doesn't quite ring true to me. I feel like Angel, even if he didn't know it was Cordelia, would know that following a young woman at night in the dark in a deserted parking lot would be scary. But obviously the writers wanted a little bit of tension there.

The One-Quarter Twist – Body Parts

At 14 minutes 24 seconds in, we get what I see as that first major turn in the story. Cordelia is trying to get out of the dumpster. She's stuck. She reaches down to free herself and pulls out a dead hand.

This definitely changes the trajectory of the story. For one thing, we ruled out zombies unless they're walking around with no hands.

In the library, our four friends show up. Angel and Cordelia are already there. Angel and Buffy have a brief exchange where he says he thought she took the night off. She tries to pretend this trip to the graveyard just came up, but he says Cordelia told him the truth.

As they talk about what might've happened, Angel says there weren't three whole girls in the dumpster. Somebody kept some parts. He also tells them that whoever cut up the girls had some skills.

The group is unsure why the body parts would be dumped five miles away from the cemetery. They conclude that whoever did it is probably connected with the school since the body parts were dumped near it.

Cordelia seems genuinely shaken. She needs to go home and burn her clothes. But she doesn't want to go alone. She asks Angel to take her. He looks like he doesn't know what else to do and lets her lead him out. She recovers and says, "Great, I'll drive," Buffy looks hurt. And Xander says he would've taken Angel for a one-woman vampire.

Chris' House – Backstory

We switch to Chris' house.

His mom is watching footage of a football game Darrell, her deceased son, was in. She ignores Chris when he goes out.

This is a nice quick way to show her grief. Plus it engenders a bit of sympathy for Chris. And I think this is a very real thing when you are grieving. It can be so hard to focus on anyone else. Partly because it might be painful to stay there in the grief, but also as you heal you feel farther and farther from the person you're grieving for.

And here, Darrell's mom is not able to do it despite that she has a son still there. So Chris is very much in the background of his mother's life. And that is literally. He is mostly in the basement, and I believe he comes out from behind the door that is behind her.

At school, Buffy and her friends are searching the lockers of the students that Willow said had the skill to cut up a body. They find anatomy texts in Chris' locker. Eric's locker has a picture of a girl, but it is created from cutouts of magazine photos. So an arm from one girl and head from another girl and so forth.

The next scene shows Eric and Chris in a large empty space that we find out later is an old science lab. A shrouded corpse lies on gurney. Eric is showing photos of the girls taken at school, which include Buffy, Cordelia, and Willow.

At school, Xander and Buffy talk about why anyone would make a girl when there are so many premade ones laying around. Xander says people don't want to fall in love with what's right in front of them. They want the unattainable. Yet another of his pointed comments about Buffy and Angel, which Buffy ignores.

Giles And Jenny Subplot

We switch to Giles walking in the hall with Jenny Calendar. He's very nervous. He stutters, he stumbles. He says words like "indecorous" and doesn't quite get to asking her out. After she rushes into her classroom, she pops back out and says that whatever he wanted to say, why doesn't he tell her at the football game?

Giles pretends that yes, of course, he was going to go to the game. And she says they can go together, and how does he feel about Mexican?

The Missing Midpoint In Some Assembly Required

The next day Eric and Chris don't come to school. This is about 23 minutes in.

We are past the actual Midpoint of the episode, so I was looking for some sort of commitment by Buffy at the Midpoint where she throws caution to the wind, fully commits to her quest, or suffers some kind of major reversal. And I just didn't see it.

This reminded me a bit of **Out Of Mind Out Of**

Sight, the Cordelia-centric Season One episode with the invisible girl, Marcy. It had a bit of a Midpoint. Buffy climbed up into the space in the ceiling and found Marcy's things. And took her yearbook, which made Marcy very angry. It also gave Buffy and her friends the information that they needed. So it was something of a commitment at the Midpoint.

Here, I just don't see anything.

I feel like this is part of why I always want to skip over this episode when I'm re-watching. Not that I think specifically of how it doesn't have a strong Midpoint. But the story itself doesn't stand out for me, doesn't make me want to watch it again. I enjoy the things like the quotes I've been talking about, the Jenny and Giles interplay, the way it moves the Angel and Buffy story a little bit.

But the actual plot of the episode doesn't really grab me. And I do think this is one of the reasons. That we just don't have that strong story structure.

The Big Reveal

Giles tells us he learned that there were three heads found in the dumpster. So the girl that is being put together is not finished.

We switch to Eric and Chris. Eric is saying, "You know what you have to do." And Chris is saying, "Please, you understand. I can't do it." He's being pushed, of course, to kill one of the girls. (I say of course because it's Sunnydale.) Eric says they need to kill one of the girls so that they have a live head.

And we get the big reveal – Darrell steps out of the shadows. He's got stitching all around his face. And he says to Chris, "You gave me your word. You promised I wouldn't be alone."

Eric argues that if you take a life to make a life it's a wash so it's okay.

Throwing Caution To The Wind

At 25 minutes in, Chris agrees to do this. So here we have a throwing caution to the wind action by Chris. If he were our protagonist, that could be the Midpoint of the story.

And sometimes you can have an episode where the antagonist is the one who commits at the Midpoint. We saw that in the Season One episode Angel. The Master, who was the antagonist, was driving the main plot. He made a commitment at the Midpoint that drove the story forward.

Here, though, it doesn't feel that strong to me.

Who Is The Antagonist?

For one thing, it isn't clear who the antagonist is here. There is Chris, who is grieving for his brother. He wants to help his brother, but he has to be pushed along.

We have Eric, who just seems like a ghoul. He's human, but he is presented just as this awful kid or young man who doesn't care about killing people. Maybe he's excited about the science of this, but I don't even get that. It seems like he just wants to do this awful thing.

And we have Darrell. Who, yes, doesn't want to be alone, so he has motivation. But I don't feel like I know enough about him to have a real feel for who he was before this terrible thing happened to him. He does drive the plot, though. He's the reason that Chris at least is contemplating killing a girl.

A Group As Antagonist

This is a good example of why it is challenging to have a group as either a protagonist or an antagonist. You can do it. There are stories that do it.

Generally, though, you need one person to be the one that the audience most identifies with or most follows. Here it's hard to truly identify with any of these antagonists. But if one of them was truly taking the lead, I think it might help make the story more gripping.

Instead we'll see that who takes the lead switches around.

Understanding The Antagonist

There is also the issue of sympathy for the antagonist. Here, I don't have it for any of them.

I didn't have sympathy with the Master in the sense that I didn't want him to achieve his goals. But the Master was trapped underground, under this church, and he wanted to get out. If you step into his shoes, you can understand his despair and his point of view. His world has been snatched from him and he is trying to get it back.

In his world, the humans are the antagonists, and he is the protagonist.

Here, I just find it hard to do that. Eric – clearly, we're not meant to have sympathy for him. He just seems awful. And Chris – yes, I can feel bad for him that he lost his brother. Also because his mother doesn't appear to know he exists anymore. I hope on some level she cares, but she's not expressing that. She's not able to get out of her grief.

And we will find out at the end that Chris brought Darrell back, and Darrell wished he hadn't been brought back. So Chris feels this responsibility.

And had I known that last element at this point, maybe the story would've grabbed me a little more. That Chris was being driven not just by his brother saying he doesn't want to be alone, but because Chris himself brought Darrell back to life, dooming him to loneliness and sadness and hiding in the shadows.

But we don't quite get that here. Maybe I should've been able to read that in but for whatever reason I didn't. So I never really feel that much for Chris.

Darrell's Perspective

And then Darrell, as I said, is someone we just don't know anything about other than that he was a great football player. And he died in this accident and was brought back.

Also, we don't see him go through any sort of struggle over the fact that he would be dooming someone else to the same fate as his. Or that he would have to take a human life.

If we saw more anger on his part it could help. A view that his life was stolen from him so young. If he had to go through this, why shouldn't someone else?

We do see some anger. But I feel like we just don't get enough for me to really empathize. And I'm not talking about empathizing as in thinking it's okay for him to do this. But to understand how he could feel it's okay.

How Darrell could justify it to himself. How Chris could justify it.

Unraveling The Clues

Back in the library, Giles and Willow figure out that the reason the villains can't use a head from a cadaver is that formaldehyde degrades the brain cells. So they know Eric and Chris need a live girl's head.

Buffy goes to Chris' to try to talk to him. Willow tells her not to be too hard on him. But Buffy, like me, has no sympathy given what Chris is trying to do. She goes to his house. The mom lets her in.

And Buffy can see that she doesn't know anything about where Chris is. She isn't paying any attention to Chris. She is still watching, or yet again watching, a football game with Darrell. She tells Buffy about it.

So Buffy does start to feel a little bit of sympathy for Chris. We can see it in her face. She notices Keep Out signs on the basement door, and she goes downstairs. She finds photos and plans. Including Cordelia's face pasted onto a diagram of a girl's body.

So she now knows Cordelia is the target.

When she hears someone or something, Buffy escapes out the window. We see Darrell behind her in the shadows.

The First Kidnapping Attempt

Cordelia is in the locker room getting ready for the game alone. Chris appears, and he distracts Cordelia. While she's talking to him, Eric throws a blanket over her from behind and they try to kidnap her.

Buffy comes in and stops it, and Eric gets away. Cordelia runs to the football field. (She has to be the apex of the pyramid, of course.)

Buffy realizes Chris is there in the locker room and she tells him she knows what they're trying to do. She asks him to stop. Chris says he has to do it "for him." Buffy at first thinks he's talking about Eric. But she realizes then that he is talking about Darrell.

This is at 31 minutes 30 seconds in and could be the next major plot turn, which typically comes three-quarters of the way through. And that plot point should grow from the Midpoint and spin the story in yet another direction.

Here, though I think it is this next scene, which is about 32 minutes in at the laboratory.

The Three-Quarter Turn In Some Assembly Required

Darrell is angry because Eric didn't bring Cordelia back. He's saying, "You promised." And Eric says they can still do this.

So this does turn the story because now Chris is on Buffy's side, and Eric and Darrell are driving ahead without Chris. There is no conscience at all left in that antagonist group.

Buffy and Chris are back to Chris' basement. But no one is there, and they realize that Eric and Darrell must be going through with the plan.

At the game, we get some nice Giles and Jenny back-and-forth about American football versus rugby. They're having fun. Xander and Willow show up. Their investigations haven't gotten them anywhere. And they sit right behind Jenny and Giles despite Giles doing his best to discourage them.

Too Late For Sympathy

Darrell is under the bleachers. He's watching the game. We get sad music. His lip trembles. I feel like this is meant for us to feel sympathy for Darrell. And I think I could in another, slightly different, story.

But I have trouble with this because right from the beginning the crime is so awful that it is really hard to feel for Darrell. We're shown so much about the crime. The empty graves, that three girls were killed, that their bodies were cut up, that someone is making this girl out of parts.

We find all of that before we know Darrell's motives. Now we see him in the shadows wishing for his former life, and it's almost too late for me to have that sympathy.

I'm sure this episode was something of a tribute to Frankenstein. And I feel like the big difference is in Frankenstein we do see so much through the Frankenstein creation's eyes and through Dr. Frankenstein's eyes. And here we don't have that.

Cordelia goes to the sides of the bleachers to get some water. Darrell kidnaps her.

In the lab, she screams when she sees him for the first time. Then she tries to convince him that she'll stay with him anyway, they don't have to do this. Of course, he doesn't buy that.

He apologizes for rejecting her in the past, saying he didn't appreciate her. But now they'll be together forever.

The Climax Of Some Assembly Required

We are 37 minutes 51 seconds in when the Climax starts.

Buffy comes in. (Chris has told her where Darrell and Eric would take Cordelia.) Buffy tries to convince Darrell to stop and tells him that Chris sent her. He doesn't believe that. As they're arguing and then fighting, gas spills. A fire starts. Flames spread everywhere.

Xander arrives. He tries to unstrap Cordelia from the gurney she's on but can't do it in time. So he wheels her through the flames and gets her out.

Eric has been knocked out, but he's not dead. Giles and Willow get him out.

Buffy and Darrell are still fighting, and he throws her on the floor. He's about to bring a desk down on her. She seems very disoriented. So we're not sure she's going to be able to get away.

But Chris comes in, and he yells, "Don't!"

Darrell backs off. He runs over to the shrouded corpse that is now in the midst of the flames, holds it, and says, "We'll be together always."

And here maybe I do have some sympathy for Darrell. This is the kind of thing that shows how desperately lonely he was. And that he didn't want to continue this existence if he had to be alone.

More On Buffy Not Killing Humans

Once again Buffy doesn't kill a human being here, even one who already was dead and was brought back to life. She doesn't kill Darrell. Darrell kills himself.

Buffy, nonetheless, as our protagonist is the one who stopped this from happening. She stopped the kidnapping of Cordelia the first time, found out from Chris what happened, persuaded him to tell her where Eric and Darrell were, and broke in and interrupted everything.

Falling Action

We now have the Falling Action, where we tie up all the loose ends in the plot and any subplots.

Angel appears. He saw the fire and figured that Buffy was there. He asks if she's okay, and she is.

Giles apologizes to Jenny. They joke about how on a second date it would be pretty hard to top what happened tonight. He's very happy that Jenny mentions a second date. So it's a nice moment with them.

Xander and Willow look around and talk about how everyone is paired up but them. Xander asks if Willow ever feels like it's a game of musical chairs and they're the only ones without a seat when the music stops. And Willow says all the time.

Cordelia comes over to thank Xander for saving her life. She's very sincere, and she says if there's anything she can do – and Xander says, "Do you mind? We were talking." After she walks away, he turns to Willow and says, "Where were we?" Willow says, "We were wondering why we don't get dates. And Xander says, "Oh yeah, why is that?"

Possible Theme – Love Makes You Do The Wacky

We switch to Buffy and Angel again in the graveyard at night. They're talking about Chris, and she says he acted crazy but it was because he loved his brother. And Angel says he took it too far.

Buffy then reiterates what Willow said: "Love makes you do the wacky."

This is the part I said I had a little bit of trouble with. I guess it goes to my whole issue with the episode. That I don't think this is enough – that love makes you do the wacky. That

Chris had this great love for his brother and that's why he tried to do this.

And I've already talked about why I feel like that wasn't enough. But it seems to be the theme that the writers were going for.

I do enjoy the Buffy and Angel back-and-forth. Angel says, in response to her comment, "Like a two-hundred-forty-one-year-old jealous of a high school junior?" Buffy says she doesn't love Xander.

The Strength Of Indirection

Something I noticed here is that we have not heard either Buffy or Angel directly say, "I love you." In the episode where Darla was killed, Darla says to Angel, "You love someone who hates us." So Buffy learned indirectly that Angel loves her.

And here, similarly, we don't hear Buffy say to Angel, "I love you." But she says, "I don't love Xander." Which implies that she does love Angel.

And this can be so strong – to have things said in an indirect way. And we don't know, maybe they have said this to each other. But I'm thinking not because of the gradual pace of their relationship and that mostly they still meet primarily to deal with terrible things happening.

Angel explains why he feels jealous of Xander. It's not so much that he really thought that Buffy loved Xander. It's that Xander gets to share her day-to-day life. He ends with that Xander gets to see her in the sunlight. Which I thought was both a beautiful metaphor for what Angel and Buffy can't have and is literally true. I love things that work on both those levels.

It's near morning, so they have to say goodbye. Buffy says, though, that she can walk him home. And they link hands.

We end on a shot of Darrell Ep's tombstone.

More On Giles

I like seeing Giles and Jenny and their relationship. In this episode I really like seeing Giles a bit awkward. We always see him so much in control, so sure of himself. It's fun to see him being a bit nervous.

I also like seeing him have a relationship with another adult. His irritation with Xander and Buffy when they're making fun of him, and the way he cuts them off, adds to what I was talking about last week. About why it isn't creepy that he's hanging out with these teenagers.

Because he doesn't engage in a serious conversation with them about his romantic life. He lets Buffy give him a little advice. He lets them tease a little. But it's very much what you could see them doing with a parent. And then he stops it before it goes very far.

A Voice Of Unflinching Truth

I also enjoy Cordelia. As I mentioned in Season One, my first time watching Buffy I didn't warm up to Cordelia until much later in the show. I just saw her as a sort of mean girl.

On re-watching, I see more and more of what's great about Cordelia.

In the book **Blood Relations: Chosen Families in Buffy the Vampire Slayer and Angel** by Jes Battis, there's a section at the start that lists all the characters. For Cordelia, it says: "A voice of unflinching truth and the embodiment of shallow materialism...."

I love that particularly – "a voice of unflinching truth." We saw a little bit more of that side of Cordelia in **Out Of Mind Out Of Sight**, but it does come through here.

Chris Again

Last thoughts on Chris: I was thinking about when we're first introduced to him.

I think that might be part of the key. The first time we see him he is with Eric, who is snapping photos of girls. And Eric is saying that Cordelia's perfect.

We don't know exactly what's going on, but already we know that Eric would really like to kill Cordelia. We need that for tension in the story.

Chris is pushing back. He's saying "No, she's alive. We can't do that." But the fact that Chris is even hanging out with this guy, Eric, already makes him an immediate bad guy in my mind.

If we saw Chris' closeness with Darrell that would help. But we only hear about it. The mom's loss is focused on her loss of the son. We don't see Chris' loss. We don't know what kind of relationship he and Darrell had.

Other than that, Chris tells us that he was trying to look out for Darrell the way Darrell had always looked out for him. But there's no way that we see that. And I don't know how you would. You'd then get into flashbacks which, as I talked about in Season One **Out Of Mind Out Of Sight**, can be tricky to use. I don't know what the answer would've been here, but I feel like if I had a better sense of how strong that relationship was I might've had a lot more sympathy for Chris.

Spoilers And Foreshadowing

CORDELIA AND XANDER

I had not realized how much the relationship between Cordelia and Xander was foreshadowed. My first time watching the series, I was taken completely by surprise. Maybe I just wasn't paying good attention. Or maybe it was just that watching it spread out over time, as it was airing, I didn't connect the dots.

But here we get Cordelia truly grateful to Xander for saving her. And she has started hanging out a bit in the library. Granted she came there for help with her science project, but now she is not afraid to be seen talking to the friends. And we have the step where she's really grateful to Xander.

When I first watched, I only read it as that – gratitude. And I think it doesn't necessarily tell you that they're going to get involved later. But it does foreshadow that there is perhaps more of a connection than we realize. It is a foundation for the start of Cordelia becoming interested in Xander. It's not so much that he saved her. Anyone, of course, would be grateful about that. But she will say later in Season Three **The Wish** that she never would've looked twice at Xander if Buffy hadn't made him, I think she says, "moderately cool by hanging out with him."

And here I think it's also that Xander is heroic. He has no special powers, yet he goes in there and he gets her out.

He does this all the time. He jumps into fights and tries to help. Even though he is very vulnerable himself.

Frankenstein And The Initiative

The other foreshadowing I did not even think of until I was looking in the book **Chosen Families** and saw an essay about Frankenstein. Buffy dealing with Frankenstein.

And my first thought was, "Oh, this is going to be about **Some Assembly Required**." I completely forgot about Season Four and the Initiative and Adam.

When we get there, maybe we'll talk about why I forgot about Adam, the Frankenstein-like creation of Professor Maggie Walsh. But the essay was in fact about Adam and

Maggie Walsh and the Initiative. Hopefully I will remember to come back to that when we get to that point.

––––––––

Questions For Your Writing

- **At the Midpoint of your story, does your protagonist make a clear commitment to the quest or suffer a major reversal? If not, what could you change so that makes sense?**
- **How many antagonists oppose your protagonist?**
- **If it's more than one, how could you combine the characters into one antagonist?**
- **If that's not possible, how can you hone in on one character to be the leader or who can represent all the antagonists?**
- **What's your antagonist's motive? Is it one you feel empathy for? If not, what can you change so that you feel more for your antagonist?**
- **Look at an important conversation where your characters' emotions run high.**
- **Do you use indirection, as this episode does, to suggest those feelings but not state them?**
- **If not, experiment. See if having**

**characters speak more indirectly
heightens the scene. (Don't worry, if it
doesn't, you can always change it back!)**

Next: School Hard

NEXT WE'LL TALK ABOUT **SCHOOL HARD**. THIS EPISODE
introduces a new character to the Buffyverse who is a very
compelling antagonist. We'll talk about why that is and about
the concept of the worthy adversary.

CHAPTER 3

SCHOOL HARD (S2 E3)

THIS CHAPTER TALKS about **School Hard**, Season Two Episode Three, written by Joss Whedon and David Greenwalt and directed by John T. Kretchmer.

In particular, we'll look at:

- **the strong story structure despite a very subtle Midpoint**
- **vulnerability as part of character building, including for your antagonist**
- **three-beats**
- **cliffhangers vs. game changers**
- **the worthy adversary as antagonist**

Okay, let's dive into the Hellmouth.

Opening Conflict In School Hard

In the opening conflict, Principal Snyder is in his office telling two students that some people say you should think of the principal as your pal. He says to think of him as "your judge, jury and executioner."

The two students are Buffy and Sheila, who we have not met before. Snyder is debating which causes more trouble. He quickly brings us up to speed on Sheila by saying that, on the one hand, Buffy has never stabbed a horticulture teacher with a trowel. Sheila smiles and tells him it was pruning shears.

On the other hand, Principal Snyder says Sheila never burned down the school gym. Buffy tries to protest, saying the fire marshal said it could have been mice.

Buffy: Mice that were smoking?

Snyder puts them both in charge of Parent-Teacher Night. The banners, the refreshments, making the student lounge friendly for adults. The winner (because they are in competition) gets to stay in school and the loser gets expelled.

Outside the school Buffy says to Sheila that it won't be so bad. They can start tomorrow. But Sheila is not interested. She waves to a guy she calls Meat Pie and disappears. Buffy looks after her and tells Xander and Willow that Sheila is what her mom sees when she looks at Buffy.

So the first two scenes set up the emotional conflict and the story arc between Buffy and her mom. While that isn't going to be our main plot, it is really the heart of the story. And it does cross over into the main action plot, though that takes a while to happen.

At 3 minutes 20 seconds in we switch to the Sunnydale Welcome sign. A classic old car runs it down. We're looking at the ground and we see someone step out. We see boots, a long black leather coat, and we pan up to peroxide hair.

Spike Starts A Spark

This is Spike, although we don't know who he is yet. But

it is a vampire who says, "Home Sweet Home." And we go to the credits.

Usually the Inciting Incident – or Story Spark as I think of it – that sets off our main plot happens at 10% in. So this is about a minute early. You could see it as the Story Spark, though, because Spike comes to Sunnydale.

Without that we would still have a story, but not the specific one we get.

As soon as we get back from the credits, we see the Anointed One in what looks like a warehouse. This child, who was the favorite of the Master, now seems to be leading the vampires. A large vampire claims he can kill the Slayer. And when he does, it will be amazing. He compares it to the crucifixion and says he was there.

At 5 minutes 8 seconds in, from behind the vampire, Spike laughs and says if every vampire who claimed to be at the crucifixion was there it would have been like Woodstock. Which Spike was at. He says something about feeding on a flower child and spending the next however long just looking at his hand moving.

No one knows Spike. He is the interloper.

So this I think is the Spark. When Spike comes into this group of vampires that is trying to figure out how to kill the Slayer. He just barges in. Then he says he can kill the Slayer, as he did a couple others.

Spike: I don't like to brag...Who am I kidding? I love to brag.

From behind him, Drusilla walks in. She's in this long flowing dress and has long black hair. She looks haunted I guess is the best word to use.

Spike turns and says she shouldn't be walking around. Dru says that the little boy (the Anointed One) has power. And she goes up to him and says:

Drusilla: Do you like daisies? I plant them but they always die. Everything I plant in the ground dies.

Even the Anointed One seems slightly spooked by Drusilla.

A More Nuanced Vampire Character

Drusilla's cold, so Spike gives her his coat and calls her a princess. They put their faces together and turn towards the Anointed One. And Spike says, "Me and Dru, we're moving in."

This is such a nice moment. This interplay between Spike and Dru.

First, we have him breaking into this group. He's the stranger. He's full of confidence. He's bragging. He seems powerful. Dru walks in, and he turns and expresses such concern for her. It is a side that we have not seen from vampires before this. What seems like a very human love and concern for another.

Spike asks the Anointed One if the Slayer is tough.

Not-So-Tough Buffy

We cut and we are at Buffy's house. She's saying "Ow: as she combs her hair because her cream rinse is "neither creamy nor rinsey."

Joyce has a flyer about Parent-Teacher Night. She suspects Buffy was not going to tell her about it. And they have a back-and-forth on what the teachers are likely to say. Joyce picks up that it probably will not be positive.

Joyce: We moved once because you got in trouble. I had to start a whole new life and a whole new business.

Buffy: And you don't want to do it again.

Joyce: What I don't want is to be disappointed in you.

I feel like this is so much worse than if Joyce had yelled at Buffy. Because we know Buffy does not want to disappoint her mom. She tells Joyce she has a lot of pressure on her, and

Joyce says, "Wait 'til you get a job. Buffy says to herself, "I have one."

Warning About St. Vigeous

That night at school, Buffy, Willow, and Xander are painting banners. Sheila is nowhere to be seen. Giles and Jenny come in talking about the night of Saint Vigeous.

Because we are approaching about 11 minutes in, this could be the first major plot point. This usually comes one quarter through, spins our story in a new direction, and raises the stakes. But I think that comes quite a bit later.

Buffy is focused on Parent-Teacher Night. She's worried about getting that done. And Giles chides her about this, saying it's more important that there might be this mystical night coming up. But she points out she can't get expelled from school. And promises to focus on the night of St. Vigeous after she gets through Parent-Teacher night.

Giles says they'll need a lot of preparation. And Xander says they can all help. They can whittle stakes or get weapons ready, whatever they need.

Principal Snyder comes in. He glares at Xander and Willow and asks if they're helping Buffy. Willow says something like, "No, no helping. We're hindering." Buffy covers for Sheila, claiming she went to get paint. And Snyder says everything better be perfect on Thursday.

Sheila appears a couple moments later. She looks really out of it, maybe high, and she thanks Buffy for covering for her. Buffy is clearly irritated with Sheila, but she doesn't say anything.

The One-Quarter Twist: Spike Sees Buffy

At the Bronze later on, Willow and Buffy are studying French and talking about how Angel didn't show up. Xander persuades them to take a break. All three of them dance. It's a really nice moment. They're having fun together.

At 14 minutes 10 seconds in Spike walks in and sees Buffy. I see this as what really turns the story and raises the stakes.

Spike studies Buffy. I feel like he is captivated by her. Fascinated. And he tells another vampire with him to go out and get something to eat.

Spike (loudly): Someone call the police. There's a guy biting someone out there.

Buffy, of course, runs out. She starts fighting the vampire and yells at Xander and Willow to get the girl he was biting away. And Buffy says something like, "A stake would be nice."

The vampire tells her he doesn't need to wait for St. Vigeous, and he says, "Spike, give me a hand." But Xander has tossed Buffy the stake. She dusts the vampire.

Spike comes out and claps. So he does give Buffy a hand, something that I don't think I noticed the first time. He says, "Nice work." She asks who he is, and he says she'll find out Saturday.

Buffy: What Happens Saturday?

Spike: I kill you.

This emphasis on the days I'm sure is purposeful. Earlier we had Snyder say this better be ready on Thursday. Now we have Spike talking about Saturday. Which we know from Giles is the night of St. Vigeous.

We flip to Sheila. She's walking in an alley with two guys saying she hopes they really have a Cadillac. They disappear one at a time. Spike appears. She asks who he is, and Spike says, "Who do you want me to be?"

Buffy, Angel, Spike

In the library Giles says, "Spike? That's what the other vampires called him?" He and the others are researching in the books. Giles says he can't be worse than other creatures

Buffy has faced. But Angel comes in through the library door. As is often the case, no one heard him walk in. Angel says Spike is worse. Once he starts something he doesn't stop until everything in his path is dead,

Buffy, though, asks Angel why he wasn't at the Bronze. And he points out she only said maybe she'd show. Buffy says he's been dating for two hundred years. He doesn't know what it means when a girl says maybe she'll show?

Willow says something like, "Wow two centuries of dating. Even if that's only two dates per year, that's – "

Buffy shoots her a look and she stops.

Exposition And Story Questions

Back at the warehouse, in what seems to be an underground room that Spike and Dru moved into, Dru lines up dolls and talks to them. She's got them blindfolded and she turns one of them around.

Spike urges her to eat something. And she says she's not hungry and she misses Prague. He says the mob nearly killed her there, and this is the place to be. The Hellmouth will restore her.

So we get some exposition through conflict, as so often is the case in **Buffy**. Before I started this podcast, I always admired the writing in **Buffy** and the dialogue. The structure of the story and the characters. I hadn't really focused at how good the writers are at getting that exposition out there without just downloading a bunch of information to us in a way that's boring. It almost always comes in through some kind of conflict like this.

Also, this dialogue is intriguing because it raises a story question about what happened to Drusilla. What is wrong with her? What are she and Spike trying to fix?

And it raises a more general question.

Before this, I don't think we had any sense that a vampire

could somehow be ill. My idea was wherever you were when you became a vampire, you froze there. So it seems that that's not true. That something happened to Drusilla as a vampire that affected her either mentally or physically or both.

In the background, we hear the other vampires chanting. Dru tells Spike to go, that the boy doesn't trust him and the other vampires all follow the boy.

Spike: All right. I'll go up and get chanty with the fellows.

That is, he'll go if Dru will eat something,

Then we see that Sheila is tied up and gagged. Dru bites her after telling her doll Miss Edith that if she'd been good, she could've watched.

Vulnerability And The Nature Of Vampires

This whole relationship between Spike and Dru is a character shift for vampires in the Buffyverse. Even Darla was limited as a character. She wanted Angel back, and we knew they had this history. But I didn't get that feeling of her really having that concern for Angel.

Spike and Dru have a connection. And Spike has so much emotional vulnerability. We can see the way that he loves Dru, his concern for her. And Drusilla has both physical and mental vulnerability. She's not weak, but she is somehow not right, somehow impaired. She gets cold. Spike is worried about her walking around.

And yet she is also very powerful. She has insights and visions.

Spike is powerful as well. Though he is not as big as the other vampires, and we haven't yet seen him fight, his very confidence tells us that he is a formidable fighter. I don't mean confidence based on his swaggering around or saying he doesn't like to brag then admitting he does. But the fact that he can have fun.

He is playful and joking, and it tells us he is not worried.

He's not worried about any of these other vampires taking him down. He's not worried about Buffy winning the fight. He can afford to have fun.

So they are both very powerful and vulnerable, which makes them fascinating characters to me.

About 21 minutes in we are at the library again. Giles is reading up about the night of St. Vigeous. Buffy has a weapon, this giant cleaver, and we see her swing it. But she's chopping vegetables and stressing about Parent-Teacher Night. Not getting ready for a fight, though her friends around her are whittling stakes.

A Subtle Midpoint Commitment

This is the Midpoint of the episode in terms of time. And usually at the Midpoint we see some sort of major reversal for the protagonist. Or a strong commitment to the quest. Or both.

Here I had to go back and really look to see if Buffy committed to anything.

I think we have a very subtle commitment. In the midst of Giles doing this research and Buffy now knows there is a specific vampire out there who plans to kill her on the night of St. Vigeous. Also, Spike worked out a plan. He sent this other vampire to lure her out. He watched her fight to study her. She also heard what Angel said about the threat Spike poses.

Yet despite knowing all this that she is up against, Buffy is committing to Parent-Teacher Night. First take care of that, then deal with this new threat. And while that was her plan earlier, she didn't have all the information then. Now she does. So I see this as her commitment.

If you had asked me before I sat down and looked at this episode whether you could have a Midpoint Commitment that was almost unobtrusive (though not soft because it's serious for Buffy) and have it still drive a strong story I might've been a little skeptical.

But it turns out that while it is subtle, it works really well here.

Comic Relief

Next we get a little comic relief where Cordelia says she is tired of whittling stakes. And Xander says she's only been at it for a couple minutes.

Cordelia: If this Spike is as mean as you all say it'll be over really quick anyway.

Everyone glares at her and she says of course she's rooting for Buffy. And she would help on Saturday if she didn't have a leg wax.

Buffy goes out. She remembered she needs to make punch. Later Willow joins her and Buffy says she made lemonade.

Willow: How much sugar did you put in?

Buffy: Sugar?

Willow, who has just sipped it, makes a face, kind of holds back choking, and says, "It's very good."

The Lemonade Three-Beat

This is the first joke about lemonade, and it's the beginning of a three beat. I mentioned this in Season One. It's where you have the same line or the same theme coming back three different times in three different ways.

Buffy tells Willow she has to keep Snyder and Joyce apart. Joyce walks in, and Buffy offers her the punch. Behind her, Willow looks at Joyce and shakes her head, which is the second beat of the joke – warning Joyce.

Snyder appears in the background. So Buffy has Willow hurry Joyce away. Snyder comes up. Buffy pretends her mother doesn't speak English anyway and she accidentally spills lemonade on Snyder. Truly accidentally.

Later, Joyce and Willow come back. Joyce comments that all the teachers magically have gone as soon as she gets to the classroom. Despite all Willow's and Buffy's best efforts, Snyder finds them. He tells Joyce, "We need to talk." They go off to his office.

Cordelia tells Buffy that when that talk is over, by the time they get to their tenth high school reunion she'll still be grounded. And Willow says to Cordelia, "Cordelia, have some punch," which pays off the joke.

The end of the three beat.

Snyder Turns Out The Lights

In the library, Giles tells us that Spike, who is also known as William the Bloody, got his nickname by driving railroad spikes through his victims' heads. He also says that Spike fought two Slayers and killed both. So now we know that Spike's bragging to the Anointed One was true.

Snyder and Joyce return to the student lounge. Joyce tells Buffy to get in the car. She is not happy. Snyder starts turning off the lights, which is really weird because there are still people milling around the lounge. I like to think it's because Snyder accomplished part of his purpose already. He got Buffy in trouble, and in his view now it's time for everyone to go home.

But it probably also is in the script for a practical reason. It's scarier.

Because Spike bursts through the window a couple seconds after that with a group of vampires.

Another Turn In School Hard

Spike says he couldn't wait for Saturday. This is all about 26 minutes in, and it could be the next major plot point. That usually comes at the three-quarter mark through the story, spinning the story in yet another new direction. It should grow out of the protagonist's commitment at the Midpoint.

And here in a way it does because Buffy is so committed to Parent-Teacher Night that she is here in the student lounge. She's not out of the way in the library preparing.

But I do think the Three-Quarter Turn comes a little bit later, though this is the beginning of it.

Willow and Cordelia run one way. I love that we get a moment where vampires chase them and Willow grabs this bust of some old guy and swings it at a vampire and knocks him over. She and Cordelia lock themselves in a closet and hide.

The Three-Quarter Turn In School Hard

Buffy directs the others, including Snyder and Joyce, into a classroom and barricades the door.

So this I see as the Three-Quarter Turn because Buffy is now taking charge. She is the one directing her mom and Principal Snyder despite that up to this point she's been struggling to keep them apart.

They in a way have been running the show in terms of the Parent-Teacher Night. Buffy's been reacting to their demands. But now she is the one who knows how to handle this.

She says, "Get in here," and people listen. Because she has that authority of seeming like she knows what to do.

A vampire tells Spike he doesn't know where the Slayer went. Spike is angry and he says – because Spike is a bit of a showman – that this vampire is too old to eat. But he twists the vampire's neck and says, "But not to kill. I feel better."

Giles, Joyce, Snyder

In the library, Giles tells Xander to go out, there's an exit behind the stacks, and find Angel.

In the barricaded classroom someone comments, "Did you see those guys' faces who broke in?"

Snyder says he's seen it before. It's a gang on PCP. They have to get out.

Buffy: No, you can't do that. You'll get killed if you leave here.

Snyder: Who do you think you are?

Buffy: I'm the one who knows how to stop them.

Buffy tells Joyce not to worry and climbs up into that drop ceiling (where we found Marcy's things back in Season One Out Of Mind Out Of Sight).

Spike is out in the hall. He's calling out to Buffy. Another vampire hears her. They figure out that she's somewhere up in the ceiling, but she crashes down into the library just as Giles was about to go out and help fight. She tells him she wants him to stay in the library because she has to go fight, and if she doesn't make it she knows he'll make sure her mom gets out.

Back in that classroom, another man wants to go out the window. He's panicking. Joyce tells him not to be an idiot. And Snyder says something like he's starting to see where Buffy gets it.

More Vampires Attack

Vampires are using an ax to break through the door. The guy who was panicking goes out the window. Immediately, a vampire grabs him. Joyce barricades the window again.

Outside the school we see Angel vamp out and grab Xander.

Then quickly we are back inside. Buffy kills a vampire in the hallway. The one who was trying to get into the classroom. Joyce only sees part of it. She doesn't see that he's a vampire.

Dramatic Irony

Sheila appears. She's not in vamp face. She pretty much looks like when Buffy last saw her. And it's not strange to

Buffy that she just turns up because that's what she did before.

So she says there's these weird guys outside. And Buffy says, "Yeah I know. They're trying to kill everyone." Sheila grabs the ax and says, "Oh, this should be fun." She's behind Buffy.

So we have here dramatic irony. Where we as the audience know something that Buffy does not. We know she's in danger immediately from Sheila.

Spike's History With Angelus Revealed Through Conflict

Angel drags Xander into the school and brings him to Spike. And Spike says, "Angelus. I'll be damned." Angel kind of scolds Spike for not guarding his perimeter and says he taught them better.

So again we're getting that bit of conflict that tells us exposition. That Angel and Spike know each other, and Angel somehow mentored Spike.

Spike asks him about the new Slayer. Angel says she's cute but not too bright. She fell for the tortured puppy dog act, and he says it keeps her off his back when he feeds. And Spike laughs and says people still fall for that Anne Rice routine?

This back-and-forth also raises some great story questions. Because yes, we know there's a connection between these two, but we don't know what it is. Also, there's a tension. Because we don't know for sure that Angel is just trying to fool Spike.

I feel like when I first watched this, I felt fairly certain about that. I don't think that I thought that Angel was truly evil and had been hiding it all this time, but I really can't remember.

Xander, though, definitely believes Angel is evil Because he's saying, "I knew it. I knew it."

Xander: Undead liar guy.

Angel offers Spike a bite of Xander's neck. He says they can drink together.

We switch back to Buffy. Sheila is about to attack, but through that hole in the door Joyce sees it and warns Buffy. Buffy fights Sheila and slays her. Then she gets everyone out of that classroom.

Buffy herds them out of the building, but she won't go herself. She still has to help other people.

Spike's Insight

Back to Spike and Angel. Spike is asking why is Angel scared of the Slayer and whether the tortured thing is really an act. And Angel says he saw Buffy kill the Master. That's why he's afraid of her or would rather avoid her.

Spike pretends he's going to drink. They both lean in, but Spike punches Angel. He says something like, "You think you can fool me? You were my sire. My Yoda." And I love that Spike knows that Angel is conning him even though it's clear that Spike and Angel have not seen each other forever. Probably for a hundred years.

So we see that Spike has a lot of insight into people.

Spike sends the other vampires after Angel and Xander. They run out of the school. Later we will see them fighting on the lawn. So Angel is not available to help Buffy.

Spike Appreciates Human Lives

Spike: Fee, Fi, Fo, Fum, I smell the blood of a nice ripe girl.

Buffy is behind him. She has the ax, and he has some kind of weapon. And Buffy says, "Do we really need weapons for this?" Spike kind of laughs and says no, but he likes them. They make him feel all manly.

And again Spike is fun, and he's kind of poking fun at himself and at the other vampires. He throws down his weapon. So does Buffy. Which tells us something else – that Buffy has rules when she fights. If she says we don't really need weapons and he throws his down, she doesn't then go ahead and use hers. She throws her weapon down as well.

Spike says the last Slayer begged for her life, but Buffy doesn't seem like the begging type.

Buffy: You shouldn't have come here.

Spike (laughs): No, I messed up your doilies and stuff.

I also like this about Spike. I feel like the vampires we've seen to this point don't really pay that much attention to what humans are doing in terms of knowing what's happening in their lives.

Or they only pay attention so they can hunt the humans and kill them. The Master focused a lot on Buffy. But we don't get the feeling he appreciated what day-to-day human life is like or that he cared.

And I find it interesting and fun that Spike is also kind of saying, though he's going to kill Buffy, that messing up her little Parent-Teacher Night was kind of mean of him. And he says as a favor, he'll make it quick. It won't hurt.

Buffy: No, Spike. It's going to hurt a lot.

The Worthy Adversary

Watching this made me think of the concept of the worthy adversary. When writing notes for the podcast, I couldn't recall exactly the definition or where I had heard the phrase. But it is not a unique phrase to Buffy and Spike. I looked around and I did find on TV tropes.org a definition of the Worthy Opponent:

"When the hero and the villain clash repeatedly over time they may develop respect for their opponent's abilities. After all, their adversary is able to keep rising to oppose them battle after battle. In the heat of battle the hero or villain's true capabilities and determination could be revealed. Or perhaps one of them was simply looking for a challenge. For whatever reason, the battles have created a sense of respect."

And later it goes on to say:

"What matters is that the character in question acknowledges and respects their opponent for their skill. Should one side actually come out on top or find the other has fallen, it may lead to sympathy for the devil or sympathy for the hero."

I feel like that is what we are starting to see here with Buffy and Spike. This respect for one another.

While I did not think of it when I was writing my **Awakening** series, I suspect this is part of where one of the adversaries for my main character Tara started developing and became a worthy adversary. He was barely a character in the first book. And then each book after that he became more and more interesting to me and more and more of a focal point. He is the one person who truly treats Tara, who is a young woman, with respect when sometimes even her family members and her allies don't.

So it was interesting to see this with Spike and Buffy and think about how much that might've influenced my own writing and what I did with my characters.

The Climax: Joyce Joins The Fight

We have some great fighting between Buffy and Spike. Then we see Joyce. She is about to leave the school, but she hesitates.

We flip back to Spike and Buffy. Buffy has been getting the better of the fight. At least I think so. Maybe some of it is that I'm rooting for her. Spike then grabs a board and hits her. She slams into the wall and down on the floor. He is on the upswing with this board when from behind Joyce clocks him with that ax and says –

Joyce: You get the hell away from my daughter.

Spike: Women.

And he storms off.

Before I re-watched for the podcast, I remembered Spike saying something much cooler than that. I feel like as Spike develops more as a character, he would have found something wittier to say. But we'll leave that where it is.

So that was the Climax, which is our last major plot point. I see it starting with the confrontation with Buffy and Spike. But I feel like the real resolution is Joyce hitting Spike. She gets to be that pinnacle of the story and protect her daughter.

So we resolve both the main plot of Spike trying to kill Buffy, and the main emotional plot – I'll call it that rather than trying to call it a subplot – of Buffy and Joyce.

Falling Action: Joyce As Protector

Joyce then says to Buffy, "Nobody lays a hand on my little girl."

And I love this moment. It's rare that we get to see Buffy being protected by anybody. In particular, we're so aware that Joyce really cannot protect Buffy. She is trying to figure out how to guide her daughter who has all these issues. She doesn't understand that the reality is that nearly all the time she cannot do anything about what truly plagues Buffy.

And it's so wonderful to me that here she is able to truly and directly help Buffy with them.

This is part of the Falling Action. It's the place in the story where the writer ties up loose ends and resolves any subplots that haven't been resolved. There's a lot of loose ends here to tie up.

More Falling Action

Snyder stands outside. There are cop cars everywhere. So

remember I said in Season One that eventually the cops would start showing up? Here we see them in force.

There's a guy, Bob. I think Bob's a detective because he's wearing a suit. He and Snyder talk about the bodies all over the place. Bob says one guy was pulled out a window and killed.

Snyder: I told him not to go out that window.

That line gives us even more insight into Principal Snyder. He does not hesitate to pretend he took a different position to make himself look better. I guess that didn't surprise me. We could have guessed that about him.

But here we have it made explicit.

Giles and Jenny come out of the school. He tells her he would understand if she started avoiding him. But she takes his hand instead.

Xander and Angel are kind of bickering. Xander says why didn't Angel hit Spike first? Angel says he needed to know if Spike bought his act. Xander says, well, what if Spike had bitten him?

Angel: We would've known he bought it.

Story Questions In The Falling Action

Back to Snyder and Bob. They're talking about what to tell the press. And this is probably my favorite series of quotes in this episode.

Bob: The usual? Gang-related? PCP?

Snyder: What did you have in mind? The truth?

Bob: The usual. Gang-related. PCP.

I like this so much because of the repetition of "usual gang-related PCP" but with such a different inflection. It also tells us so much about what at least some people in the police department know and don't. And about Snyder's communication with the police and the authorities in Sunnydale.

At the same time it raises story questions: Do the authorities know it's vampires? Is there a plan for dealing with this more so than just on a one-off basis?

These are interesting questions to keep us going through the series.

Cordelia and Willow are still stuck in the closet. They weren't able to see what happened. They concluded all they could do was pray. Cordelia is saying out loud a long-winded prayer, kind of rambling on tangents.

Willow: Ask for some aspirin.

Cordelia starts to include that and then says, "Hey!"

Spike Has Enough Of The Anointed One

Now we get to the last loose end to tie up, which is Spike's promise to kill the Slayer.

Drusilla asks Spike if the Slayer hurt him.

Spike: A Slayer with family and friends. That sure wasn't in the brochure.

He also asks her, "How is the Annoying One?" Which I also like because again we get that irreverence from Spike. And Dru says he doesn't want to play.

Spike says he better go in and make nice. So he goes to the other vampires, and he gets on one knee before the Anointed One and says he couldn't kill the Slayer.

The Anointed One says Spike failed. Spike says he offers penance.

Another vamp goes into this rant, saying Spike should forfeit his life. Spike starts to say that he was rash and if he had to have it to do again –and then he stops and laughs and says –

Spike: Who am I kidding? I would do exactly the same, only I would do this.

And he grabs the Anointed One, puts him in this cage (that is just conveniently, there – I don't know what it was supposed to be for), and locks it. And the cage is on a pulley system.

Spike pulls the cage up into the sunlight.

Spike: From now on we'll have a little less ritual and a little more fun around here.

And we pan up to this smoking cage.

The first time I saw this episode I did not understand what happened. Because I didn't realize the Anointed One was a vampire. Maybe that sounds like how could I have missed it? But even as I re-watch, we never see the Anointed One, I'm pretty sure, in vamp face. I thought he was just this supernaturally chosen little kid. It took me a while to figure out.

It must've been when I was able to watch the DVD and replay it that I got that Spike brought the cage into the sunlight and dusted the kid.

Dru smiles at the end of the Anointed One. And Spike says let's see what's on TV. And we end on that smoking cage.

A Game Changer

This is a game changer at the end of the episode. A cliffhanger is where you don't resolve your main plot. But you end your story anyway. So the audience or reader is left hanging and has to come back to another installment to learn the resolution.

With a game changer, on the other hand, the main plot resolves, but something major changes.

So here the plot of Spike trying to kill Buffy resolved, but everything changes because Spike kills the Anointed One. And he and Dru take over.

I really like this because we've introduced this different type of vampire. Or, really, two different types of vampires. Spike with his kind of freewheeling fun. Not about the ritual. And Dru who is both somehow not well and has some sort of second sight or visions. And they have this passion for each other.

These are very different kinds of leaders than the Master or the Anointed One who, though he was a child, was very serious all the time. I think this was a good choice for the writers. It got them into a new place where maybe on the vampire side we will have even more interesting stories.

Spoilers And Foreshadowing

EXPULSION

Snyder says in the first scene that whoever loses gets expelled. So this is the second time we've gotten that foreshadowed and it's only Episode Three. And it is Buffy's worry as she prepares for Parent-Teacher Night. One, she really wants her mom to not be disappointed in her. But, two, she does not want to get expelled.

The Tortured Puppy

We also have Angel, when he is trying to con Spike, referring to his tortured puppy act. It made me wonder if the writers already were thinking ahead to the episode **The Wish**.

In that Season Three alternate universe episode, a demon grants a wish that Buffy never came to Sunnydale. So when she does get there in that universe, Angel is locked up. The Master still exists. And Angel is referred to as the puppy, and he's being tortured. Later on, probably just because the writers like this language, when Willow is trying to talk in code about getting bitten in front of someone who doesn't know about vampires, Willow tells Buffy she got bit by an angry puppy.

It's a great example of the writers using a specific language for the show that resonates with fans. And it's sort of an Easter egg for fans like me. I felt excited when I realized the tortured puppy reference started here.

Who Sired Whom?

Going to more serious foreshadowing, there's the whole Spike-Angel-Drusilla relationship. Later, it will be retconned a bit. Here, when Angel is trying to con Spike, Spike says that Angel was his sire. Xander asks what a sire is. Which is a great way to bring out something the audience doesn't yet know. And to reassure the audience members that they didn't miss anything. That the show hadn't explained that yet.

It also raises a nice story question: What does the sire relationship mean exactly?

We get more details later, but we find out that Drusilla actually sired Spike. Turned him into a vampire. I'm thinking that the writers didn't know that part of the history yet.

Which is interesting because we will hear a fair amount about Angel and Dru in this season. But maybe they hadn't quite figured out all the interlocking parts yet.

Spike And Spikes

I love the reference to Spike driving spikes through the heads of his victims. Because we will find out that the night that Spike is turned into a vampire, while still human he read poetry to a group at a party. And it was made fun of. One of the guys who made fun of it said he'd rather have a spike driven through his head than listen. So, filling in the blanks, I'm assuming that he is one of the first people Spike sought out, and that's why he drove a railroad spike through the guy's head.

That doesn't come until Season Five. I would love to

know if maybe the writers just came up with that nickname and that bit of history to make Spike seem fierce. And then they created that backstory about the poetry later. Or whether they always knew that it was part of Spike's origin story as a vampire.

That Angel couldn't fool Spike – we will see in the coming seasons how Spike is able to read people. And how he often uses that to manipulate people. But also it helps him just survive. He picks up on what is going on around him, including in a way that many humans in the show do not.

Future Deals With Spike

The throwing down of weapons between Buffy and Spike foreshadows their dealings going into the future. When Buffy makes a deal was Spike, she keeps her side of the deal and he keeps his side of it. We'll see that so many different times. Including in the finale in Season Two when they make this pact to help each other for different reasons.

We'll also see, though, that Spike doesn't go overboard with that. As here. He's losing the fight. He threw down his weapon earlier, but he picks up a board later. And in the finale, he does what he says he'll do, but he doesn't go in to try to help Buffy fight or survive or not get killed. His view is "not my problem" and he leaves.

Also, not a foreshadowing of the finale, but just something fun that the finale will call back to. We will see that great scene at the end of the season where Joyce sees Spike again. They're sitting in her living room and she says, "Have we met?" And he says, "Yeah, you know, get the hell away from my daughter."

What's On TV

Also, you have that last line Spike has: "Let's see what's on TV." It foreshadows that Spike and TV will be an ongoing – theme is probably too strong – an ongoing aspect of his character. When he eventually moves into his crypt in a cave, somehow he gets power because he has a TV. He likes to watch his stories on the telly.

He and Joyce bond at one point over that. I think it's the show Passions. Joyce discovers he watches and says something like, "Oh, do you think Timmy will get out of the well?" This so fits Spike's character to me. He understands people. He watches people. Their relationships and their interplay with one another. So of course he likes that type of show, or maybe that's where he gets some of his insights about people.

And he is a very dramatic character. He plays for the audience. Whether it's an audience of vampires, or whether it's just for his own entertainment, Spike likes a good story.

More On Worthy Adversaries

A little more on the worthy adversary concept. Buffy and Spike are in that category for one another. Over and over they will **not** kill each other. They will try, but they won't do it.

And eventually they have this relationship. You can see part of that even from here. From that first moment Spike sees her. And from Buffy saying, "We don't need weapons, do we?"

There is a great interview with James Marsters, the actor who plays Spike, on the podcast Buffering the Vampire Slayer. (You can find a link to all my references in show notes at LisaLilly.com) If you are not spoiler sensitive, this is such a great interview with James. He talks about how Spike was supposed to die. I think it says in Season Two. Fairly early. Spike was supposed to come on, just be a villain, and get killed off pretty quickly. And he was told to play it just like that.

Just be a villain.

But James said that he figured out that to not get killed off, his character had to be something more than just the bad guy. So he did his best to make Spike come across even more vulnerable than he was written and have more personality.

The whole interview is really fascinating.

Jenny And Giles

My last little foreshadowing, very small. But we have Jenny and Giles, and he's saying, "I would understand if you started avoiding me."

Of course, we will see Jenny does exactly that when we get to **The Dark Age**, the episode about Giles' past. Jenny herself is taken over by a demon Giles raised when he was a young man. And it will be so traumatic and so difficult for both of them.

I was surprised to see that was very much foreshadowed here. We have relatively little about Jenny and Giles in each of these episodes, but the writers make such great use of the moments we do have.

Questions For Your Writing

- **In what ways is your protagonist vulnerable?**
- **Does your antagonist also have areas of vulnerability? What are they?**
- **If you're writing an installment series, what's your hook at the end of your story?**
- **Do you include a game changer? Could you?**
- **Does the worthy adversary as**

antagonist idea interest you? How could you use it?

Next: Inca Mummy Girl

NEXT WE'LL TALK ABOUT **INCA MUMMY GIRL**. IT'S A one-off episode where we get to know Xander, including his flaws, much better. We'll also talk about the emotional arcs, weaving in a new character, and foreshadowing changes for Willow.

CHAPTER 4
INCA MUMMY GIRL (S2 E4)

THIS CHAPTER TALKS about **Inca Mummy Girl**, Season Two Episode Four, written by Matt Kiene and Joe Reinkemeyer and directed by Ellen S. Pressman.

In particular, we'll look at:

- **a clear Inciting Incident**
- **how Xander, a very flawed character, draws the audience in**
- **emotional character arcs with major commitments**
- **the perils of ignoring previous developments**
- **weaving a new character into an ongoing series**

Okay, let's dive into the Hellmouth.

Opening Conflict

We start with our Opening Conflict. This is the conflict

to draw the reader into the story, whether or not it relates to the main plot.

Here, it does.

Buffy, Willow, and Xander are walking outside toward a museum. Buffy is complaining that it's so unfair she has to have a complete stranger living with her for two weeks as part of the cultural exchange program. And we can imagine it will be hard for Buffy to hide her secret identity with someone staying with her. Xander, though, thinks this melding of two cultures is beautiful.

Inside the museum, Cordelia is looking through photographs of the exchange students. She says hers is Sven, "100% Swedish, 100% gorgeous, 100% staying at my house." Buffy has not seen a photo of her exchange student.

She kind of shrugs when either Xander or Willow asks about what the student looks like. But she does say he is guy-like. Suddenly Xander doesn't think the cultural exchange program is such a great idea.

Does Buffy Always Resort To Violence?

We see a new character, Rodney. He is scraping at one of the masks on display. Xander makes some disparaging comments about Rodney's intelligence and we get the first set of favorite quotes for me from this episode.

Willow: You just don't like him because of that time he beat you up every day for five years.

Xander: Yeah, I'm irrational that way.

Buffy says she better go stop Rodney. And Willow says she'll do it because not everything is solved by violence. After she's gone, Buffy says to Xander that she doesn't always use violence. And Xander tells her what's important is that she believes that.

Willow is very nice to Rodney and gently leads him away from the idea of damaging the mask. It turns out that she tutors him, and he seems to like her. But, as we'll see, she doesn't really discourage Rodney from vandalism, and it does not end well for him.

The museum guide says that the human sacrifice is about to begin and leads them into an exhibit with the mummy. She was an Incan princess sacrificed at the age of sixteen to protect her people. A stone seal now protects her.

While they're in the exhibit and standing near the mummy, Buffy and Xander talk further about the exchange student, Ampata. Buffy says she's picking him up at the Sunnydale bus depot after everyone leaves.

Story Spark In Inca Mummy Girl

Next we get our Story Spark or Inciting Incident that sets our main plot in motion. It happens about 4 minutes 51 seconds in, so a little past 10% into the episode. Rodney has broken into the exhibit. He tries to steal that stone seal the mummy holds. It breaks.

Breaking the seal seems to free the mummy, because it grabs him and sucks the life out of him.

This is such a clear Inciting Incident for the story. We know right away what this is going to be about. And it is a classic horror movie trope – the mummy.

Buffy And Giles Argue

After the credits we see Buffy and Giles training. He's holding up these big pads. She is punching really hard, and it is obviously jarring for him. They're having an argument because she wants to go to the cultural exchange dance. He says no because she's the Chosen One.

We get another great quote.

Buffy: Just this once I'd like to be the overlooked one.

She also tells him, "Come on, Giles, budge. No one likes a non-budger."

Eventually, after more training Giles says yes. Because

Buffy makes the point that having a student staying with her means she needs to act like she has a normal life. Also, I think the training helped persuade him because we get a nice Giles comment: "I'll just go and introduce my shoulder to an ice pack."

Xander Forgets Kissing Willow?

Buffy and Xander, alone in the library, are talking about the dance. Xander wants her to go with him and Willow. If he and Willow go alone, it'll seem too much like a date. And Buffy says come on, in all this time he's known Willow he's really never thought about her lips?

Xander says, "I love Willow. She's my best friend." Which makes her not the kind of girl that he thinks about her lips very much. Willow walks in behind during Xander's lines. Her face lights up when he says she's his best friend and he loves her and then just falls when he says the part about how he doesn't think about her lips.

Alyson Hannigan is so expressive here. She tells so much through her face.

I don't like this scene, though, because we're completely ignoring that Xander almost kissed Willow in the first episode of the season. I don't buy that Xander would forget that. The way this is played, it seems like he has. I don't feel like it's directed or acted in a way that tells me Xander remembers that and feels weird about it and doesn't want to tell Buffy about it. It really seems more like it never happened.

It's one of the rare times in the series where I feel like there is still that holdover from when each episode of TV had to be self-contained and could almost ignore what happened before. When I went back and watched one of my favorite shows, The Bionic Woman, from the seventies, I saw how much of that there was. I feel like that's what's happening here.

I also am pretty sure the network must have wanted – or maybe the producers and writers wanted – to keep that Willow/Xander romantic tension spooling out. And rather than address that almost-kiss, they liked starting almost with a clean slate with Willow and Xander. As if that never happened. So we can have more tension there and not follow up on that moment.

But it makes this episode feel off, and it makes Xander seem like more of a jerk than I believe he's meant to be.

Willow doesn't say anything about overhearing. She tells them that Rodney is missing.

It Sinks In Rodney's Missing

The three of them joke around about how maybe Rodney broke in to see the mummy and it came alive and killed him. And then they all become very somber as they realize that's probably what happened, given that it's Sunnydale. Giles says he's not convinced, but they should go to the museum just to rule out evil curses.

Buffy: One day I'm going to live in a town where evil curses are generally ruled out without saying.

At the exhibit they find the stone seal is broken but the mummy is there. Seemingly from nowhere, a man with dark hair in a ponytail (who is wearing what looks to me like a white martial arts training or karate suit) comes out. He attacks them.

Then he sees the mummy and he runs away.

Everyone is really shaken. They're about to leave when Willow looks more closely at the mummy. She asks Giles if the Incans were very advanced. He says yes and she asks if they had orthodontists.

We see that the mummy has braces, which Rodney also had. They all realize that this is Rodney, turned into a mummy.

Giles takes the part of the stone seal that is still left. It has pictographs and writing on it. He says it'll take weeks to translate.

Meeting Ampata

When they're back at the library, Buffy realizes she's late. She forgot she has to pick up Ampata. Xander tries to persuade her that that's not important.

Of course, she has to go there. She's not going to leave Ampata at the bus station.

This is one of several examples of Xander's jealousy over anyone that Buffy might possibly be interested in. In retrospect, it gets on my nerves.

Here, though, it serves a purpose. Because we're going to see him fall for Ampata. So we get that switch, and I feel like that's why we need these early scenes where he's fixated on Buffy.

Changing Views Of Characters And Stories

Each time I rewatch Buffy, it's at a different time in my life. And a different time in what is going on in the larger world. I very much grew up in, I think, the same world as most of the writers in terms of the decades we were young. There was definitely that idea for girls that if a boy (or when you're older a man) was interested in you, and you didn't feel the same way, you somehow owed that person something. You owed it to them to date them and "just give it a try."

Or if you did go out for a while, and you still didn't feel that way, there was the sense that they had a right to comment on anyone you dated. If you got involved with someone and it didn't work out, there would often be an attitude of "Well, that's what you deserve because you have this great guy here and you chose someone else."

Interestingly, to my recollection, it did not work the other way. If a girl was interested in a boy and he didn't reciprocate, and she kept having these feelings or acted possessive, she was just viewed as kind of sad and pathetic.

I like to think Xander if he grew up now would behave differently. He might still have crush on Buffy, but his sense of entitlement and that she somehow owed him – or that he could criticize anything she did relating to other people she was interested in – would be different.

Nearing The First Major Plot Turn

We are now nearing the first major plot point. It typically comes about one quarter through a story. It is from outside the protagonist and spins the story in a new direction, which we will see here. It also usually makes things more complicated or challenging for the protagonist. Which is definitely the case here.

We're not there yet, though we are 10 minutes 22 seconds in and it's a 42-43 minute episode, so nearly a quarter of the way through.

We see this young man alone. Someone out of sight whispers, "Ampata." Ampata looks around, and the mummy appears and sucks the life out of him.

The One-Quarter Twist In Inca Mummy Girl

When Buffy arrives and calls out for Ampata, this very beautiful young woman steps out. And this moment is what I think of as the One-Quarter Twist. It's 11 minutes in and it really turns our story in a new direction.

Everyone is surprised that Ampata is a girl. Xander is clearly smitten with her. She finds him quite fun, and he makes her laugh. Which I can relate to. Someone who can make you laugh is wonderful thing. And she has been a mummy forever. So he's the first guy that she has talked to. She genuinely seems to have fun with him.

And Willow, we can see, feels very sad about this.

Ampata's very impressed with Buffy's house and later

Buffy's room. Buffy asks what it's like where Ampata is from. And she says it was very cramped and very dead at home.

Throughout the episode, I like that Ampata's answers are careful and honest. Everything she says is true, if you take it literally. But she answers in a way that doesn't raise suspicions. I pretty much believe she's able to do this because we're told, or we get the impression, that as she was taken around the world she listened to a lot of conversations. Learned a lot about different cultures, including the United States. So I more or less buy that she is able to put up this front.

When Buffy asks more she says, "It is just me at home." Buffy empathizes with her because Buffy so often feels isolated. And she tells Ampata she'll meet people. Ampata says she wants to fit in, be just like Buffy, and have a normal life.

Contrasts To Oz

Back at school, Cordelia is talking to Devon, a musician she's dating. Both of them are irritated with Sven, the exchange student, who is standing nearby. Cordelia is just awful. She says things to Sven almost as if he were a pet dog, like "Come, Sven." We're going to deal with that later in the episode.

After she leaves, Devon is talking to a new character, with red hair, who is winding up microphone cable. There's a guitar behind him. It's Oz. Devon asks Oz what he thinks of Cordelia. And Oz, in an ironic tone, a kind of flat voice, says yes, she's a hot girl but she's not his type.

Devon tells him he's too picky and Oz says he's not, that Devon is just impressed by any pretty girl who can walk and talk. Devon says, "They don't have to talk." We are supposed to see Devon as a jerk here. Or at least as very, very shallow.

I see Devon as clearly meant to contrast to Oz.

The Dance

Willow and Xander are talking about costumes for the dance. Xander is struggling with what to wear.

Willow: Why are you suddenly so worried about looking like an idiot? That came out wrong.

I thought that was fun. Especially because Willow just says it. She isn't saying it to be mean or because she is jealous. She's just thinking Xander never worried about looking silly before.

Buffy brings Ampata to meet Giles. Who right away asks her to translate the seal. They claim it's for an archaeology club.

Ampata tells them that the man who is pictured on the seal is something like a bodyguard for the mummy. Buffy and Giles have work to do so Buffy starts to ask Willow to hang out with Ampata. But Xander jumps in right away and says he will take Ampata around.

Willow looks after them and says, "Boy, they really like each other."

About 18 minutes in we see Xander and Ampata at the bleachers. He is explaining Twinkies to Ampata and making her laugh by showing her how to eat one by stuffing the whole thing in his mouth.

Willow Faces The Truth

Buffy and Willow are researching, but Willow is distracted.

Willow: Yes, I'm caring about mummies.

They have this great conversation where Buffy says that Ampata is only going to be here for two weeks. But Willow says then Xander will just find someone else who's not her. And at least with Buffy she knew Xander didn't have a shot.

Willow says she needs to make a choice. She can wait for Xander to go through everyone else who's not her, or she can accept that it's just not happening and move on. Buffy says good for her.

Willow: I didn't choose yet.

I love this because it is so realistic. That feeling of knowing what you need to do to move on, but just not being able to accept that and make that choice.

The Bodyguard Attacks

Based on Buffy's research, Giles thinks the killer is probably the mummy and it can feed on a person's life force. But they don't know how to find the mummy or to kill it.

Back at the bleachers, about 20 minutes in – so we are getting near the Midpoint of the episode – the bodyguard appears and attacks Xander, saying Xander had the seal.

But then the bodyguard looks closely at Ampata and says, "It's you."

I don't think Xander really picks up on that.

Back in the library, Ampata is very shaken up. She tells them they should destroy the seal, that someone could die. They are talking in code about what's going on. She gets very upset because she senses they're not telling her everything.

A Series Of Midpoint Commitments

This is very near 21 minutes, almost exactly the Midpoint of the episode. At this point, I expect to see some kind of major commitment by the protagonist or a significant reversal.

Here, what we see instead are a series of very significant commitments by the other characters. And I feel like that works. So I learned something here – that it doesn't always have to be the protagonist. Although, generally, I think that is the best route, particularly if you are telling a single story, one novel, or even one novel in the series. Then we want our protagonist to be the one driving that Midpoint.

But not something like a television series where you have

a twenty-two-episode arc or even a twelve-episode season arc. Then you can have an episode (or two or three) that are more focused on the other characters.

Here, first I see Ampata making a commitment when she says, "You're not telling me everything." Because she's letting her emotions show through. And she will make a more major commitment very shortly.

Xander is first to throw caution to the wind.

Xander: You're right. We're not telling you everything. And it's time we do.

He is about to say that Buffy's the Slayer. But Giles clears his throat, and Buffy glares at Xander. And they switch and say, okay, it's not an archaeology club it's a crime club.

A Reversal For Ampata And Willow Commits

Ampata goes out to the hall, very upset. She says she just wants a normal life. This is a reversal for Ampata. She really thought she could have a normal life, at least for a little while. And now she has this bodyguard coming after her and these friends that she's made are getting close to what's really going on.

Next Willow makes a major commitment.

She comes out into the hall. Ampata is at the drinking fountain. Xander tells Willow why Ampata is so upset, and Willow says Xander should take Ampata to the dance. I really like that. His response is, hey, we'll all go, and it'll be great. But Willow says no, he should just take Ampata.

Xander: But you were all excited about it.

Willow says no, just the two of them should go and she'll see him there.

This was so wonderful for Willow and so sad. It is her making that choice. She is looking at both what's good for Xander and what will be good for Ampata. But it is also what is good for her. She is saying, "Okay, this is how it is. You guys go to the dance." And I feel that this is a big moment for her. That she is moving on.

I think she'll still have her feelings for Xander. But this is a new direction for her. And Xander says to her, "You're my best friend," and she says, "I know."

Again, Alyson Hannigan's face – so expressive – tells us everything about how Willow feels.

Buffy Commits, Too

Buffy and Giles decide they should go back to the museum that night to see if the other pieces of the seal are there. And Buffy seems very pleased for a moment, saying, "I came up with a plan." And then she says something like, "No, wait. I have other plans. Dance plans." Then she frowns. "Canceled plans." That's about 23 minutes in.

I see that as a commitment by Buffy.

In the beginning, she was fighting so hard to go to the dance. And here she is saying, okay, she really wanted to go to the dance and have that normal life part but now she can't. It's her duty.

Ampata Throws Caution To The Wind

Ampata is really happy when Xander asks her to the dance. And they both confess that they like each other. So of course something terrible happens right away.

In the Women's Room, the bodyguard confronts her. Ampata begs him not to kill her. And he says she's already dead. She argues that she was innocent, she was sacrificed and it wasn't fair. But he points out that the people she kills now are innocent. She must die. She's the chosen one, and she has no choice.

At 25 minutes in, she throws caution to the wind, puts her hands on him, and sucks the life out of him. And kills him.

This is a very serious commitment to the quest by our antagonist.

Buffy And Ampata Hide Their Secrets

At the house, Ampata is getting ready for the dance. She asks Buffy for a lipstick. She's also asking why Buffy's not going to the dance. And Buffy says she has work to do.

Ampata tells Buffy that Buffy reminds her of the story from her people about the Incan Princess. Because Buffy always puts others before herself. Ampata relays the story of the sixteen-year-old being sacrificed to protect her people. Buffy resonates with this, for obvious reasons. As they are talking, Buffy is starting to open Ampata's backpack, which was sent over from the train station.

She almost sees boys' clothes in there. But at that same moment, Ampata is opening a drawer of Buffy's dressing table. There are stakes inside. Buffy runs over to close it and hand Ampata a lipstick. So they've almost seen each other's secrets.

Then Buffy starts to open Ampata's trunk. And we can see there is a mummified body inside but the doorbell rings.

Buffy leaves to get it, and Ampata locks the trunk with a padlock.

The Costumes

Xander arrives. He looks like one of many characters Clint Eastwood played in what were called spaghetti westerns (because they were filmed, I guess, in Italy) and he jokes about that. And this further confirms my view that someone in the writers' room was a Clint Eastwood fan.

At the dance, Devon's band is playing. He's the singer. Oz is in the background playing guitar. Cordelia is wearing what looks almost like a bathing suit with a sort of skirt bottom and a flower in her hair. Willow, on the other hand, is wearing a fur coat with the hood up around her face and holding a spear.

Cordelia looks at her and says as a joke, "Oh, I almost wore that."

Later when Ampata comes in, she compliments Willow on wearing an authentic costume, and she seems genuine about it. Willow, seeing Ampata's beautiful dress, says to herself, "I guess I should have worn something sexy."

We see Cordelia complaining to her friend about Sven. How he follows her around and he doesn't understand anything. And she says to him something like "Get punchee" and "Get fruit drinkee." So obnoxious.

Later Cordelia's friend is nice to Sven and is talking with him. And he says in perfect English, "What is wrong with Cordelia? Is she even from this country?"

Three-Quarter Turn In Inca Mummy Girl

We are moving toward the Three-Quarter Turn. This plot turn spins the story in a new direction though it grows out of the Midpoint. And here it starts around 31 minutes 36 seconds in.

Giles shows up at Buffy's home instead of meeting her at the museum. He tells her the bodyguard was found mummified in the restroom. And unlike what Ampata told them, the man in the stone seal is not a bodyguard for the mummy. He's a guard to keep the mummy from escaping.

Buffy checks Ampata's trunk and finds the mummified corpse.

Buffy: What kind of girl travels with a mummified corpse and doesn't even pack a lipstick?

This is a major new direction for our protagonist because she and Giles realize Ampata is the mummy. We knew that, but Buffy did not.

Who Is That Girl?

Back at the Bronze, Xander and Ampata are dancing. They both seem so happy. As they start to kiss, her hands start to mummify. Xander doesn't see it, but she feels it and runs away from him.

Before that, though, Oz and Devon are on stage. Oz says, "Who is that girl?"

Devon thinks he means Ampata and tells him about her being a foreign exchange student. But Oz is pointing to Willow, and he's definitely very taken with her.

Giles and Buffy are on their way to the museum but realize that Xander is in danger. So Buffy decides to go to the Bronze. Giles will head to the museum alone.

Ampata, at the Bronze, finds this high school boy who looks a little bit lost and lonely he sitting by himself. I think he is wearing some kind of cowboy hat. She draws him into some isolated area of the Bronze. They start to kiss, and she starts to suck the life out of him.

He does ask her before they kiss isn't she with Xander. And she says, "Does it look like I'm with Xander?"

Stay tuned for Spoilers about this boy. For now, he is saved when Xander calls to Ampata, distracting her. The boy runs off.

Xander In Danger

Xander asks why Ampata ran away. She starts to cry and tells him she's very happy and very sad but she can't tell him why. It's a secret. Now they do kiss. Her dried hands grip his face as she starts to suck the life from him. It's like she can't help it.

And we cut to a commercial. Another great hook before that commercial comes in and you potentially lose the audience.

Afterwards Ampata does break away from Xander. She

says, kind of under her breath, "No, I can't." She tells him she's sorry.

Giles is at the museum fitting the seal together. He's very close to finishing it. Ampata somehow feels this. She runs away, leaving Xander.

Buffy comes into the Bronze. She finds Willow and tells her Ampata is the mummy. Willow says at first, "Oh good," and then she says, "Xander!" They run to find Xander.

Oz comes up and is about to talk to Willow. But she has disappeared with Buffy. And he says to himself, "Who is that girl?"

Heading For The Museum (And The Climax)

Willow and Buffy find Xander and they all head for the museum. Giles is there alone. He is still fitting that seal together.

If you look too closely, the timing doesn't work here. There aren't that many pieces to the seal. I suppose Giles could have been hunting for it and gradually piecing it together. But it seems kind of crazy that Ampata was at the Bronze, we had all these things happening, and somehow she gets to the museum before Giles finishes.

But it does make for a good Climax. He is just about to put the last piece in. Ampata sneaks up on him and tries to kill him. We are getting our climax of the main plot (to stop the mummy). But also of Xander's emotional arc and Ampata's as well.

Buffy interrupts. She stops Ampata from hurting Giles. They fight. Ampata throws Buffy into the coffin and closes the lid on her.

The Climax Of Inca Mummy Girl

Xander and Willow arrive. Ampata grabs Willow and tries to suck the life out of her. Xander yells at Ampata to let Willow go. Ampata says that they can be together. She just needs this one more. Let her have this one. Otherwise she'll die and that will be it.

42 minutes, 5 seconds in, Xander says if she wants a life, she'll have to take his and can she do that?

This is the true climax. The pinnacle of the story. Ampata says yes. She grabs him and starts to suck the life out of him.

Buffy frees herself and pulls Ampata away as she is disintegrating.

I like that Xander stands up to Ampata. We see not just that he will protect Willow, but that he is not willing to be happy at the expense of other people.

I don't think we ever thought that Xander would make a choice to say, "Okay, I'll be with this mummy girl who has to kill people to stay alive." But it is in the heat of the moment. It's good to see that Xander does not hesitate even for a second to stop Ampata. To basically sacrifice himself in Willow's place, though he probably thought Ampata was going to say that no, she couldn't take his life.

But I believe he really meant it. "If you want to take someone's life, you have to take mine."

Falling Action In Inca Mummy Girl

We have a very short Falling Action section. Less than a minute where we tie up loose ends.

Willow comforts Xander at the museum. The next day, Xander and Buffy are walking together. He says he has the worst taste in women ever. And either here or earlier in the episode he calls back to having fallen for the teacher who was a praying mantis.

Buffy, though, tells him Ampata wasn't evil. That she really cared about Xander. She also says Ampata got cheated. She had her life taken away from her. Buffy remembers how she felt when she found out she was chosen, and says she wasn't exactly thinking about doing the right thing.

Xander points out that she did and that she gave up her life. Buffy says, "And I had you to bring me back."

And that is the end.

Xander-Focused Episodes

I find it interesting how many episodes in these early seasons focus on Xander. On the one hand, as I mentioned in earlier episodes, he's not quite a sympathetic a character, especially when we view him two decades later.

In other ways, though, there are aspects that I think everyone can identify with. Everyone has fallen for someone who doesn't return their feelings. Which we also have with Willow.

And I think everyone has had that feeling, especially during high school years, that they will never figure these things out. Xander has this feeling not just that Buffy's not interested, but that he is rejected over and over again. His fear is that this this is what his life will be. And then at the end we get that fear that okay, here was someone who did want him, but there was something so wrong with her. And his feeling that, "Okay yeah. When I do find somebody, I choose someone who's evil."

All of these things are things that audience members can identify with.

We also have some great things to model in Xander even looking back two decades. I love that he admires Buffy's strength. I'd love to say that of course any guy should be comfortable with a strong woman. But we really had few representations of that in our stories at the time.

Spoilers And Foreshadowing

Jonathan

The boy we saw Ampata try to kill at the Bronze is Jonathan. He will turn up several different times in the series, including at the end of the next episode, **Reptile Boy**. That's the first time we'll learn his name.

He becomes increasingly more important.

At first, we keep seeing him as sort of the butt of jokes. Mostly, though, we see him as a sort of generic victim, or the generic nerdy high school boy. Which is what will happen in **Reptile Boy**.

Eventually, he will drive some very pivotal episodes in **Buffy**. Including in Season Four when he alters the entire world for an episode and gets to be in the credits looking very cool.

But the first time he really comes into focus for the show is in Earshot, in Season Three, where we think at first that he's the villain of that piece.

Later, Jonathan will become an actual villain in Season Six. I find his character arc the most interesting of the trio of the villains in Season Six because we do see him so early on as both a victim and a fairly nice guy just trying to get by. And because, even as a villain, he's the one who seems not to grasp the true darkness and evil of what he's doing until it's too late. I think he tells himself that he's having fun, getting back at people who hurt him or at least realigning his position in the world, and that's all okay. It takes far too long for him to see that he's one of the bad guys. Yet, I feel some sympathy for him all the same.

Oz

The other major character who comes in here is Oz. I

love this subtle introduction of him. I don't know if I picked up on how important he would be when I saw this episode the first time. But I really like that he is this very reserved young guy who doesn't say a lot and has this dry wit. And that he is so taken with Willow from the moment he sees her.

It's so much fun the next time they cross paths in the Halloween episode where she's wearing the ghost costume. They literally cross paths, but he doesn't recognize her. Not until he sees her much later, at the end of the episode, without the costume.

I'm also looking forward to talking about Oz and that relationship. It will be key this season, and in Season Four will give us one of the most heartbreaking episodes of **Buffy** ever. Make that two of the most heartbreaking episodes. One when he leaves and one when he comes back.

But there's a lot to go before we get to that, starting in the next chapter with **Reptile Boy**.

Questions For Your Writing

- **What sets off your main plot? Is it clear?**
- **Do your key characters have flaws? What are they?**
- **What aspects of those same characters might your readers empathize with?**
- **Are there ways that more than one of your characters can make a major commitment toward the middle of your story?**

- **If you're writing a series, or a particularly long novel, how are you tracking important developments? (So you don't "forget" about something like that almost kiss between Xander and Willow.)**

Next: Reptile Boy

NEXT WE'LL TALK ABOUT **REPTILE BOY**. WHILE IT'S A Cordelia-focused episode that at first appears self-contained, it includes a key development in Buffy's relationship with Giles.

CHAPTER 5

REPTILE BOY (S2 E5)

THIS CHAPTER TALKS about **Reptile Boy**, Season Two Episode Five, written and directed by co-executive producer David Greenwalt.

In particular, we'll look at:

- **universal themes**
- **the effect of major plot turns in unusual places**
- **how the story prompts a key change in the Giles and Buffy relationship**
- **when you can have a character tell the moral of the story**

Okay, let's dive into the Hellmouth.

Opening Conflict

The opening conflict is a quiet one. Xander and Buffy are braiding Willow's hair as the three friends try to figure out what's happening in an Indian soap opera they're watching on TV. The dialogue is in Hindi, and there are no subtitles.

Willow and Xander sort of complain about having no money and nothing to do. Buffy, though, says she's happy because it's quiet all over Sunnydale.

We then move on to a violent conflict. About 2.5 minutes in we see a large house. A girl crashes through an upper-floor window, climbs down, and runs. Someone in a monk-like robe follows her, chasing her. She runs through the trees and climbs a wall to go into one of the many cemeteries in Sunnydale.

In the cemetery, three guys in robes chase her. Yet another one appears in front of her and grabs her. He calls her Callie and tells her she can't get away. After taking his hood off, he looks right at the camera. He's blond and good-looking and appears to be around college age.

This moment could be our Story Spark or Inciting Incident. This is a little bit early because normally that comes at about 10% through our story. Here, while it does set off a story, it does not set off the true arc of the episode. That arc has to do with Buffy and the choices that she makes.

And we will see that happen a little later.

For now, we switch to credits. And come back to see Cordelia practicing a fake laugh in the hall. She explains to her friends that Doctor Debbie says to draw in a boy or man, you need to make serious eye contact and really listen. And laugh at all his jokes.

As they walk down the hallway, Buffy tells Willow about a sexy dream she had about Angel. Willow says something like, "Oh, you two are so right for each other, except for –" And Buffy says except for him being a vampire, and she's the Slayer.

Willow says they could go out for coffee. It's not a date, it's a caffeinated beverage, "non-relationship drink of choice."

Xander: What's like a relationship?

Buffy: Nothing I have.

Xander overhears Cordelia talking about how she's dating college guys only, and they make fun of one another. Cordelia gets in the last insult.

Cordelia: I just know your pizza delivery career will take you so many exciting places.

Story Spark In Reptile Boy

Around 5 minutes 59 seconds in, so a little bit later than 10%, we get what I see as the true Story Spark or Inciting Incident of the episode.

Buffy tells her friends Giles won't be upset that she's a little late for training because things have been so quiet. Giles takes a completely different position. Just because things are quiet doesn't mean Buffy can slack off. Now is the time to patrol even more and train even harder.

And Buffy says something like, "Okay, in the five minutes between seven and seven-oh-five in the morning, can I do what I want then?"

I see this as the Inciting Incident because it will drive the choices Buffy makes. She feels very frustrated at being treated like a child. She can be ordered around by everyone at the same time as she has all these adult responsibilities. So it will set her off to accept when Cordelia later invites her to a fraternity party.

Greenwalt's Take On The Theme

I had already been thinking this moment was the Inciting Incident, and then I watched the episode again with the DVD commentary by David Greenwalt. He said that he thinks Buffy is at its best when the theme is clear. Here, he says the theme is Buffy feeling like she's being treated like a child by the adults in her life. And she rebels against that and it has terrible repercussions.

Also, he sees Buffy being, like many teenagers, at the cusp of adulthood and yet still a child.

And in my view it's even tougher for Buffy because she has more responsibility than most adults ever have.

That Greenwalt sees this as the theme of the episode – and what drives the story – confirms for me that this is the Inciting Incident. Giles is pushing and pushing and pushing Buffy. Also ordering her around. She's kind of pouting and he says this isn't getting to him. And he tells her: "We all have to do things we don't like and you will come for hand-to-hand training and you will patrol."

He really does speak to her as if she is a little kid who is just being difficult and refusing to listen. He also ends by saying she needs to be there after school and "don't dawdle with your friends."

Buffy Dawdles With Her Friends

Of course, the next scene is Buffy outside after school. Willow and Xander are chatting with her. And they say, "Hey, what are you doing?" And she responds: "I'm dawdling. With my friends."

A very nice car pulls up. I wish I could tell you what type, but I'm just not a car person.

Richard is driving. He is the guy we saw in the cemetery where we got such a great look at his face. So we know it's him. He has a friend, Tom, in the passenger seat. Cordelia runs to the car. She does her fake laugh when Richard asks her to come to a little get together at "the house."

Tom sees Buffy and is interested.

Richard (to Cordelia): Who's your friend?

Cordelia: She's not my friend. (Catches on that Tom

wants to meet Buffy.) She's more like a sister. We're that close.

Cordelia, looking unhappy, goes over to Buffy and says the guys want to meet her.

Buffy: I don't really want to meet any fraternity boys.

Cordelia: And if there was a God, don't you think he'd keep it that way?

She drags Buffy over. Richard calls her sweetheart and is generally a jerk and she turns to walk way. But Tom intervenes.

Tom Flirts With Buffy

Tom apologizes for Richard. He makes few jokes and is kind of self-deprecating. He says he feels like a dolt standing there, yet here he stands in all his doltishness. Xander is watching and saying "she's gonna walk away, she'll never fall for that."

But Buffy seems to like Tom, who's a history major and a senior in college. He tells her he only joined the fraternity because it meant a lot to his father and grandfather. He asks her to come to the party. But Buffy says she can't, she's seeing someone.

Tom jokes about talking too much and rambling.

Buffy: You know, people underestimate the value of a good ramble.

Nearing The First Major Plot Turn Of Reptile Boy

Giles comes out and points to his watch, irritated. Buffy goes inside.

We are nearing the first major plot point that turns the story in a new direction. In my book **Super Simple Story Structure** and in the templates that I have available, I call it the One-Quarter Twist. Because quite often you see it exactly at one quarter through a movie or book.

Here, I think it comes quite a bit later, although there are some shifts here that could qualify.

First, we see Buffy in the graveyard. She finds a broken bracelet. Angel appears and tells her there's blood on it. He can smell it. (There isn't enough to see.) This is about 11 minutes 31 seconds in, so that is a quarter way through roughly this 42-43 minute episode.

And we have this shift or turn in the emotional story because Buffy says something like, "Wouldn't it be funny to see each other when it wasn't about blood and violence?" Angel says, oh, she means she wants to date, and pretty soon she'll be asking him for coffee.

Buffy: Coffee?

They have a back-and-forth. Angel is saying he's two hundred forty-one years old, she's sixteen. She says she can do the math. But he's telling her she's young, she doesn't know what she's she wants. He's trying to protect her. He also says things could get out of control.

Buffy says isn't that how it's supposed to be? Angel warns her that it's not a fairytale. When he kisses her, she's not going to wake up from a deep sleep.

Buffy: No, when you kiss me, I want to die.

They have this very dramatic moment and she runs away.

Overdramatic Line?

That line really is not one of my favorites. I wish I could remember how I felt when I first watched it.

Now it seems over-the-top and overdramatic. But it is probably accurate to the very dramatic situation Buffy is in. And that she's sixteen, and this is the first time she has really fallen in love.

In the scene-by-scene commentary director and writer

Greenwalt said this was one of his favorite lines. And he pitched it to Joss Whedon and was so pleased when Joss agreed to use it. So he obviously felt this was a great line.

No One Takes Buffy Seriously

The argument is a significant turn in the Buffy-Angel relationship. They have indirectly talked about their feelings towards each other, but this is the first explicit conversation about dating or having a relationship. Even the word dating tells you a lot. Because for Angel, what would that mean? He can't take her to a movie or take her out to dinner.

So it truly highlights the difficulties.

And it is a turn because this is a second person who is important in her life, whom Buffy loves, who is saying: You're a kid. You're too young. You don't understand what's going on.

Which is really frustrating and upsetting. It makes her feel no one is taking her seriously. I still think, however, that our first major plot turn comes a little bit later.

Cordelia Asks Buffy To The Party

At 13 minutes 52 seconds in Cordelia finds Buffy alone at school and says something like: "Did you lose weight? And your hair – " And then she says, "Okay, I respect you too much to lie. And the hair – well, that's not the point."

Cordelia explains that Richard's fraternity needs some sort of balance at the party. But Cordelia was so busy really listening that she didn't hear exactly what that's about. All she knows is Buffy has to come or Cordelia can't go to the party.

She tells Buffy she's not being selfish. She's thinking of all the good she could do with the money because this is Richard Anderson of Anderson Farms, Anderson Aeronautics, and Anderson cosmetics. Which brings Cordelia near tears.

The One-Quarter Twist

I see this invitation, and Buffy's acceptance, as the One-Quarter Twist because it's coming from completely outside of Buffy. It's also something we wouldn't expect to see before this episode. Cordelia inviting Buffy, not just to a party, but somewhere where she really wants to make an impression. Because while she liked Buffy in the beginning, and she does seem to admire her, she also views Buffy and her friends as outcasts. She called them lepers at some point. Or one of her boyfriends did.

So we wouldn't expect Cordelia to invite Buffy to something where Cordelia wants to build her own popularity.

But she does so, and at 14 minutes 36 seconds in Buffy says she'll go. And this takes the story entirely in a new direction. Because even though the finding of the bracelet would presumably prompt Buffy eventually to investigate, she wouldn't be at the fraternity party.

Naming A Demon

Next we see all these fraternity boys in the basement wearing robes. Doing this ritual. They're pledging themselves to Machida.

In the commentary, David Greenwalt said that it was really hard throughout the show to keep naming all these demons. He was really excited about what a great job he did coming up with Machida. And then later he saw that name on some of the tools that the grips were carrying around. Even though he spelled it differently.

(I looked it up in on IMDB and then I searched Google. And there is a toolmaker Makita, which has to be what Greenwalt was referring to. And, interestingly, they spell it the way I saw the name in my head: M A K I T A.)

Bad Things Happen There

Our fraternity guys are chanting, going through these

rituals. Then they break out the beer when they're done. And we see that Callie is chained up in the basement.

We switch to Buffy, Willow, and Xander talking. Buffy says that she's going to a fraternity party with Cordelia. Willow says, "Cordelia?" and then asks if she sounded jealous. Because she's not. She also says she is worried about Buffy going. She's heard things about fraternity parties. That there's lots of drinking and maybe orgies and bad things happen there.

Buffy, though, is focused on her feeling that nothing happened with Angel and nothing ever happens because he treats her like child. Xander chimes in about how terrible that is, criticizing Angel. Until he realizes she's going to the party with Tom. And he says something like: "Buffy, really? Frying pan, fire."

So we have a little more of jealous Xander, though I feel like he is funnier here in that he is so open about it.

Lies In The Library

In the library, Buffy shows Giles the bracelet. Xander jumps in and says "she" should patrol that night and the rest of them should research. Giles agrees that "she" should do that.

Buffy: She's standing right here, and she's not available.

Then she tells Giles that she doesn't want to patrol tonight because she has a lot of homework. And her mom isn't feeling well, and, well, to be honest, she's not feeling that well herself.

I really like this line because it's the sort of overkill that someone who feels guilty about lying might do. She gives not just one excuse but three of them.

Also, she throws in "to be honest." Which, as a lawyer, when you're learning about preparing witnesses to testify, you learn that often "to be honest" or "to tell the truth" is a cue the person was lying before or is about to tell a lie. Because most of us, if we are generally honest, don't walk around telling people how honest we are. We don't need to do that.

It also can be just a verbal tic for some people. All the same, I tell my witnesses to try not to say that.

Giles, though, says of course she should stay home. I love that he's very concerned about Buffy.

Willow is really upset about this. She doesn't tell on Buffy. But when they're out in the hall she says, "You lied. You lied to Giles." Buffy says she just wants to have some fun for a change. So we get one of those cuts that I love where we pick up on that line.

Because Cordelia says, "This isn't about fun. It's about your duty." The duty to help Cordelia achieve prosperity. She gives Buffy a list of rules to follow. What she can wear. What she can say.

Buffy bangs her head down on the table.

The Rule Of Three

Xander decides to go to the fraternity party to keep an eye on Buffy. And Willow says, "You want to protect her? Show you're as good as those rich guys? And maybe catch an orgy." And he agrees.

These lines show the Rule of Three, which is that, often, to say three things is very powerful. For whatever reason that kind of sticks with people, it resonates. That also could be part of why we got three excuses from Buffy.

Here, Willow has three things she says. And the last one is kind of the payoff of her joke. For whatever reason if you try it with four or with two it just doesn't work quite as well.

Transparent Richard

At the party, Richard comes up with drinks for Cordelia

and Buffy. Buffy asks if there's alcohol in the drink. And he says, "Just a smidge." So she doesn't want to drink it.

Richard: I understand. When I was your age I wasn't into grown-up things either.

This is so smarmy and it's such a transparent attempt to manipulate Buffy. I'm glad that she doesn't fall for it, even though it hits on exactly what has been bothering her. That she has all this adult responsibility yet is being treated as a child.

I like to think it's because Richard is so transparent, and Buffy sees what he's doing.

Buffy Sips A Drink

Cordelia and Richard disappear, leaving Buffy alone. She is standing there kind of awkwardly. A guy across the room lifts his glass to toast her. And she picks up her glass and sips it.

This happens around 23 minutes in. As I talked about last chapter (and talk about every week on the podcast), usually at the Midpoint in a well-structured story we will see the protagonist fully commit, throw caution to the wind or suffer a major reversal.

You could see this as that sip as throwing caution to the wind because Buffy is doing something she just refused to do. But it doesn't feel big enough to me. I read it as she feels really awkward and alone. She'll take this little sip of the drink because at least someone has sort of said hello to her, and she'll look like she's fitting in a little more.

But I don't see her as deciding, "Okay, I'm going to drink at this party."

Another obnoxious fraternity guy intervenes. He yells, "New girl," and charges drunkenly toward her.

Tom "Rescues" Buffy

Tom appears and kind of sweeps Buffy away and they dance.

In the meantime, Xander sneaks in a window. He looks more polished than we usually see him. He's got his hair combed back. He's wearing khakis and a polo shirt. And he almost blends in at this party. He just misses seeing Buffy.

About 25 minutes in, as they're dancing, Tom says how glad he is Buffy came to the party. And we again feel like maybe he is kind of a nicer guy. Because he can clearly see that Buffy is not happy about being there. And he remembers she said she was seeing someone. She hesitates before answering.

Tom: You're not seeing someone?

Buffy: Someone's not seeing me.

So he asks why she shouldn't be there. She's tries to explain, but of course she can't really. So she's talking vaguely about responsibilities and obligations. And he says he likes that she's mature, but there is such a thing as being too mature.

Tom Manipulates

I love this manipulation by Tom. I don't mean I love that he does it. But I like the way this is written. Years and years ago I read a book **The Gift of Fear: Survival Signals That Protect Us from Violence** by Gavin de Becker.

In it, the author (who I believe ran a security company) was giving advice about how to avoid dangerous situations and how to spot predators. One of the things he highlighted is that this is the kind of thing a predator will do. Acknowledge that you are being smart or cautious or whatever it is (or mature). But say that you can overdo that.

So if someone you don't really know offers to help carry something for you, you might say, "I don't really know you." And the person would say, "That's good you're cautious about strangers. You should be. But there's such a thing as being too cautious, and then you don't let anyone help you." It's a manipulation technique that often works.

Here we see Tom doing that. We don't know yet that he is one of the guys who worships Machida. He has hit on what will work with Buffy, though. Because she says, "Oh, you think I'm too mature?" So much better at it than Richard who tried to make her feel like a child.

Xander At The Party

We switch to Xander, who is joking with some girls. Richard and his friends see him. One of his friends is that same obnoxious guy who yelled at Buffy. They start yelling, "New pledge. New pledge." Later we'll see that the frat boys' idea of humiliating Xander is to dress him up in wig, put lipstick and a stuffed bra on him, and make him dance.

I like Xander in this episode. He puts up with this when he could just leave. But he really did come to see that Buffy and Cordelia are okay. And he has not seen Buffy yet, so he is staying despite that you can tell he does not want to be here and is uncomfortable.

Buffy walks outside onto the terrace and steps on some broken glass. She looks up, sees the boarded-up window. And she's holding a glass shard. When Tom and Richard come out behind her, though, she drops the piece of glass.

Richard hands Buffy a drink. And Tom makes a toast to maturity.

Buffy Really Throws Caution To The Wind

Buffy says, "What the hell. I'm tired of being mature." And she downs the drink.

This is almost 27 minutes into the 42-43-minute episode. This is pretty late to see this throwing caution to the wind by the protagonist. But this to me is the moment because although she doesn't grasp how much danger she's putting herself in, she drinks this whole drink. And we definitely get the idea Buffy has not had much alcohol up to this point. She was going go to this party to have fun, but not to drink.

So this choice is the Midpoint Commitment.

My view on this was confirmed when I listened to the Greenwalt commentary. He called this a crucial turning point.

He also mentioned that the network wanted to cut some of the Xander parts of the story. And that Greenwalt was very happy that he was able to fit in the scenes showing the way Xander gets treated.

I can't help wondering, though I do like the Xander side of the story, if that's what throws off the structure here. I like this episode, but it rarely stands out for me as a particularly strong one, and the structure is part of why. Particularly this Midpoint Commitment coming so late.

I'm not saying that this doesn't work at all. In fact, I think it's a good example to show that whatever structure you use, there is always flexibility.

I talk about the structure I describe in my book **Super Simple Story Structure** because it works for me to look at major plot turns. Generally, if you put them at the one quarter, one half, and three-quarter marks you keep your story moving along and you avoid the kind of sagging that can happen at the middle. A lot of writers know their story's beginning and its end. But they hit the middle and feel stuck and don't know where to go.

But if you focus on that major commitment or major reversal for the protagonist at the halfway mark, it ensures that your story becomes more gripping at that point rather than flagging.

The Bracelet

Back at the library, Willow and Giles are trying to figure

out where the bracelet came from. Willow discovers there is a missing girl from Kent Prep School. And we see a picture of Callie.

They also eventually realize that one girl has been missing at the same time every year. So it's some sort of anniversary for that.

At the party, Buffy is stumbling. She's alone, she's near the stairs, and she seems very drunk. Much more than anyone could be from one drink. She can't really see where she's going. Everything is fuzzy.

She sees Xander dancing, wearing that wig, but she doesn't recognize what's happening. She's bumping into things, and she climbs up the stairs and passes out on a bed.

Richard comes in, turns her on her back, and touches her neck.

Tom appears in the doorway and yells at him to stop. And for a second we're meant to think he's a good guy. He's stopping Richard from assaulting Buffy.

Three-Quarter Turn In Reptile Boy

Well, Tom is stopping Richard, but not because he's concerned about Buffy. He says Buffy is not there for Richard but for the pleasure of the one they serve. He says that's also true for the other one. And we see Cordelia on the floor.

That is 29 minutes 39 seconds in.

This to me is the next major plot point. Usually it comes around three quarters through. It generally arises from that Midpoint either commitment or reversal, but it spins the story in yet another new direction. Here, it clearly comes from Buffy downing that drink, and making that commitment: "I'm tired of being mature. I'm going to do what I want."

Turning The Story On Its Head In Act Three

Greenwalt also commented on this point. He said in the

best stories, Act Three turns the story on its head, gives us this complete flip. He says the best example is **The Witch** (from Season One), where we learn that it's not Amy doing these spells and things to the other girls. It's her mom in Amy's body.

I agree that this is great way to look at the shift to the last part of the story. Whether you divide it like I like to do in quarters so you have this flip it on its head for that last quarter or you view it as a three-act structure.

In the three-act structure, Act One includes roughly the first quarter or third of the story. Then there is a turn. Act Two spans what I would see as the middle two quarters, and then there's Act Three, which is that last third or last quarter of the story.

So he's talking about that structure and saying at the end of Act Two you should have something that turns the story on its head. I really love that because I have always just thought about another new direction. Now I think I will look at it more as he does.

And ask if I can make that last major plot point just turn the whole story on its head.

Here, there is definitely a turning of the story on its head. Greenwalt makes the point that we find out that Tom, who seems like the nice guy, is actually scarier than the scary guy (Richard). Because Tom is a true believer.

We find out the fraternity and their alumni get all the success and money because they keep making the sacrifices. So I read Richard as doing all this to get the benefits. But Tom seems like he really believes in Machida. He wants all the benefits, but he also is truly devoted.

Willow Keeps Buffy's Secret

At the library, Giles is telling Willow they need to call

Buffy. Willow says no. Remember, Buffy's sick. And her mom is sick.

But when they find out about more girls missing, Giles is more determined to call Buffy. He wants to know where was that bracelet found. Willow says, "Call Angel. He'll know. He was with Buffy."

So she is still keeping Buffy's secret. But we see her feeling more and more kind of frantic about it and struggling to come up with how to do it.

Back at the frat house, we see Xander being thrown out. The frat guys give him back his clothes, but they throw him out the door and make fun of him some more.

Buffy Became Vulnerable

In the basement, Buffy and Cordelia are awake. But they're chained up next to Callie. Buffy tells Cordelia that those drinks were drugged.

31 minutes in we see a ritual with three stones in a bag. The frat boys are pulling them out. At first it seems like maybe they're going to choose one of the girls. But then it's clear that it's just what order they'll be sacrificed in. There's this pit towards the back of the wall. Cordelia is worried about being thrown into it, but Buffy figures out that some sort of demon is going to come to them.

A Fuzzy Three-Quarter Mark

This comes at the actual three-quarter point of the story. So you could see this as the Three-Quarter Turn, but I do think that happened when Buffy passed out on the bed. Because that's when she became so vulnerable. That's what arose from the commitment she made to down that whole drink, and it's what puts her in this position where she cannot fight the way she normally could – not only to protect herself, but to protect these two other girls. And I believe it's the only way these frat boys could ever have gotten an advantage over Buffy.

Though you could also see the real turn as the discovery that the frat boys are sacrificing girls to a demon. That does switch the story from dealing with the frat boys to dealing with this demon. We did, however, as the audience know about some sort of demon worship all along, even though Buffy didn't know it.

This question is another example of where the structure in the story is just a little bit fuzzy. It's not as clear of a turning point as we usually see in **Buffy**.

But we do see definitely that there is an escalation of tension, conflict, and danger.

Raising The Stakes

The stakes have to become higher and higher in whatever story structure you use.

Generally, you'll start with conflict. And whether it's the same conflict that escalates or you have increasingly serious different conflicts, you will see that increasing tension, increasing danger, throughout the story.

There may, though, be some ups and downs. Moments where you have comic relief or you give your characters a little bit of a break. But overall if you were to graph out the conflict, the line should be going on a diagonal heading up.

And that is happening here. Because now we have these three girls chained. This demon is going to rise. And Buffy's in this position where she is weakened.

Calling Out Angel

At the library, Giles has called Angel. Angel appears in person. He tells them that Buffy found the bracelet in the cemetery near the fraternity house.

Here is where Willow finally tells Buffy's secret. Because

now she has to protect Buffy. And she says Buffy's there and she went there with Cordelia.

Giles: She lied to me?

Willow: Well –

Angel: Did she have a date?

Willow kind of hesitates and then she gets mad at both of them. And says Buffy only went there because Angel brushed her off. And she turns to Giles and tells him that he is pushing Buffy too hard. Yes, she's the chosen one, but he's killing her with all the pressure. She's sixteen going on forty.

And then Willow turns back to Angel and says –

Willow: And you. I mean, you're going to live forever and you don't have time for a cup of coffee? Okay, I don't feel any better, and we still have to help Buffy.

Greenwalt said he loved seeing this side of Willow. That he always enjoys being able to show a new aspect of the character that we know well. And we see her getting angry and really telling off Giles and Angel. Telling them things that they need to hear.

The Team Goes To The Fraternity House

They go to the fraternity house and run into Xander. He is wearing one of the monk-like robes. He found it in the trash.

Just before that, we had a really nice moment where he was walking and grumbling to himself about how one day he'd have money and prestige and on that day those guys would still have more.

And then he saw Cordelia's car. (She has Queen C on her license plate, which I love.) So he stayed around. He looked in the windows. And he tells the others he saw the guys in robes in the basement, or heading for the basement. He put the robe on thinking it will get him back into the house.

Angel vamps out. He's ready to fight. And I love that Xander looks at him and expresses admiration for him. And respect. It's really nice to see that because he has been so petty and jealous about Angel. And I love seeing him realizing, hey, this is someone we want on our team.

Fighting The Frat

Xander's monk robe does get the guys inside to open up the door. Xander punches the first one he sees. It hurts his hand, but he gets a good punch in. And there is fighting among all of them. Giles also is fighting.

There's a funny moment where Xander is just wailing on the big obnoxious guy and yelling something like, "This is for the lipstick, and this is for the bra, and this is for the last sixteen years of my life."

In the basement, a giant snake demon has arisen from that pit. Buffy tries to distract him from Cordelia. Tom tells her she can't speak to Machida. No woman is allowed to speak to him. Buffy finally breaks the chains.

Upstairs Willow is yelling at everyone something like, "Snake. Basement. Buffy." Because Xander, Giles, and Angel have all gotten a little too absorbed in that fight with the frat boys. They start running down the stairs.

The Climax: Buffy Fights Tom And The Demon Snake

In the basement, Buffy frees herself. Tom is fighting her. He's got a sword, and he's saying he's going to serve Buffy to the demon in pieces. Buffy tells him, "Tom, you talk too much." She defeats him, but the snake still has Cordelia.

Buffy uses the sword to sever the demon snake from the rest of his tail. And Machida falls to the ground.

So our climax started with the fight when the demon arose and Buffy struggled to free herself. And it played out through her both confronting Tom, who is the one who brought her into this, and the demon itself and slaying it.

Falling Action

Falling Action wraps up whatever we have left hanging from our plot.

So first we have Cordelia and a little bit of comedy. She says, "You did it. You saved me." She runs toward Buffy. Except Angel has come down the stairs. Cordelia isn't thanking Buffy, she's thanking Angel. And she hugs him.

Cordelia: You guys. I just hate you guys. The weirdest things happen when you're around.

And she tells Tom he's going to jail for "fifteen thousand years."

This is where I still have mixed feelings about Cordelia. On the one hand, this whole episode (and Greenwalt mentions this) includes a theme of men sacrificing women to maintain their control and enhance their power. And now we have Cordelia still buying into this. She is the one who wanted to go to the frat party in the first place. She is all about achieving prosperity – and Cordelia seems pretty prosperous already – by getting this frat boy to like her. Now she's saved, and she attributes it to Angel, who has done little more than walk down the stairs.

And yet I do love that she turns to Tom and says, "You're going to jail for fifteen thousand years."

I also give Cordelia a tiny bit of a pass because she was quite traumatized. Maybe she didn't see what happened. So maybe she does think that Angel, Giles, and Willow burst in and saved the day. (Probably not though.)

When You Can State The Moral Of The Story

The really emotional Falling Action here, and I so love it, is between Buffy and Giles. Buffy says something like, "I told one lie. I had one drink." And she's looking very sheepish.

Giles: Yes and you were very nearly devoured by a giant demon snake. The words "let it be a lesson to you" are a tad redundant at this juncture.

I think that has to be my quote of the episode. It is yet another favorite Giles quote.

In the commentary Greenwalt also noted this line. And he said, yes, it is outright stating the theme or the moral of the episode. But he doesn't mind doing that if it has been earned emotionally.

I think that is such a great point because normally I don't like when we get a story and then the writers have one of the characters tell us what it all means. Here, though, I think it works for the exact reason that Greenwalt said. Because we have earned it emotionally. We've seen Buffy go through this, and Giles saying it seems so very true to his character and their relationship.

Also, the other reason I think it works is that line is not the end of it. That is not the only lesson from this. Because Buffy says she's sorry, and Giles says he is sorry, too.

That makes this moment a huge turning point for Giles and Buffy. He tells her he drives her so hard because he knows what she has to face. But he's not going to be so demanding in the future. He's not going to order her around. He realized he has been doing that too much, so he says he'll just do an inordinate amount of nudging.

It is perfect parenting. I know Giles is not really her dad but he is taking that role, and he could just be angry. And it's a normal thing because you fear for that person you love after they have been in danger. They've almost died, and you're so afraid. It's like when you see a kid run into the street and the parent gets them back and yells at the child.

And a lot of this is coming from that fear of what could have happened. So Giles could have reacted that way.

Instead, he didn't just scold Buffy and point out what happened.

He also examined himself. He examined his role and whether the way he was treating her contributed to this. And he grasped that if he stayed with that approach he might harm Buffy. Because basically, Willow was right. She can't be nothing but the Slayer. Buffy needs to have more in her life.

Giles to some extent has certainly recognized that before. But here he really sees that his desire to protect her and help her can be counterproductive. And that he can't keep behaving this way.

I love that he is willing to admit that he made a mistake. And to tell Buffy that, and tell her he will change.

Cordelia And Jonathan At The Bronze

At the Bronze, the boy from **Inca Mummy Girl**, the one the mummy lured into the back and was going to suck the life out of, is getting a cappuccino. He brings it to Cordelia. She chides him a bit because it is not quite perfect. It doesn't have the extra foam. So he goes back to get it.

She says, "Thank you, Jonathan." So we find out his name. And she tells her friends that young men are the only way to go.

Angel, Buffy, Frat Fallout

At a table, Xander is reading the paper. All the fraternity boys (in an example of very speedy justice) have been sentenced to consecutive life sentences. Also, the past fraternity members who were uber wealthy are now going broke. Their corporations are losing profits. There are boardroom suicides. So we know that they were successful because of all the sacrifices.

Xander: Starve a snake, lose a fortune. I guess the rich really are different.

Willow then asks if Buffy has heard from Angel and says how upset he was when he thought Buffy was in danger.

Xander: Does every conversation we have have to come around to that freak? (sees Angel has walked up to the table) How you doing?

I really like this Xander. I like that he is still a little snarky about Angel. But he's not hiding that from Angel. But he also accepts Angel as part of the picture. As part of the group.

Angel says to Buffy that he noticed they serve coffee here and maybe she'd like to go out for coffee sometime.

She says, yeah, sometime, she'll let him know, and walks away. And that is the end of the episode.

Spoilers And Foreshadowing

XANDER'S FUTURE WORK

When Cordelia makes that comment "I just know your pizza delivery career will take you so many exciting places" it foreshadows the struggles that Xander will have later on. Unlike his friends, he doesn't go to college. We see him in a variety of jobs. I don't know if he ever delivers pizzas, but he drives an ice cream truck. He tries selling protein bars. He does a number of things to figure out how to make a living and get out of his parents' basement.

It is such a scathing comment from Cordelia, the way she delivers it, which also foreshadows that Xander will feel he doesn't fit in with his friends when they go to college and he is not there.

Snake Monsters And Alcohol

Machida is one of many demon snakes that we will see in **Buffy**. (Also lizards that look like snakes.) Including the

Mayor in Season Three, who will turn into a giant snake demon. So it's fun to see that so early in the series.

Also, this clearly foreshadows other episodes about the evils of alcohol, particularly one of my least favorites, Beer Bad. Which, like all the **Buffy the Vampire Slayer** episodes, has some great moments. But unlike all the **Buffy** episodes, it's one that I almost never want to re-watch. Usually when I do, I still find it fun, but it is quite heavy-handed with the "alcohol bad" message.

Reptile Boy is a sort of an early version about how bad it is to drink.

History Majors And Defaults

I noticed something early on with Tom. He says he's a history major. Well, who is the other guy Buffy becomes interested in who is a history major? Parker Abrams? Who is such a jerk. And also a frat boy. While as far as I know he did not worship a demon snake monster, he treats Buffy terribly.

It makes me wonder if somebody in the Writers' Room had something against history majors.

Or is it just one of those default things that comes to mind?

We all have those as writers. Things that we put in for backgrounds of characters and don't always realize that we are repeating.

Here, it's that Tom, the supposed nice guy, is so much like Parker. Both pretend to be nice, and funny, and self-deprecating. And they're both major manipulators. And history majors.

Jonathan

Of course, the biggest foreshadowing is Jonathan. Green-walt in the commentary said that Danny Strong, who plays Jonathan, is a great comedic actor and he was a lot of fun to work with. So after the first time they kept asking themselves as writers where else could they use the character of Jonathan so that they could have Danny back.

I also looked up Danny Strong and Jonathan on Wikipedia and here is what Strong said about the character development. He said he initially auditioned for the role of Xander, but he lost out to Nicholas Brendan. He appeared in the unaired **Buffy the Vampire Slayer** pilot in a bit part. And he said: "I think everyone is sort of like Jonathan. Either they're like Jonathan or they're trying to cover up their Jonathan qualities."

Questions For Your Writing

- **What is the theme or point of your story? What conclusions might your readers draw about life from it?**
- **Is your theme one that you think will resonate with a lot of readers?**
- **Does your story include strong major plot turns at the expected spots? If not, why not? What effect do your plot turns have on the story's momentum?**
- **Do important relationships change in your story? If yes, do the events of the plot justify the change?**
- **If one of your characters states the moral of (or the theme of) the story, does that make the story stronger?**

Might it be stronger if you left it for the reader to figure out?

―――――――

Next: Halloween

NEXT WE'LL TALK ABOUT **HALLOWEEN**, INCLUDING SIDE stories and story questions that keep the audience coming back for more.

CHAPTER 6
HALLOWEEN (S2 E6)

THIS CHAPTER TALKS ABOUT **HALLOWEEN**, Season Two Episode Six, written by Carl Ellsworth and directed by Bruce Seth Green.

In particular, we'll look at:

- **an intriguing trickster antagonist**
- **story questions that keep viewers hooked**
- **small progress in character throughlines which also help keep viewers coming back**
- **why Buffy is the protagonist though another character saves the day**

Okay, let's dive into the Hellmouth.

Opening Conflict In Halloween

We start with our Opening Conflict. We see a sign that says Pop's Pumpkin Patch. Buffy is thrown on the ground.

Hay and pumpkins are all around. She fights back against a vampire by throwing small pumpkins and gourds at him.

As they are fighting the viewpoint shifts. We see a vampire holding a video camera. He is recording the entire fight from a safe distance. Buffy finally uses another sign on a wooden stake to dust the vampire. Despite that she won, she leaves looking fairly disgusted.

This is about 1 minute 36 seconds in, and we go to the credits. After the credits we get to the conflict that is at the heart of the story.

Remember, our Opening Conflict can hint at our main plot or it can be completely unrelated conflict that's there just to bring the reader into the protagonist's (or another character's) ordinary world.

Here, we had both in the pumpkin patch. This definitely brought us into Buffy's ordinary world – yet another night of fighting vampires. We will also see right after the credits how that plays into the emotional conflict of the episode, which is the heart of the plot.

Angel Alone At The Bronze

We switch to the Bronze. But we see Angel, not Buffy. Angel is alone at a table, looking very awkward. He's glancing around, his elbows on the table. Cordelia joins him. She is waiting for Devon (who was mentioned, I think, a couple episodes ago). He is the lead singer she's dating, and it appears he is late. Or just not showing up.

She says something about how Devon thinks being in a band gives him an excuse to treat her badly. And she says to Angel, in my first favorite quote of the episode:

Cordelia: His loss is your incredible gain.

Buffy shows up a few moments later. She sees Cordelia and Angel together. He is laughing at something Cordelia said. As soon he sees Buffy, though, he heads over to her. He picks a leaf out of her hair.

Cordelia comes up behind him and says something snarky like, "Love the hair, Buffy. It just screams street urchin."

The Inciting Incident Or Story Spark In Halloween

Buffy says she needs to go. Angel tells her she looks fine but, at about 4 minutes in, she says dates are for normal girls. Ones with time to think about nail polish and facials. She thinks about things like ambush tactics and beheadings. Not the things dreams are made of. And she leaves.

This take on romance and relationships is somewhat shallow or superficial, but Buffy is only sixteen. And she is really struggling with that feeling that having fun and dating is something that maybe just can't be part of her world anymore.

We're coming to our Story Spark or Inciting Incident. That normally comes about 10% into the episode, sometimes a little bit later. Here, we are right about 10%.

These comments from Cordelia, and Buffy feeling like she just can't be in that world of dating, socializing, and having fun – which she so longs to be part of – is the Story Spark. It both sets off Buffy's emotional arc in the episode, and is why she later chooses the costume that she does for Halloween. Without that we would still have a Halloween story, but it wouldn't be this story.

After Buffy leaves, Cordelia comes up behind Angel with a large cup and says, "Cappuccino?"

Trick Or Treat Orders

At 4 minutes 29 seconds in, so a little bit past or probably right at the 10%, we are back at Sunnydale High.

Lots of Halloween decorations are everywhere. Principal

Snyder is "volunteering" students, which means requiring them to sign up to take little kids trick or treating. You can imagine that living somewhere like Sunnydale you definitely wouldn't want your little kids going trick-or-treating alone. He ropes Buffy, Xander, and Willow in though he instructs Buffy not to speak to any of the kids because they don't need her influence.

Snyder tells them that costumes are mandatory.

So this, too, could be seen as the Story Spark. Because if Snyder didn't require costumes, we also probably wouldn't have this story. Maybe the answer is we need them both. These things have to combine to incite this story.

Giles Expects A Quiet Night And Xander Gets Mad

We learn that Giles has told Buffy that, contrary to what we all might think, Halloween is generally pretty quiet. As Buffy puts it, it's dead for the undead.

Xander puts money in the vending machine. Before he can get his soda a new character, Larry, walks up and asks Xander if he thinks Buffy might go out with him (with Larry). And Larry says he heard she was fast. Xander gets angry. He grabs Larry, who is much bigger than him, and threatens him.

Larry reaches his arm back to punch Xander. But Buffy grabs Larry's arm, twists it behind his back, and shoves him up against the vending machine. And gets a free soda for her trouble. She tells Xander, "You're welcome."

But Xander is angry.

Xander: A blackeye heals, Buffy, but cowardice has an unlimited shelf life.

What Is Angel's Type?

Buffy feels bad that she has unwittingly broken the guy code. She and Willow commiserate. Buffy also tells Willow about being late for her date and says Angel wasn't mad. In fact, he was unmad, probably because he was with Cordelia.

Willow tries to reassure her, saying Angel would never fall for Cordelia's act. And Buffy says something like, "You mean showing up wearing a stunning outfit and embracing personal hygiene act?"

Buffy goes on to say she really doesn't know Angel's type. They have not talked that much. He doesn't overshare.

Willow gets an idea. And then we get a fun exchange between them where the dialogue shows what in a novel might be the characters' inner thought processes. But even there, it would be so much better this way, where our two friends play off each other.

Willow: Too bad we can't sneak in and read the Watchers' Diaries. They're full of fun facts to know and tell.

Buffy: Oh, they are, and it's too bad because they are private.

Willow: Yes, and they're also in Giles' office in his personal files.

Buffy: Most importantly, it would be wrong.

Distracting Giles

Of course, our next scene is Willow and Buffy peering through the little window in the door to the library. Buffy goes in. Giles then surprises her by coming out of the book cage.

He starts talking to her. She does her best to distract him while Willow sneaks in and goes to his office to get the diaries. Buffy runs through all kinds of topics, including asking more about Halloween. Which is a really nice way to give the viewers a little bit more information while there is tension. Because we don't know if Giles is going to turn around and see what Willow is doing.

Finally, a truly desperate Buffy blurts out that Miss

Calendar said that Giles was a babe. She is clearly making this up. Giles, though, is distracted, so she achieves her goal.

This also has the effect of reminding viewers about Giles and Jenny Calendar. We are going to see her in this episode, and it's a very nice way to say hey, remember how Giles and Jenny have this relationship starting out?

As viewers, we listen to these bits of exposition and aren't bored because we still feel the ongoing tension of Buffy trying to distract Giles from Willow's actions.

There's also some humor. Because after Buffy leaves, Giles looks bemused. I expected he was going to comment to himself about how strangely Buffy acted. Instead, he says, "A babe. I can live with that," and kind of laughs.

Nearing The First Major Plot Turn

We're now nearing the one-quarter point in the episode. Usually at that point we will see some sort of event that spins the story in a new direction and raises the stakes. It typically comes from outside our protagonist.

Here, Willow and Buffy are in the Girls restroom. They're looking through the diaries. Now, they did decide to steal the diaries, so in a way this comes from Buffy's actions. But she didn't know what she was going to find there.

What takes her attention is a drawing of what is probably a noblewoman. She is in this beautiful gown. It's from 1775 when Angel was eighteen years old and still human.

Buffy exclaims at how beautiful the woman was and says how amazing it would be to have lots of gowns and servants and go to balls. Willow argues she prefers being able to vote, or at least she will when she is old enough.

This longing Buffy has for this other life, and this fear or feeling that perhaps this is the kind of young woman that would attract or appeal to Angel, could be our One-Quarter Twist. I definitely think it is for Buffy's emotional arc.

I'm not sure by itself it is enough to turn the plot, though. That comes a little bit later.

First, Cordelia comes in. She taunts Buffy about how she kept Angel company after Buffy left. Cordelia does not believe Willow and Buffy when they tell her Angel is a vampire. She reads this as Buffy being jealous.

Cordelia: Oh, he's a vampire. Of course, but the cuddly kind. Like a Care Bear with fangs.

She then tells Buffy that Buffy may know all about this demon stuff, but when it comes to dating, Cordelia is the Slayer.

Choosing Costumes

At 12 minutes 50 seconds into the episode, so a little more than a quarter way through, Xander, Willow, and Buffy go to the costume shop.

Willow chooses a ghost costume, which is basically a sheet with eyeholes that goes over her head, completely covers her, and has the word Boo written across the chest in big letters.

Buffy tries to convince her she's missing the point of Halloween. That she'll never get any attention if she keeps covering herself up and hiding. Willow is not at all comfortable with that idea of dressing up sexy and wild, so she buys her ghost costume.

Xander gets a toy gun and says he has fatigues at home to complete his costume. Clearly, he wants to be tough and what he sees as manly. Buffy apologizes for the incident with Larry and promises to let Xander get pummeled in the future. He says okay.

The One-Quarter Twist In Halloween

Xander is still talking, but Buffy stops listening. She's distracted, drawn to a beautiful gown with a small waist and a huge skirt. It's very much like the one in the drawing.

This is 14 minutes in. I think this is the true One-Quarter Twist in the episode. The first major plot turn. It spins the story in a new direction because it ensures that Buffy will be weak during the coming chaos. Which also raises the stakes.

Xander looks at the dress and kind of scoffs. He says he prefers spandex.

The store proprietor comes out and says she looks like a princess. Buffy can't afford the gown, but the proprietor tells her he feels quite moved and will make her a deal she can't refuse.

Spike Admires Buffy's Fighting Style

We switch to Spike and the vampire who made the video of Buffy. Spike is watching Buffy fight and admiring her style. He says she's tricky.

Spike: See that? When she stakes him with that thing – that's resourceful.

Dru wanders in and she's talking about Miss Edith, her doll, needing tea. And then she asks Spike does he love her insides, "the parts you can't see?"

Spike: Eyeballs to entrails, my sweet.

He tells her that's why he has to study the Slayer and kill her. So that Dru can have the run of Sunnydale. Which I'm pretty sure he calls Sunny Hell.

This is another example of great exposition through conflict. We get very quickly that there is something wrong with Dru and that Spike is hoping that killing the Slayer will somehow restore Dru. Or at least put her in a place where she's able to feed and terrorize people and perhaps heal.

Dru tells him don't worry, she has seen everything. That something is changing and it makes Buffy weak. And Spike says, "On Halloween? Nothing happens on Halloween." But Dru says someone has come to change it all.

We're about 16 minutes in, and we see the proprietor of

the costume shop, Ethan. He cuts his hands, dabs blood on his face, and says something about chaos and calls himself "thy Faithful Degenerate Son." He is in front of a statute of Janus, a two-faced god. It looks really creepy. We see one side and then the other with two very different expressions.

Costumes On

Next we're with Buffy in her bedroom. She's wearing a black wig, lots of curly hair piled up on her head, and she's in that fancy gown. She mentions that her mom is gone for the night, and she tells Willow to come out. She can't hide all night long.

Willow emerges. She is wearing a black leather skirt and boots, a shirt with a plunging neck line and a bare midriff, and much heavier make up then we usually see. Lipstick, eyeliner, eyeshadow. She looks great, but it's clear she feels very awkward by her body language. She crosses her arms over her stomach as if to hide it as Buffy leaves to answer the doorbell.

Xander is there in his army fatigues. Very impressed with Buffy, whom he calls the Duchess of Buffonia. He says he hereby renounces spandex. She is excited for him to see Willow and says, "But wait till you see – Casper." Because Willow has come down the stairs, but she put her ghost costume on. We can't see anything of Willow. She's completely covered by that sheet.

Character Throughlines

At school, everyone gets their groups of little kids separately. We see Cordelia walking through the hall. She's wearing a tight-fitting leopard print cat costume with fuzzy ears.

Now the episode continues some character throughlines that have been going for the season: Cordelia and Devon and Oz and Willow.

Oz is putting away his guitar in front of his locker. Cordelia asks if his band is practicing that night. And will he see "Devon I'm a lead singer and I'm so cool I don't have to show up for my date or even call?" Oz says yes, but he's just going by Devon now. Cordelia tells him to tell Devon she doesn't care that he didn't show up, and she didn't even mention it, and in fact she didn't even see Oz.

So he asks well, what do I tell him? And she says something like, "Nothing! Get with the program." As she stalks off, Oz says to himself, "Why can't I meet a nice girl like that?"

Willow, in her ghost costume so nobody can tell who she is, comes around the corner just as Oz is starting down the hall. They almost collide.

And we have this wonderful back-and-forth as they are both moving to try to get around each other. It's not going so well. And we get this exchange (sorry you can't see/hear the inflection on the page):

Oz: Oh, I'm sorry.
Willow: Sorry.
Oz: I'm sorry.
Willow: Sorry.
Oz: Sorry.

And Oz walks around her. Such a nice way to further that Oz and Willow throughline the slightest bit. And again using humor and conflict so that we are intrigued and not bored.

It isn't even like we really have an Oz-Willow subplot just in this episode. It's more like we have an Oz-Willow subplot they're very slowly building. Starting with **Inca Mummy Girl** and moving just the tiniest bit in each of these episodes.

Trick Or Treat – Midpoint Reversal

Everyone is trick-or-treating. The kids are in all kinds of different costumes. Separately, we see Ethan chanting in what I think is Latin in front of the statue and a bunch of candles.

A group of little kids rings a doorbell. An older lady answers. She tells them they are adorable.

We are at 22 minutes in, so the slightest bit past the Midpoint. And we get such a strong Midpoint Reversal for Buffy. There's this wind as Ethan is chanting. All the candles blow out, and Ethan says, "Showtime."

So we also have our antagonist, Ethan, committing in full to the quest. He's clearly been preparing this, setting things in motion. Doing this ritual. And now he has thrown all in and is ready to see what happens.

It's really nice when you get that combination of this significant reversal for the protagonist and a very strong commitment by the antagonist.

All the little kids turn into real monsters and attack the old lady.

Willow tells the kids with her to stop, but she can't stop them herself. She staggers back and falls onto the porch, unable to breathe. A second later she stands, but she rises right out of the ghost costume. It remains laying on the porch. She is in her leather skirt and boots and her shirt with a bare middriff. So she didn't change out of that. She just put the ghost costume over it.

She looks down at herself and says, "Oh my God, I'm a real ghost."

Then she hears a machine gun firing, says, "Xander!" and runs to find him.

Xander does not know who Willow is. But when she walks right through him, he becomes convinced that she is really a ghost. Which makes him a little bit more inclined to believe the other things she's telling him.

A monster approaches. Xander starts to shoot. Willow

yells at him, "No, no guns. That's still a little kid in there."
She also says they just need to find Buffy.

And Buffy is in fact close by. As the monsters converge,
Willow turns to her and says to Buffy, "What we do?"

Buffy passes out, and we get another series of nice quotes:

Willow (to Xander): She's not Buffy.

Xander: Who's Buffy?

Willow: Oh, this is fun.

When Buffy wakes up, we find out she thinks it's 1775.

Wish Fulfillment

I've watched this episode so many times. Yet this is the
first time that, because I was taking notes, I realized the year
Buffy names is the same year of that drawing in the Watchers
Diaries. This underscores what Ethan will tell us later – that
this is all about wish fulfillment. (Which we will see again in
Buffy, as I'll talk about in the Spoilers.)

They go to Buffy's house because it will be safer. Buffy
doesn't recognize the house. She's very confused when she
sees photos of herself in casual clothes. She says she just
wants to go home.

Willow: She couldn't have dressed up like Xena?

Cordelia's Dialogue Holds Clues

From outside we hear Cordelia screaming. Xander lets
her into the house. Willow assumes Cordelia won't know
who she is either. And she runs through this thing, saying,
"You're name is Cordelia. You're in high school. We're your
friends. Well, sort of."

Cordelia is irritated because she knows exactly who she
is. She is not confused at all, and she doesn't know what's
wrong with Willow. And she's complaining about how her
costume got ripped and Party Town probably won't give her
deposit back.

This dialogue is such a great example of working in a

detail that the characters will later need. Willow will use it to help figure this all out. And it's done in a way that seems very natural. It comes in through Cordelia's character. It's exactly what we would expect from Cordelia. She's upset about her costume getting ripped and not getting her deposit back. Not about monsters chasing her.

So we get that little detail about Party Town.

And this is a great way to do that if you are writing a mystery. Or any story where you need to weave in clues for the reader or for your main character to figure out without making it obvious that's what you're doing.

We next see Spike roaming the streets with a group of monsters, saying how this is just neat.

Willow goes to the library to try to research and get help from Giles. She startles him by walking through the wall.

Angel comes to Buffy's house. Buffy and Xander have no idea who he is, and Cordelia tries to explain.

The lights go out. Cordelia and Xander go upstairs, or maybe to the basement, to check the electrical panel. And Buffy goes with Angel into the kitchen. The back door is open. A monster attacks. Angel vamps out. Buffy screams and runs out the door.

Three-Quarter Turn In Halloween

This happens about 31 minutes in, so it is roughly three quarters through our episode. This is usually where we see another major plot point. It typically grows from Midpoint and spins the story in yet another direction.

Here, I think it is Buffy running out the door. Despite that she is not quite herself, she makes that choice, and it comes from that reversal at the Midpoint. That costume that turns her into this noblewoman who is no longer the Slayer and doesn't remember being one. So of course she is frightened when Angel shows his vamp face, and she runs.

We also get a twist, or movement of the plot, in that Giles and Willow start to figure out what's happening. Also a nice quote from Giles, but it does inadvertently make Willow feel bad.

She says something about she's having trouble reading because she's a ghost, and she can't turn the pages. Giles looks at her and says, "The ghost of what exactly?"

Willow becomes self-conscious again and once more crosses her arms over her bare stomach. Something she had not been doing since she realized she was a ghost. Since then we have not seen her have any self-consciousness about how she looks or what she's wearing. She's been focused on helping and saving people. On solving the problem. Now suddenly she feels awkward again.

This line isn't here just to make Willow feel bad, though. It propels a conversation that leads to solving the problem.

Willow: This is nothing. You should see Cordelia's costume. It's a unitard with all these cat things.

Giles: She became an actual feline?

And Willow says she didn't. And they figure out that Cordelia got her costume at Party Town, but everyone they know who changed bought their costume at a new place. Ethan's.

This is 32 minutes and also turns the story. We don't realize it yet, but the name Ethan's means something to Giles.

Searching For Buffy

Angel, Xander, and Cordelia are on the streets looking for Buffy. So this is that new direction to the plot, this new part of the episode, where they have to find Buffy and protect her.

One of them, maybe Xander, says Buffy will be okay.

Angel: No, Buffy would be okay. But now she's helpless.

Spike overhears this and tells the other monsters all they

have to do is find Buffy first.

Giles Confronts Ethan

Giles and Willow go to the new costume shop. It's dark, and they find the statue of Janus with the face on both sides. Giles explains it represents a division of self. Male and female, light and dark.

Ethan walks out of the shadows and says, "Chunky or creamy. Oh, sorry, that's peanut butter." And he calls Giles by his first name, Rupert. Giles tells Willow to leave. He's very intense about it, so she does.

Giles: Hello Ethan.

Ethan: Hello Ripper.

This is the first time we've heard Giles called Ripper. And it is this hint about Giles' past that raises the first of several story questions about Giles and Ethan. Those are in there, I think, to keep the viewers coming back for future episodes and to make us wonder about Giles.

Pirates And Good Vampires

Our group finds Buffy just as Larry, now a pirate, is trying to assault her. Xander grabs him and punches him out. Buffy is afraid to go anywhere with Angel and Cordelia because she says Angel is a vampire.

And this is kind of funny because Cordelia still doesn't believe that's true.

Cordelia (to Angel): She's got this thing where she thinks – forget it. (turns to Buffy) Angel's a good vampire. He would never hurt you.

Buffy is sort of reassured. She goes with them. They want to find somewhere to hide. And they go to what I can only imagine is one of many, many creepy giant deserted warehouses in Sunnydale.

Xander says he has a weird sense of closure after beating up that pirate.

What They Wished For

Back to Ethan and Giles. Ethan says, "What, no hug?" And asks if Giles isn't pleased to see his old mate. Ethan also says the spell is the very embodiment of be careful what you wish for.

This made me think about Willow. Willow didn't wish to be a ghost, but she did wish to be hidden or invisible. The Janus statue, that idea of the division of self, really fits here.

On the one hand, I see Willow as wanting attention. Specifically, she has wanted Xander's attention, but I think she has gotten past that. Or accepted that that isn't going to happen. Xander really saw her and knew her, but we get the feeling she doesn't feel like anyone else does. While she wants attention and wants people to see her, she simultaneously feels uncomfortable about that and prefers to be invisible.

So in her two costumes we get both sides of that. Her conflicting desires.

Xander's wish is clearer. He wanted to be strong and able to fight and feel manly. So he became a soldier. Which for him is the epitome of manliness. We saw in the pilot that Xander equated not being able to fight vampires the way Buffy did with not really being a man.

And Buffy is also very clear. She wants just for a little while to be a girl who thinks about nothing but gowns and looking pretty and balls and romance. That is something that she feels was taken away from her. So her character completely embodies that.

Story Questions About Giles

Giles tells Ethan the spell is brutal and it harms the innocent. Ethan taunts him about being the protector of all things pure and good and how it's quite a little act Giles has going. And Giles protests that it's not an act.

But Ethan says that these kids have no idea where Giles came from.

Giles then punches Ethan when he refuses to end the spell. We don't see all of it. But as we shift back and forth from Ethan and Giles to Buffy and her friends, we get the feeling that Giles is really beating up Ethan.

Ethan's lying on the floor. It's pretty clear Giles has been kicking him. Anthony Stuart Head plays this really ominously.

When I first saw this episode, it made me wonder about what sort of dark past Giles had. And whether he was fooling everybody. He certainly seems to be on Buffy's side and helping her, but we don't really know that much about him.

Which is a great way to keep your readers or viewers wondering. And wanting to find out the rest of that story, even when the main plot in a particular episode, installment of your series, or chapter ends.

The Climax Of Halloween

We're now reaching the Climax at about 38 minutes in. So this will resolve the main plot.

Spike and the monsters break into the warehouse. The monsters are able to subdue Angel and keep him restrained. Which seems unlikely. Given what we've seen of Angel so far, he is stronger than this. But it is a great example of how as a viewer I'm willing to choose to believe for the moment that these monsters can hold Angel back because I want to see what happens.

Buffy is crying as Spike pushes her down on a table or counter. He grabs her hair, and he's ready to bite her.

Willow tells Xander, "That one you can shoot." Because she has been restraining him from shooting any of the monsters.

We switch to Ethan and Giles. Giles has finally beaten

Ethan enough, or Ethan is just ready to end this game. He tells Giles he can break the spell by breaking the Janus statue.

Giles does just that. It shatters.

We flip back to Xander, who is trying to shoot his gun. But it turns back into a toy. Buffy's black hair in Spike's hand becomes a wig again. So Spike is left holding this wig and is very startled. Buffy pops up and says, "Hi, honey, I'm home."

The two of them fight.

Buffy: You know what? It's good to be me.

Spike runs away.

So this is our Climax. We get Giles being the one to end the spell. He prevails over Ethan and breaks the statue. Buffy has her fight with Spike and repels him. And they're all able to turn those monsters back into kids.

Falling Action Begins

At 39 minutes 40 seconds in we start our Falling Action. This is where we tie up the loose ends of the plot. And there is quite a bit here to tie up.

Buffy and Xander both remember what happened. Xander says it was creepy, like he was there but he couldn't get out. Buffy agrees. Cordelia starts talking with the two of them, but Angel comes up to ask how Buffy is. Angel and Buffy walk away.

Cordelia says she thought she was talking, and it was like they didn't hear her. Xander tells her she'll never get between the two of them. He knows.

I like this because it suggests that Xander is building on what happened in **Inca Mummy Girl** and **Reptile Boy**, as he is gradually accepting Angel as part of their group. He doesn't like Angel, but he is with Buffy. That's how it is. And he can joke around a little bit about it.

They look around for Willow, but she's not there.

Willow's New Confidence

Willow is now lying on the porch. And she is in her ghost costume, just as she was when she staggered back and fell. She struggles to stand and starts to take the sheet off. Then she suddenly looks awkward and nervous again and starts to pull that sheet down over her body again.

Next, we have this wonderful moment where Willow kind of freezes and shrugs. It's like she collects herself, and maybe realizes that she's been walking around without the sheet and doing all these things and it's been fine.

So she takes it off. She walks down the stairs, drops the costume onto the railing, and leaves it behind.

Alyson Hannigan is such an amazing actress because we of course can't get into Willow's head in a TV show. And yet I feel like I did. Because of Hannigan's body language and her movements and how she plays it. I'm sure also some credit goes to the director, Bruce Seth Green who, by the way, is not the Seth Green that plays Oz, for that. And likely to the writers as well, as I'm sure Willow's actions were in the shooting script.

A Hook: Oz Sees Willow Again

Willow is looking very confident as she walks down the street. A van drives up. It has black and white zebra stripes all over it and Oz is driving. Willow crosses right in front of him.

Oz: Who is that girl?

And that is our little hook and the tiny continuation of the Willow and Oz throughline.

Buffy and Angel are in her bedroom. He asks why she thought he'd like her better looking like a noblewoman. She's wearing her sweats, and I think a tank top. Casual clothes. And she says she wanted to be a real girl. The kind of fancy girl that Angel liked when he was her age. He tells her he was bored by those girls. He always wished he could have someone exciting. Interesting. And they kiss.

Is Ethan A Game Changer?

Now we get the last part of the Falling Action. It is daylight. Giles goes to the costume shop. It's now deserted. The glass counters are empty. There are dress racks with nothing on them. And there is a note on the counter. It says, "Be seeing you."

And that is the end of the episode. So it ends not with a cliffhanger – because we did resolve our main plot – and maybe not even a game changer.

A game changer changes the whole world after you resolve the main plot. So it's not a cliffhanger, which leaves the plot unresolved to (hopefully) prompt the audience to return next time. But it does show that things will be different from now on. We don't quite have that here because we don't know if this is going to change the world.

But it is a little hook to make us wonder what the deal is with Giles and Ethan. And it tells us we will probably see Ethan again.

Character Arcs In Halloween

One of the things I love in this episode is how well it handles multiple story and character arcs. It's clear that Buffy is the protagonist, even though you could argue that Willow has the strongest emotional arc.

Buffy realizes that Angel loves her for who she is. And she doesn't need to be someone else. She doesn't need to fulfill some idea she thinks he has, or her own idea, of what being a real girl is.

Willow goes from truly being afraid to be seen, afraid to get attention, to feeling confident showing who she is. And also being able to be different ways at different times. I still think she would wear that same costume to the cultural dance, though it covers her up, because she was trying to go with the theme of the dance. But she now also can dress in a different way. She can wear something she feels is sexy and feel okay with that. Feel good about it.

So she has really expanded.

Who Is The Protagonist?

Also, it's interesting that our protagonist doesn't really save the day. Giles saves the day by figuring out it's Ethan and breaking that statue. And Willow had a huge part in that. She's the one who gave Giles the information he needed and figured out that crucial distinction about the costume shops.

Yet Buffy is clearly the protagonist. The protagonist should be our main viewpoint character, and should have an active goal that she strives to reach. Also, she should have the most at stake if she loses.

Here, Buffy has all those things.

She is our main viewpoint character. Yes, we spent some time in Willow's point of view in particular, and a little bit in Giles'. But Buffy is the one that we start out with, stick with, and keep coming back to.

She has an active goal. From the moment that she leaves the Bronze, she wants to be what she calls a real girl. She wants to be able to have fun and romance. And she actively pursues that and steals the Watchers Diaries. She chooses the dress that she thinks will make her look like the kind of girl she thinks Angel wants. Just for Halloween, she can be that girl who thinks about nothing but balls and gowns and romance.

So she pursues that and she becomes it. And she finds out it's not what she thought it would be. She eventually learns that she is happy to be who she is and where she is, but she pursues the goal throughout.

Buffy also has the most at stake if she loses. What Willow had at stake is she could've not grown as a character. She could've stayed where she was.

Buffy could've died. Because as the Slayer, when she becomes weakened she is the target. She's the one Spike wants to take out.

The Trickster Antagonist

Ethan is such an interesting antagonist.

He is the trickster archetype. Not necessarily inherently evil. Evil in itself is not his goal. But he doesn't care if he creates chaos that hurts people. His goal is chaos. He likes to watch it. He delights in it.

This makes him a very interesting antagonist because we just don't know what might happen. I feel like Ethan might've been just as happy if his chaos created problems in the demon world and they all killed each other. So it's not that he is necessarily trying to kill human beings or hurt human beings. Or even, as Giles says, hurt the innocent.

Giles' point is that hurting humans is the result. Ethan's goal could just be to confuse everyone, but that is the result.

Unanswered Questions

Ethan's also intriguing because he presents wonderful unanswered questions. We don't need them answered for the plot, which is why it's okay to leave them hanging out there. We don't know at the end if Ethan, before he set up his costume shop, knew that Giles lived in Sunnydale. He didn't seem super surprised to see Giles. So I think the answer might be yes.

Did he know Buffy is the Slayer and Giles is her Watcher? Not clear.

Was his goal to draw Giles back in? Was he doing this in part to lure Giles to him? Maybe.

All these things create great questions not just about Giles but about Ethan.

Spoilers And Foreshadowing

Darla In The Drawing

First, the drawing in the diaries looks a lot to me like Darla as we will see her in Becoming Parts One and Two, the Season Two finale. That's where we get the flashbacks of how Angel became a vampire. The face in the drawing doesn't necessarily look like Darla. But the hair, and particularly that dress, its style, evokes for me that image of Darla.

Also, Angel tells Buffy that when he was her age, he wanted to meet someone exciting. Interesting. That is exactly how Darla seems to him in the flashbacks. That's what lures him into the alley – he sees this woman and he follows her.

And it's the promise Darla makes to show him the world, or show him amazing things, that drives him to trust her. To allow her to turn him into a vampire.

Cordelia Highlights What Buffy Lost

The Cordelia-Buffy interaction also foreshadows quite a bit. Cordelia's says that Buffy may know all these things about demons but when it comes to dating, Cordelia is the Slayer. This foreshadows an ongoing clash between the two of them.

I feel Buffy is much more aware of it than Cordelia. For Buffy, Cordelia in many ways represents what she lost when she became the Slayer. She doesn't get to be the prom queen anymore. She doesn't get to just think about flirting with boys and looking pretty. Instead, she has to slay vampires and save the world.

And you can argue that in many ways this has made Buffy a stronger and kinder person with more empathy for others. I like to think Buffy had most of those qualities anyway, but it certainly brought them out in her. I think Buffy appreciates that.

But she does mourn the loss of that life, and it creates tension with Cordelia.

Cordelia on her side often seems oblivious to that.

We saw in Out Of Mind Out Of Sight that she didn't believe that Buffy was ever popular like her. Or at least she expresses that. I think she does believe it, and her putting Buffy down is a way to reassert her own position. As in, hey, this is what I'm good at, this is my world.

So I believe Cordelia has some amount of envy of Buffy. She will claim she doesn't, and she will even say, "I'm not like Buffy," more than once.

But I think part of Cordelia does want to be like Buffy. She wants to be able to fight. She wants to be part of the team against the forces of evil. Even as she denies it during the run of **Buffy**, later we will see her on **Angel** embracing that. And clearly being part of the team.

Spike And Dru

Spike and Dru – also tons of great foreshadowing there. When Spike is watching that video of Buffy and admiring her resourcefulness, the way she fights, Dru comes in. And she asks him if he loves her. This is such a strong hint of what is to come.

I did not pick up on it on my first watch of Season Two (or on several re-watches), but it really foreshadows our end of Season Two where Spike goes to Buffy for help against Dru and Angel.

He tells Buffy, and I believe he means it, that it's because he wants Dru back. He is jealous of Angel and Dru, and he wants it back to just the two of them. Also, Spike loves the world. He doesn't want the end of the world. He wants it to continue.

But I do think there is that continuing respect for Buffy. And later, I think in Season Five, we learn that Dru feels that some of the choices Spike made came from feelings for Buffy. She says something like Buffy was in his head, or Buffy is all around him. The Slayer is all around him. And Drusilla breaks up with Spike.

So this early moment with Spike studying Buffy, admiring Buffy, and Dru saying, "Do you love me?" is so telling. (She says "Do you love my insides?" but she's really asking, "Do you love me?")

Wishes In The Future

Foreshadowing Season Three is this idea of be careful what you wish for.

I find it so interesting that of our core characters, the high school ones anyway, the one who doesn't get a wish fulfilled is Cordelia. And then next season we will get **The Wish**. Which is all about Cordelia's wish being fulfilled and the terrible consequences of it.

I wonder if the writers knew that was coming and that's why Cordelia doesn't get a wish here. Or maybe it was just more fun to have her still be herself.

Also, at this point I don't think Cordelia really has anything strong that she wishes for. She seems to be on top of her world.

In Season Three, there will be many things Cordelia wishes for. When her father's in trouble with the IRS, there's no longer money for Cordelia. She can't go to the colleges she got into. She can't afford her prom dress. Everything goes wrong with Xander. And she makes that wish that Buffy never came to Sunnydale.

Here, I don't know what wish we would've given her. And I'm happy we didn't. I love the way this episode plays out. And I love that Cordelia will get an entire episode for her wish. (**The Wish** is one of my favorite **Buffy** episodes ever.)

Leading To The Dark Age

Finally, of course, Ethan and Giles. Not next episode but the following one is **The Dark Age**. Where Giles' past literally comes back to haunt him. And we will see Ethan again.

Many of the questions raised here will be answered in **The Dark Age**. Had we not had this back-and-forth with Ethan here, and this run in, I feel like **The Dark Age** would've come too much out of the blue. It would've felt more like the writers just decided to invent this back story for Giles, just to create more tension. It would feel like they pulled it out of thin air.

This way it is really led up to and built up.

One more thing about Ethan. I talked about him being the trickster. We will continue to see that about him in Band Candy, another of my favorite episodes.

There, Ethan basically gets paid to be a trickster. That scheme in Band Candy has to just be his idea of heaven. Because he's part of this game. He's paid to distribute this candy that turns all the adults basically into teenagers and creates chaos. It's like whatever your favorite thing ever to do is and someone is willing to pay you to do it.

And then down the road, of course, we will see him and Giles interacting again. We think they are bonding, and probably they are, in Season Four. But that doesn't stop Ethan from slipping something into Giles' drink that turns him into a demon. I look forward to talking about that, to talking about what Ethan's motivations were.

So much coming with Ethan. I really enjoy him as villain.

Questions For Your Writing

- Does your antagonist embody an archetype? Which one?
- Whether or not you draw from an archetype, what motivates your antagonist?
- Can you include questions early on to keep your readers turning pages? At the end of the story to engage your readers' minds and bring them back to your next installment (if you're writing a series or planning a sequel)?
- If you're writing in installments, are there character throughlines you can develop?
- Is it clear which character is the protagonist? Why or why not?

Next: Lie To Me

NEXT WE'LL TALK ABOUT **LIE TO ME**. INCLUDING WHY sometimes it's stronger if characters don't talk about what upsets them and a theme that encapsulates much of the philosophy of the entire **Buffy the Vampire Slayer** series.

CHAPTER 7

LIE TO ME (S2 E7)

THIS CHAPTER TALKS about Season Two Episode Seven, **Lie To Me**, written and directed by Joss Whedon. In particular, we'll look at:

- **a two-part Inciting Incident or Story Spark**
- **a Midpoint Reversal that Buffy only recognizes after the fact**
- **the way the characters' indirect dialogue indicates intense conflict**
- **a theme that expresses the philosophy of the series**
- **how Buffy and Spike serve as reflections of one another**

Okay, let's dive into the Hellmouth.

Opening Conflict

Our Opening Conflict occurs in a dark, deserted playground. There is a spinning merry-go-round, which we'll learn is never a good thing on Buffy. And there are swings with creaky old chains.

A little boy is alone. His mom is late. Drusilla, in a long gauzy white gown, asks the boy if he wants her to walk him home. And she sings a creepy sort of song that she says her mother sang to her. Or maybe the song is fine, it's just the way she sings it.

Drusilla: What will your mummy say when they find your body?

Luckily for the boy at 1 minute 22 seconds into the episode Angel appears. He gets between the boy and Drusilla and tells the boy to run home. Which, quite sensibly, he does.

Drusilla says, "My Angel," and seems surprised to see him there. Angel tells her to leave Sunnydale. To take Spike and get out of town. When she asks if he'll hurt her if she doesn't, he looks down. We can tell Angel feels guilty about whatever past the two of them have.

The Story Spark Part 1

Buffy is walking in an area of ground above the playground, so Angel doesn't see her. But she sees him just as Drusilla leans close and whispers into Angel's ear that this is just the beginning.

I see this as part of our Inciting Incident or Story Spark, which is what gets the plot of the story moving. Usually that happens about 10% into an episode, a book, or a movie.

Here it comes in two parts.

This part is at only 2 minutes 47 seconds into the 42-43 minute episode, but it does give us the first half of what sets the story in motion. Based on that moment she sees, Buffy suspects a relationship between Angel and Drusilla.

We will see the second half of the Spark a little over 6 minutes in. For now we shift to the credits.

When we return, Jenny is telling Giles that it's a secret. She won't tell him where they're going on their date tomorrow night. Buffy appears and tells Giles that nothing vampiry happened last night. He notices Buffy seems a little blue and suggests she take the night off.

So he is taking his own advice from back in **Reptile Boy** to stop driving her so hard. Buffy's okay with taking the night off, but when Giles says she could spend some time with Angel, she says he might have other plans.

Later she tells Willow about seeing Angel with this woman and says she doesn't know if the woman is a vampire.

The Story Spark Part 2

Now, at 6 minutes 30 seconds in, is what I see as the second half of that Inciting Incident or Story Spark. Billy Fordham (whom Buffy later calls Ford) walks up behind them. Buffy's been talking to Willow and Xander about feeling a little blue. Xander wants her to cheer up by coming to the Bronze.

Ford jokes that he'd suggest Oreos dumped in apple juice, but Buffy probably isn't into that anymore. It turns out Ford was Buffy's fifth grade crush. They also started high school together.

Ford tells her that his dad got transferred and now Ford is attending Sunnydale High.

Buffy invites him to join them that night at the Bronze. And we get some great dialogue.

Ford: I'd love to. But if you guys already had plans, would I be imposing?

Xander: Oh, only in the literal sense.

That night at the Bronze, Willow, Xander, Buffy, and Ford play pool. Ford jokes that he knows all of Buffy's darkest secrets.

Xander: Care to wager on that?

Angel Lies To Buffy

Angel is at the bar when Buffy goes to get a soda. She asks what he did last night. Angel lies and says he stayed in and did nothing. Which of course only makes Buffy angry and more suspicious. She walks away. He follows. She introduces Ford and Angel, but almost immediately asks Ford to walk home with her.

After she leaves, Angel looks concerned. In another wonderful quote for the episode, Xander says, "Okay, once more with tension."

Outside, Buffy is explaining to Ford that maybe Angel is her boyfriend. But she hears noises. She can tell someone's being attacked, so she asks Ford to go back into the Bronze, claiming she left her purse.

Partway there, he stops when he hears a woman crying. The woman runs out and past him. We hear other sounds that tell us that Buffy is slaying a vampire.

Ford Knows Buffy's Secret

When Ford finds her, no one else is around. Buffy tries to cover for the commotion by saying that there was a cat that fought another cat and it was bad and now it's gone.

Ford: Oh, I thought you were fighting a vampire.

This could be our first major plot turn. The turn that comes from outside the protagonist and spins the story in a new direction. Usually we see that a quarter of the way through an episode or a book.

This is a little early. At 9 minutes 48 seconds in, he tells her he knows that she is the Slayer. So that could certainly turn the story in a new way. However, I think the first plot turn comes a little bit later than this. I'll get to it in a moment. It shifts the story in a completely different way.

Later that night on the phone, Buffy tells Willow that it's sort of neat that Ford knows about her being a Slayer. She didn't have to deal with whether or not to tell him. He just knew and now she doesn't have to spend all this effort and energy hiding her secret.

Since Buffy is happy, we know something bad will happen. And it does in what I see as the actual first major plot turn.

The One-Quarter Twist In Lie To Me

Ford is knocking on what looks like a warehouse door. He goes down some stairs. Inside is a hidden club. All of these people are enamored of vampires.

This comes from outside our protagonist, Buffy, and spins the story in a new direction, which is what the One-Quarter Twist should do. Just Ford knowing Buffy's secret wouldn't necessarily be a problem. But Ford knowing Buffy's secret and being part of this club that is fascinated with vampires – that's a problem. It also raises the stakes, as it puts Buffy in danger.

In the background, vampire movies are playing. A guy wearing a cape that looks like he got it at the Halloween store comes up to Ford. His name is Marvin, but he calls himself Diego now. He asks how it went with Buffy. Diego also reminds Ford that the lease is almost up for this place, something that's important later.

Ford swallows some pills. A young woman, thin with long blond hair, is also talking to them and saying that she can't wait. Ford reassures her and Diego that pretty soon they will all do what all teens should do. Die young and stay pretty.

He then repeats the words from the vampire film that's playing in the background. (I was not sure what film this was. But according to a Buffy fandom wiki, it is the 1974 version of Dracula.)

Angel Asks For Willow's Help

At 14 minutes 20 seconds in, Willow is home, and there is a knock on her door. She's in her bedroom. The knock comes not from inside the house but from her doors to the patio.

It's Angel. He tells her she has to invite him in, and she does. She's wearing a long night shirt. She quickly hides her bra and socks, obviously uncomfortable he's there. And she tells him she's not supposed to have boys in her room.

Angel wants her help to research someone on the Internet. Willow is happy to do that – until she hears the person he wants to research is Ford. She very carefully suggests that Angel might be jealous.

He tells her he never used to get jealous. He spent a hundred years isolating himself, feeling guilty.

Angel: I really honed my brooding skills.

He admits, though, that now he does get jealous. But his gut tells him that something is off about Ford.

Willow says okay, "but if there isn't anything weird – hey, that's weird." She has discovered with a few keystrokes that Ford is not in any of the school records. He's not registered at Sunnydale High.

Angel asks her not to mention anything about this to Buffy until they both know more.

Willow is clearly uncomfortable about that. That's obvious again the next morning at school. Buffy and Ford come up to talk to Willow. And she stutters and stumbles. Happily for Willow, Buffy thinks it's because Willow was drinking too much coffee again.

Buffy And Ford Fight Vampires

That night Buffy gives Ford a walking tour of Sunnydale. They see two vampires. She hands Ford a cross and goes after the male vampire, fighting and killing him. While she's otherwise occupied, Ford corners the female vampire and threatens her with a stake.

He tells her he'll let her live if she tells him what he wants to know.

This is about 19 minutes in. So we are nearing the Midpoint of the episode.

A Near Midpoint Reversal

Buffy has killed the vampire. She returns to Ford. He pretends to be shocked that he was able to kill the female vampire and claims that she turned to dust.

Usually at the Midpoint of a well-structured story we either see the protagonist fully committing to the quest or a major reversal for our protagonist.

While this is still a little bit before the Midpoint, I see this as the Reversal for Buffy, though she is unaware that it has happened. She thinks Ford really has dusted the vampire.

We find out later that he made a deal with her, and that deal is to give Buffy to Spike. Clearly a major reversal for Buffy.

Meanwhile Willow, Angel, and Xander find the warehouse and the vampire club in it, called the Sunset Club.

Willow mentions this address is the only thing she was able to find on the Internet about Ford. That makes me think perhaps the lease Diego mentioned is in Ford's name. And I really like that because it's a minor detail that was thrown in that supports the idea that Willow was able to track this place down.

Later we will find out that Ford wanted Buffy to figure out what was going on to some extent and to come to the club. So perhaps he left that breadcrumb for Buffy to follow.

They go into the club after claiming to be friends of Ford. Xander and Willow comment on the "Vampires, Yay" theme.

The Lonely Ones

Chanterelle, the young woman with the long blond hair, welcomes them and tells them it's okay that they're new. She calls vampires the Lonely Ones and says people misunderstand them. They don't want to harm anyone. The vampires are exalted, above humans.

Angel, clearly never having read How To Make Friends And Influence People, tells her that she's a fool. He also tells Xander and Willow that these people don't know anything about vampires, including how they dress. Just as, of course, a guy walks past them wearing exactly the same clothes that Angel is wearing.

At 21 minutes 45 seconds in, Diego watches them leave.

When I initially watched this for the podcast, I thought maybe this was the Midpoint Reversal. Because perhaps Diego seeing Buffy's friends and maybe realizing they are out of place was the reversal for her. But since we later find out that Ford wanted her to figure out what happened, this isn't really a reversal.

Not A Great Date For Giles

Giles and Jenny are in the library with Buffy. She called them away from their date. Giles pretends that he's upset at leaving the monster truck rally, but he doesn't do a very good acting job. And Jenny tells him they could have just left.

Ford isn't with them. Buffy sent him home.

As they're researching, Buffy comes across a photo of Drusilla in a book. Giles tells her Dru is the sometime paramour of Spike who was killed by an angry mob in Prague. Buffy says they don't make angry mobs like they used to because she saw Drusilla the other night with Angel.

Jenny says isn't he supposed to be a good guy?

Thieving and Lying

As they're talking, the female vampire, the one that Ford

supposedly killed, breaks in and steals a book from the library. I love that Giles is outraged that she took his book.

Everyone is surprised because that isn't typical vampire behavior. Buffy is especially surprised because she recognizes the vampire. It's the one Ford claimed he killed.

This is 23 minutes 37 seconds in. I see this as Buffy recognizing the Reversal that happened. Now she knows that Ford is lying to her and plotting something.

We switch to the warehouse where Drusilla and Spike live. She is trying to get a dead bird to sing to her. It's lying on the bottom of the cage, and she's promising it seeds if it will sing.

Spike asks her if she met anyone interesting, like Angel, when she was out and about the other night. He wants to know what they might have talked about. And he says it's a little odd her talking to Angel, him being the enemy and all.

Drusilla ignores him and keeps talking to the bird.

Spike loses his temper and tells her the bird is dead. She left it in the cage and didn't feed it and it died. Just like the last one. The scene always makes me sad. Drusilla seems so upset about the bird being dead.

What The Fight's Really About

This dialogue between Spike and Drusilla is a wonderful example of conflict where the character who is really upset is not saying what he's upset about. Spike snaps at her about the bird when he's really angry about her seeing Angel and lying about it.

Spike to some extent realizes it's not about the bird. And he says he's rude and he's a bad man and he's sorry. However, he still doesn't admit that the issue is him being jealous of Angel.

Instead, he talks about her being too weak to be out alone. Now that may be true, and we'll find out later that Drusilla is vulnerable. But that is not the heart of what Spike is angry about.

Nonetheless he does apologize. To try to make her feel better, he says, in another great dialogue line –

Spike: Would you like a new bird, one that's not dead?

Reflections

In this way, Spike and Drusilla are a reflection of Buffy and Angel. Spike is jealous and worried about Drusilla talking to Angel. Buffy likewise is upset, jealous, and suspicious of Angel because he was talking to Drusilla.

Also, both Angel and Drusilla do not tell the people who love them about their encounter, making it more suspicious.

Ford Makes A Proposal

At 25 minutes 20 seconds in, Ford walks in on Spike and Drusilla. He says he came looking for Spike. Spike's upset that no one is guarding the place. But the female vampire that Ford made the deal with comes in. She has brought Spike that book from the library. He takes a quick look and says it will be very useful.

Ford then says he has an offer for Spike. But he wants Spike to say the dialogue lines from the Dracula movie -- that Ford has thirty seconds to convince Spike not to kill him. Ford says it's traditional.

Spike says he's not much for tradition and grabs Ford to bite him. But Drusilla stops Spike. Ford insists Spike has to say the line. After he does, Ford tells Spike that he wants to become a vampire.

In another great line, Spike says –

Spike: I've known you for two minutes and I can't stand you. I don't really feature you living forever.

But Ford offers him a trade. He will hand Buffy to Spike on a silver platter if Ford can become a vampire. We cut to a commercial. Great hook before that commercial break.

Buffy And Angel Finally Talk

When we return, Buffy is home. Angel comes to the door. As he did with Willow, he asks if he can come in. Buffy says sure, but once he's invited can't he always come in? And he says yes, he was just being polite.

This is a nice, funny line, and it gives us the new rule we haven't heard before. That once a vampire is invited, it can always come back into the house.

Angel tells her Ford is not what he seems and reveals that Willow and Xander helped him check things out.

Buffy's mad that they all went behind her back. But unlike Spike (and unlike when she talked to Angel in the Bronze) she goes right to the point of what she's angry about. She asks Angel who is Drusilla and says don't lie to her. She's had enough of that.

Angel: Sometimes a lie is better. If you live long enough you realize that.

Then he asks if she loves him.

Buffy: I love you, but I don't know if I trust you.

He says maybe she shouldn't do either.

Angel tells her that he did many unconscionable things as a vampire but Drusilla was the worst. He was obsessed with her. First, he made her insane. He did every kind of mental torture he could think of, including killing everyone she loved. She finally fled to a convent. The day she took her vows he turned her into a demon.

Then he tells her that Ford belongs to this vampire cult.

Buffy Surprises Ford – Or Does She?

Buffy and Ford meet the next afternoon in front of the school. He wants to take her out again and says he'd like to surprise her. Buffy says, "I like surprises." They agree to meet later.

In the next scene Ford is at the Sunset club. Diego asks

Ford what about his friends, are they coming? Ford seems a little worried and angry that Diego didn't mention the friends before. But he says that everything is fine.

From upstairs, Buffy says, "No, it's really not."

Ford tells Diego it's drafty in here. Diego disappears up the stairs.

Buffy calls Ford a lying scum bag, and he admits that he will become a vampire and that's what he wants. She realizes that he must have offered her as a trade because vampires are kind of particular about who they turn.

She asks what's going to happen. He laughs and says it's already happening. We hear the door swing shut upstairs. So that's why he said that it was getting drafty – so that Diego would know it was time.

The Three-Quarter Turn In Lie To Me

Ford tells Buffy that door can only be opened from the outside. He also reveals that the club used to be a bomb shelter. There's three feet of concrete in all the walls. No one can get out. At sunset the vampires will come. They will open the door from the outside.

I see this as the last major plot turn.

Usually that's about three quarters of the way through, so this is right about on target. You could see the major turn as being earlier when Buffy arrives. However, I see it as a much bigger shift that she is now locked in with all these people, including Ford, who want to be vampires.

Ford says it's sunset.

Spike Plans The Battle As Buffy Confronts Ford

We switch back to Spike and Dru. He's organizing everyone, and he says the Slayer is the priority. He asks Dru if she's up for this, is she sure? Drusilla says she needs a treat.

Buffy, inside the shelter, is hunting for another way out

and can't find one. She tries to reason with the others and then with Ford.

He reveals that he is dying. He has brain tumors and only has months to live. It's very painful. That's why he wants to be a vampire. She tells him it's not like it will be him. She says a demon sets up shop in your body. It remembers your life. It walks and talks but it's not you.

Ford says that's better than what's in store for him otherwise.

Central Theme Of Buffy The Vampire Slayer

Buffy tells him she feels sorry for him, but what he's doing is still wrong. When he claims he has no choice, we get a great dialogue line that encapsulates much of the theme of the entire series.

Buffy: You have a choice. You don't have a good choice, but you have a choice.

We hear car sounds from outside. He admits to her that everyone else is going to die. The deal is only for him. But he views the others as sheep. You can tell he thinks they are kind of pathetic, and he just doesn't care what happens to them. Or at least that's how he acts.

The Climax Of Lie To Me

We're 38 minutes 41 seconds in. The Climax of the episode starts. Ford knocks Buffy down the stairs. Chanterelle looks a bit shocked at that. All the same, she ascends the stairs to meet the vampires. She looks very Gothic in her long evening gown.

Spike comes in, yells to the others to take them all but save the Slayer for him. He bites Chanterelle. Buffy sees vampires attacking humans everywhere. For a second, she looks lost as to where to start.

Then she spots Drusilla alone on a catwalk up above,

watching everything. Buffy leaps up next to Dru and grabs her. She puts a stake to her heart and yells to Spike to stop.

Spike lets go of Chanterelle and tells all the vampires to stop, which they do.

Buffy demands that he let everybody go. He tells them to do it. The humans are all allowed to leave except for Ford, who at some point got knocked out. He is down on the underground level passed out.

Buffy tells Spike to back down the stairs. She's making sure that he won't be able to get to her or anybody else. When she lets go, she throws Drusilla at him and runs out. Buffy slams the door, sealing all the vampires inside.

Falling Action

Spike: Where's the doorknob?

We're now in the Falling Action. This is where we tie up loose ends after the Climax. The main plot has resolved. Buffy defeated Ford's plot. She defeated Spike, and she saved all the humans except for Ford.

I think part of why Ford is shown as not caring what happens to all the other people, and having sold them all out, is that we don't want to feel bad that Buffy was not also able to save him. She definitely feels sad about it, though.

Angel, Willow, and Xander meet her outside. She tells them the vampires are contained. But they should come back for the body later when the vampires are gone.

Inside, Ford wakes up and asks what happened.

Spike: We're stuck in a basement.

Ford: Buffy?

Spike: She's not stuck in a basement.

Ford nonetheless tells Spike that he delivered and handed him the Slayer, so he wants his reward. We fade out on Spike going into vamp face.

The next day the door's been broken open at last from inside. The vampires got out during the night and are gone.

Buffy finds Ford. It looks like he's dead.

At The Graveyard

That night at the graveyard Giles and Buffy wait. She brought flowers. She says it would be easier if she could just hate Ford. And she thinks he wanted her to hate him, that it made it easier for him to do what he was doing if he saw himself as the villain.

Buffy says nothing is ever simple anymore. Who to love or hate or trust. And the more she knows the more confused she is. Giles tells her it's called growing up. Buffy says she would like to stop and asks if it ever gets easy.

Ford, as a vampire, bursts from the grave. Buffy stakes him.

Giles says, "You mean life?" And Buffy says yeah – does it get easy? Giles asks what she wants him to say, and she says, "Lie to me."

He gives a half smile and tells her something like, yes, life is simple. The good guys are always stalwart and true, the bad guys are easy to identify with their black hats, and no one ever dies. Everyone lives happily ever after.

Buffy says, "Liar." And that's the end.

Keeping Your Word

Something I noticed on this re-watch: Spike and Buffy both do what they said they would do.

Buffy threatens Drusilla and says or implies she will let Drusilla go if Spike lets the humans go. They are out the door, and she still has Drusilla and a stake. Buffy could've killed Drusilla. But she made the deal with Spike, and she flings Drusilla at him.

Likewise, Spike does what he said he would do. Ford says, hey I gave you the Slayer, I can't help it if you messed it up. You promised me immortality. And Spike follows through.

When I first watched, until the graveyard scene I thought that Spike had killed Ford. But he did turn him into a vampire. Now maybe he figured Buffy would then kill Ford. But Spike did what he agreed to do, despite that there would be no consequences for failing to do that.

Practicality Or Honor?

You can argue Buffy was being practical in keeping her deal was Spike. She may have to deal with him over and over in the future. Honoring her promise means that she may be able to get out of other confrontations with him or get the better of him because he knows she will do what she said.

There was no downside for Spike killing Ford, yet Spike had made a deal. So he went ahead with it. That plays into something I'll talk about further in the Spoilers. Even though this episode doesn't seem like it does much to move our season-long story arc, it does.

Spoilers And Foreshadowing

FUN AND DOORS

We'll start with a very short and fun foreshadowing that I felt was unintentional. After Angel and Ford meet, it's a very awkward moment, and Xander says, "Okay, once more with tension."

A little foreshadowing of the title of the musical episode **Once More With Feeling**.

However, I doubt that any of them were thinking about that at the time.

Another thing is Willow's patio door. We will see her

bedroom again in Season Three. In Gingerbread, the parents in Sunnydale are infected by a paranoia demon. They go after all the teenagers they think are involved in the occult. Which includes Buffy and Willow.

Willow's mom will lock her in her bedroom. And the bedroom looks pretty much the same as it does here, except there is no patio door. There is only the door to the inside of the rest of the house, which is locked. So Willow can't get out. One of those convenient TV things that I guess we are not supposed to notice.

Trusting Jenny

Jenny tells Giles "you just have to trust me" when he's nervous about her choice for the next night's date. She is joking. But I find it interesting that we are linking trust and Jenny. Particularly in an episode that is all about who to trust and who not to trust.

And remember in the Season One finale Prophecy Girl, Giles said to Jenny, "How do I know I can trust you?" So here we have this little echo of that in a light, funny context. I do think it is part of weaving through some subtle hints that maybe we can't trust Jenny.

Also, when Buffy says she saw Angel with Drusilla, Jenny says, "I thought he was one of the good guys."

This makes me wonder – is she rethinking her mission about Angel? Or already disagreeing with that mission? I love the line because it's just quickly thrown in there. There's no reason for viewers who don't know what's coming to fasten on it, but it is consistent with what we later learn about Jenny being there to watch Angel. And ensure that the curse continues to haunt him.

Who Chanterelle Will Become

We also meet Chanterelle in this episode. She will return at the beginning of Season Three in the pilot episode. She's living on the streets and going by the name Lily.

In that episode, she remembers Buffy, but Buffy doesn't remember her at first. At the end, Buffy, who has been working as a waitress to support herself, tells Lily that she's arranged for Lily (if she wants) to take over Buffy's job. And she gives her the one room she's been staying in and her uniform. Buffy has a name tag with it because she's been going by her middle name. The name tag says Anne.

Lily asks if she can be Anne. And the next time we see her, which is on **Angel**, she's introduced as Anne. Nothing is said about her past or knowing Buffy. But she is running this shelter for homeless teens, and she knows about vampires. She's very practical about the dark side of living in Los Angeles.

I love that she went through this character growth. And that only viewers of both shows will know about her backstory.

Spike, Dru, And Angel

Spike, Angel, Dru, and Buffy – lots of foreshadowing here of the Season Two story arc that involves all of them. Particularly Spike feeling jealous over Drusilla talking to Angel. That jealousy of Angel and that connection between Drusilla and Angel will drive the climax of the season.

On a smaller scale, we have this female vampire bringing Spike this book. I'm not sure that I noticed on first watch that Spike looked through the book and said, "Oh, this should be helpful."

I didn't focus on why he wants the book. But later we'll find out he is looking for a way to restore Drusilla. That angry mob in Prague didn't kill her, but the implication is whatever happened there is why she's so weak now.

In a few episodes we'll find out the book showed Spike

how to restore Drusilla. And that what they need is Angel's blood because he is her sire. That also makes Spike's comment about Angel being the enemy and all even more telling. Because they're going to need to drain Angel's blood.

The Rules And Surprises

As I mentioned, we get these reminders about the rules about vampires. Angel tells Willow she has to invite him in. We hear when he talks to Buffy that once you're invited in you can always come in. And if you were a new viewer or you forgot what happened before, you are also reminded that Buffy already invited Angel in. So he has access to her house.

This foreshadows the fear that Buffy and her friends will have when they realize that Angel can get into their homes.

There's also a line of dialogue that I wonder if was done on purpose. I am guessing yes because everything about Buffy seems so well crafted and planned. When Ford doesn't want to tell Buffy what they're going to do that night and says he wants to surprise her, Buffy says, "I like surprises."

And of course the episode where Angel changes at the end and becomes evil is called Surprise. I don't think it can be accidental that Buffy says this line in the context of a boy that she had romantic feelings about, in an episode that is all about whom to trust and whom to love.

No Black And White Answers

Which leads me to that conversation with Buffy and Giles over Ford's grave. I always found it very moving. It sums up so much of the show itself.

Buffy moving toward adulthood. Having to take it on too quickly and facing all these complicated questions. Which is part of what makes the show so good. It could easily be just a monster fighting show. Good versus evil. I don't think if it was, it would've lasted this long.

One of its strengths is that sorting out good and evil is not black and white. Is not simple. So that conversation conveys the struggle Buffy has and Giles' efforts to help her deal with it. Wishing he could lie to her and just make her feel better.

Hints Of The Dark Age

That's how I saw that conversation the first time I watched the episode (and probably on several re-watches). It is only watching it for the podcast and looking ahead to what's next that I realized how much it foreshadows the very next episode, **The Dark Age**.

In that episode, Giles will be one of the people that Buffy is unsure if she can trust. And his comment about how you can always tell the good guys from the bad guys by the black hats also is so telling. Because we find out Giles was not always the good guy.

Also telling is that they have this conversation about adulthood when in the next episode, Buffy will have to grapple with things Giles did before he became an adult.

Buffy And Spike

On Buffy and Spike both doing what they said they would do:

Weaving this in early, showing us this about both characters, is what persuades us as viewers when we get to the season finale that Buffy and Spike really would make a deal with each other. They have reasons to trust one another. When Spike offers his help, Buffy doesn't completely trust him. But she does know from experience that Spike does what he says he will do.

Likewise, when Buffy sets certain conditions on Drusilla being allowed to live (as an undead person), and Spike and Drusilla being allowed to leave Sunnydale, Spike knows that Buffy will honor that.

Questions For Your Writing

- Is there a reversal at your Midpoint? When does the protagonist recognize it happened or how important it is?
- Find a section of dialogue where a character is upset or angry about something important. If the character says exactly why they're upset, can you revise it so the character talks about something else? Does that make the scene stronger?
- Do any of your characters serve as reflections of one another the way Buffy and Spike do?

Next: The Dark Age

NEXT WE'LL TALK ABOUT **THE DARK AGE**, INCLUDING seeing a different side of Giles and whether the episode is a coming of age story.

CHAPTER 8

THE DARK AGE (S2 E8)

THIS CHAPTER TALKS about **The Dark Age**, Season
Two Episode Eight, written by Rob DesHotel and Dean
Batali and directed by Bruce Seth Green.

In particular, we'll look at:

- **an unexpected side of a well-known
  character**
- **a subtle Midpoint Reversal, followed by
  a Commitment**
- **the elements of a coming-of-age story**
- **two clear, key character arcs from one
  story with one protagonist**

Okay, let's dive into the Hellmouth

Opening Conflict

We start, as we should, with conflict. A man in a suit
hurries across the darkened schoolyard. He asks a custodian

where to find Rupert Giles. The custodian tells the man that Giles is the librarian and directs him to the library.

This is a nice way to establish through conflict who Giles is (for new audience members).

Why do I see it as being through conflict? Because the man is clearly distressed as he rushes across the schoolyard. He's anxious to reach Giles.

A woman appears and shuffles toward the man. Her eyes flash. Her face is decaying. He says, "Diedre?" And she says, "Philip." This, too, is a good way to get names in through conflict.

Philip bangs on the door as Diedre moves closer.

But inside the library, music is blasting. Buffy, in workout clothes, is doing step aerobics. I have to agree with Giles, who is holding his ears, that the music is just noise. Specifically, he says it's not music because it has no notes.

Buffy, though, says she needs a beat to aerobicize.

Outside, Diedre reaches Philip and starts to strangle him. He falls to the ground. Her body sort of melts to the ground and turns into this shadow that oozes out toward him. That is at 2 minutes 41 seconds in.

It's a great hook, and we go to the credits.

The Story Spark

Usually our Story Spark or Inciting Incident, the event that sets off the story, comes about 10% into an episode, book or movie. In **Buffy**, that's typically around 4.5 minutes in, as most episodes are about 43-44 minutes.

Here, though, I think the moment of Diedre choking Philip before he could reach Giles, and then this shadow reaching Philip, all amounted to the Inciting Incident. Because that sets off our main plot.

After the credits, we see flashes of symbols and tattoos

and long-haired guys with tinted glasses. And we hear screaming. Giles awakens.

This could also be the Story Spark because it tells Giles that the demon (who we will learn is called Eyghon) has returned. But I see that more as simply giving Giles information.

As I'll talk about later, this episode is primarily Buffy's story. So what sets this plot off is Eyghon being passed from Diedre to Philip in that first scene. Though technically I suppose the Story Spark started before this episode began with whatever it is that brought Eyghon back in the first place.

Anywhere But Here

Willow and Buffy are at the school in the sun. They are playing Anywhere But Here, a game where they tell each other stories about where they would rather be. Xander appears and joins the game. The three joke about whether Giles ever played this game. Xander is certain the answer is no and that Giles is still bitter about there being only twelve grades in school.

Buffy says Giles probably sat in math class thinking that there should be more math.

Giles joins them. He tells her about a delivery of blood to the hospital. Buffy says, "Vamp Meals on Wheels." Giles seems concerned she's not taking it seriously enough.

Buffy: Have I ever let you down?

Giles: Do you want me to answer that or should I just glare?

This is a great quick back-and-forth that emphasizes the nature of their relationship. He is the adult, the parent, telling Buffy what needs to be done and pointing out that she needs to take it seriously. And yes, she has on occasion let him down. But they are joking, and we know that this is overall a good relationship.

Jenny And Giles

Jenny joins them. She says she's holding a class reviewing computer basics on Saturday and Willow is assisting her. Xander makes fun of the students who have to attend until he finds out he's one of them, and Cordelia is the other.

When Jenny and Giles are alone, Giles asks if she wants to go out that weekend. And she says no, she'd like to stay in. They kiss as the bell rings.

In the library, having had a nice moment with Jenny, Giles now faces a serious obstacle: the police. They are in the library, and they tell him there was a homicide on campus the night before. The victim had Giles' name and address on a piece of paper in his pocket. (These days I suppose it would be on the guy's phone.)

Cordelia comes in through the doors.

Cordelia: Evil just compounds evil, doesn't it?

But she is not talking about the homicide, which she knows nothing about. She's talking about having to go to the computer class tomorrow and on top of it to get a book for it.

Cordelia: There are books on computers? Isn't the point of computers to replace books?

She sees the police. Giles is quite irritated with her when she tries to get one of them to fix a "bogus" ticket. And he says, "Cordelia!" And she says why does everyone always say her name like that? "I can take a hint. What's the hint?"

He tells her the hint is to come back later.

At the morgue, Giles identifies Philip's body and admits that he knows him. He says they hadn't spoken in twenty years. That they were friends back in London. But he claims he doesn't know anything about the unusual tattoo on Philip's arm. Even though that is one of the symbols that we saw in Giles' dream.

Reminding The Audience

At 10 minutes 16 seconds in Buffy waits outside the hospital. Giles is a no-show. She sees the vampires meet the van bringing in the blood. She fights them.

Angel appears from nowhere to help her. When she asks how he knew he says everyone knows about delivery day. She tasks him with getting the blood to safety because she's worried about Giles.

At first Angel downplays her worries about Giles. But she points out Giles is never late for anything.

This Angel appearance serves two purposes. One, it gives a reason for us to see Angel, to remind us that he is around. And he is important.

Also, I see it as a way to get Buffy's worries about Giles out there and to make clear how unusual this is for Giles. If you're a regular watcher, you would know that already. But with network TV at the time, people often jumped in and out of the season. Or they might just start watching in the middle. So this is a good way to inform new audience members.

It also tells us Buffy's thoughts in a way that you can't otherwise do on television. In a novel you could simply show Buffy's thoughts. However, in one of the writing classes I took, the instructor (and I wish I could recall who it was) said to cut out all the scenes where a character sits and thinks. There's just not enough happening there.

So even in the novel, having this other character there to create a small amount of conflict, to disagree with the protagonist or strongly disagree, is a good way to bring out a character's thoughts.

One caveat: In a novel, I wouldn't bring in a brand-new

character to just walk on and do that. Adding more characters than you truly need gives your reader too much to remember and think about. But if you have a character like Angel who is ongoing, whom the reader or the audience member already knows, that can be a good character to help turn internal thoughts into dialogue.

The One-Quarter Twist In The Dark Age

So we are now moving toward our first major plot turn. It usually comes about a quarter of the way through a book or movie, which is why I think of it as the One-Quarter Twist. In TV it sometimes comes a bit later. Here it is about 12 minutes 47 seconds in.

Giles answers the door looking rumpled. And there's something else we have never ever seen before – his tie is loose. With anyone else, no big deal. With Giles, very disturbing. He tells Buffy he forgot about the hospital, which is even more disturbing. And he's very vague about what he's doing now.

He asks Buffy if she was hurt. When he's sure she's not, he tells her he'll see her Monday and basically slams the door in her face. That shutting of the door on her I see as the One-Quarter plot turn.

From this moment on, Buffy will move forward in a new direction. As it should, this first plot turn came from outside our protagonist, and it spins her in a new direction.

Here, that direction is figuring out what is wrong with Giles.

Giles Crosses Off Names

Before we follow Buffy, though, we see Giles, looking distraught, on the phone. He apologizes to the person who answered, saying he knows it's 5 AM there. But he's looking for Diedre and learns that she died. Giles tells the person he and Diedre were friends when they were young.

Now he crosses off Diedre's name on a handwritten list of five people. Only two are left. Ethan Rayne, whom we saw in **Halloween**, and Giles. Giles rolls up his sleeve and looks at his tattoo, a match for the one we saw on Philip. And he looks in the mirror and says to his reflection, "So you're back."

At the morgue, Phillip opens his eyes and takes the sheet off himself. His eyes flash. Next time we see him, he'll attack the morgue attendant.

Saturday Morning

On Saturday morning, Jenny is opening up the computer lab. She's wearing a sweater and pants. I am pretty sure we've never seen her wearing anything but a skirt before, and I don't think we'll ever see her wear pants again. This is most likely to accommodate the stunt person later.

Also, that person is larger than Jenny, and it adds to this unsettling feeling when the demon takes over. Because the demon looks a bit like Jenny and is wearing Jenny's clothes.

Buffy interrupts the computer tutorial to talk to Jenny. She's worried about Giles. So this is what I mean about Buffy going in this new direction. Now she's trying to find out what's wrong with Giles.

Buffy tells Jenny about the night before and adds that Giles was drinking alone. And everyone more or less gasps. (Personally, I'm more worried about his tie.)

Buffy asks if anyone else noticed anything strange about Giles. Cordelia says no, he seemed normal when he was talking to the police. After a few more questions she says oh, she thinks it was about a homicide.

Everyone is a bit irked at her, to say the least, that she didn't think to mention this before.

Buffy goes to the library to call Giles. Someone is lurking in the stacks. It's Ethan Rayne. He tries to push a bookcase down on her.

She corners him and recognizes him as the person who sold her the dress and almost got everyone killed on Halloween. And she punches him and threatens to call the police for him trespassing. But he tells her that Rupert will need to answer so many questions.

He also says he and Giles go way back and asks if she knows where Giles is.

Reversals

We see these disturbing dreams again, and a ringing phone wakes Giles. He has his head down on his desk. So he apparently passed out there.

(I love this phone. It's an old-fashioned dial phone that is sitting there on the desk. I'm pretty sure at that point only my parents still had dial phones, although theirs were even more classic. They were wall-mounted. Of course Giles would still have this type of phone.)

It is Buffy calling him. He tries to tell her he'll see her Monday, but she says, "What's the mark of Eyghon?" When he realizes Ethan is there, Giles tells her she has to get away. She's in grave danger.

At 21 minutes in, Phillip bursts into the library. Either of these two things could be that reversal that we often see at the Midpoint of a well-structured story. Buffy finding out she's in great danger because of something connected to Giles, or Philip coming in at that moment. But Buffy fights these types of – or all types of – monsters all the time. I think the real reversal comes just a little bit later.

Buffy fights Philip and kicks him into the book cage. She locks him in.

Xander, Willow, Jenny, and Cordelia have come into the library. Buffy yells at them not to let Ethan get away. They stop him. Willow says Philip looks dead though he is walking and moving. Ethan confirms that yes, Philip is dead.

Giles arrives.

Giles: It can't be.

Ethan: Hello Ripper.

Then we have a nice moment that very quickly gives us a little back story.

Cordelia: Why did he call him Ripper?

She says this just as Giles grabs Ethan by the back of the head, lifts him out of the chair, and says he told him to leave town. And Cordelia says, "Oh."

Ethan tells Giles that he's having the dreams, and they both know what's coming.

The Midpoint Reversal In The Dark Age

Here we are getting to what I see as the Midpoint Reversal. At 22 minutes 45 seconds in, Philip breaks out of the cage. Buffy kicks him. He falls, and his body sort of melts the way Diedre's did. That shadow oozes towards Jenny, who was knocked out in the fight and is lying on the floor.

This is a significant reversal despite that we don't know it when it happens. Jenny has now been infected just as Philip was. Ethan gets away during the chaos. Jenny wakes up. She seems out of it. She and Giles hug, and he comforts her.

Her eyes flash, but no one else sees. This tells the audience that the reversal happened.

This also is an example of dramatic irony, which we saw in previous **Buffy** episodes. That is where the audience knows something that the characters don't. And here we know Jenny is now in danger. And is a danger to Buffy and everyone around her. Particularly to Giles, who is taking Jenny home.

Buffy wants to know what's happening, but Giles says it's private and it's his battle, not hers.

At the Midpoint, we often see either this type of reversal

for the protagonist, or the protagonist fully committing to the quest. Sometimes we see both.

A Post-Midpoint Commitment

Here, we see Buffy commit in full to helping Giles. This comes slightly after that Reversal, and in some ways is triggered by it. Though Buffy was already on this path, she is now determined. It's 24 minutes 51 seconds in. She's determined to help Giles despite him telling her it's not her battle.

She tells Willow to research in the books. Find out what the mark of Eyghon is. She tells Xander to go through Giles' personal files and look for anything that would shed some light on this. Cordelia then gives Buffy a hopeful look. And Buffy kind of stares at her.

Cordelia: What about me? I care about Giles.

I love this. I see this as even more evidence that Cordelia truly is part of the group now.

The old Cordelia – or maybe not "old" Cordelia, but initially Cordelia would've just left at this point. Or she wouldn't have stuck around in the first place. But she really wants to help. Except that Buffy tells her to work with Xander. She hesitates, but Buffy says, "You want to help or not?" So she does it.

At Giles' apartment, he gives Jenny a drink and apologizes. She more or less tells him it's okay. The two of them are involved, and she's part of his world. He says that he's not safe to be around right now.

Jenny: Nothing is safe in this world, Rupert.

At the library, Willow found information about Eyghon, a demon known as the Sleepwalker. He can exist only in a dead body or an unconscious person. But the dead body can't handle it and will decompose. Which is what we've seen. Also, if Eyghon stays in an unconscious person too long, the demon takes over for good.

At first the three say it's okay because there was no one dead when Philip disintegrated. But –

Buffy: No one dead, but someone unconscious.

Eyghon Attacks

Jenny disconnects the phone from the wall. Giles brings her tea, not knowing what she's done. She wants to stay the night and she kisses him. He's hesitant. He doesn't want to take advantage.

Now Jenny starts to behave differently. She says he just never changes. And she mimics him. "It's not right. It's not proper." And she tells Giles, "You never had the strength for me. You don't deserve me, but you've got me under your skin."

As she is saying this, she's embracing Giles but also morphing, looking more and more like a demon. Her voice changes and becomes very low. On "under your skin" it sounds really frightening. I found it very disturbing.

Obviously more disturbing for Giles. He fights her off and Eyghon says, "I'll rip out your stomach."

Buffy Saves Giles

Buffy kicks in the door. She came in person because she couldn't reach him on the phone. She's able to repel Jenny, or I should say Eyghon, because it's not really Jenny anymore. Eyghon kind of shrugs, says, "Two to go, and leaves.

This is 30 minutes 27 seconds in. Giles says he's sorry to Buffy. Buffy says what I find to be an amazing line.

Buffy: Don't be sorry, be Giles.

She tries to reassure him that this is what they do, they fight monsters. Giles says it's different because he created this demon.

At the library, Xander has found in Giles' personal files a photo of a long-haired young-looking Giles, holding an electric guitar.

The Three-Quarter Turn In The Dark Age

These two back-to-back scenes I see as the next major plot point, which is usually at the three-quarter mark. It spins the story in yet another direction and it should grow out of our Midpoint.

Here, it comes from Jenny being possessed, which we saw at that Midpoint Reversal, and Buffy committing to help Giles. It's a new direction because now Buffy learns at last what's wrong with Giles. And she will move forward to stop it and protect him.

So we have shifted from figuring out what's wrong to protecting Giles and also saving Jenny.

Giles tells Buffy that when he was studying in Oxford he felt all of this pressure of his destiny to be a Watcher. He dropped out and fell in with the worst people who would take him. They practiced magics. He says at first it was small things, and it was pleasurable. Then he and Ethan discovered Eyghon. Their group did rituals. One went into a deep sleep and the others summoned Eyghon. Giles says it was an extraordinary high, but they were so stupid.

One of their members died when they tried to exorcise the demon from him.

Giles thought they were through with Eyghon after that. But now Eyghon is back. Giles wants to go with Buffy to try to help Jenny. To try to fight. But she says she has to go alone. He's barely mobile right now and he'll slow her down.

Giles, looking so broken, says he doesn't know what to do, how to stop Eyghon without killing Jenny. Buffy tells him that everyone is working on a way to save Jenny.

Buffy then goes to the costume shop and tells Ethan she is there to help him. But it's not for him. It's for Giles.

Ethan pretends to be relieved and grateful, but he maneuvers himself behind Buffy and knocks her out. When she wakes up, she is face down on what looks like a massage table. (Maybe Ethan just keeps one in the back of the costume shop.) He tattoos the symbol on her, telling her it's nothing personal. He likes her, but it's him or her and he likes himself better.

He uses acid to burn off his own tattoo.

Willow Takes Charge

In the library, Cordelia and Xander are bickering. Willow yells at them. She tells them there's no time for this. Their friends are in trouble. And she orders them out of her library if they can't cut it out.

This reminds me of that scene with Angel and Giles when Willow yells at them that Buffy needs them.

I have to think part of why Willow asserts herself the most in this space is that the library is where she feels most confident. This is where she knows her stuff. And also, as we've seen before, Willow is far more apt to intervene forcefully when her friends are in danger than any other time.

Cordelia and Xander look sheepish and apologize.

Based on the research, Xander says if only they could get another dead body for Eyghon to go into. Willow says that wouldn't kill the demon just give it a change of scenery. But then she has an idea.

Again, we see these flashes or visions Giles is having. He sees Buffy with the tattoo, the mark of Eyghon. And he knows what Ethan has done.

The Climax Of The Dark Age

So we are at the climax. Eyghon breaks into the shop. Now he is looking as tall or taller than Ethan. Broad shoulders, still looking faintly like Jenny and in her clothes, which makes it all the more disturbing. Eyghon goes after Ethan but turns to Buffy at the last second, sensing the tattoo.

At that same moment, Buffy finally breaks her bonds and is able to get off of that table. She fights Eyghon.

Giles bursts in and says, "Take me instead." Buffy tries to stop Eyghon, but Eyghon sends her flying without even touching her. Eyghon stands over Giles. He is lying on the floor.

Angel bursts through the door, Willow and Xander are with him. Angel starts choking Jenny.

Giles is distraught, but Willow tells Buffy and Giles to trust her, it will work. The demon, in peril as Jenny is being choked, jumps into Angel.

Angel's face distorts, he's thrown all over from the inside. It's very dramatic. Eventually Angel passes out. When he opens his eyes. All is calm, and the demon is gone for now.

Falling Action In The Dark Age

At 40 minutes 13 seconds in we're into the Falling Action stage of the story. The Climax resolved our main plot. The demon was defeated. Jenny and Giles were both saved. This section, the Falling Action, will resolve the loose ends and explain what happened.

So Jenny is herself again. Buffy is talking to Willow and says, "Oh, you knew that if the demon were in trouble it would jump to the nearest dead person. Which would be Angel." And Angel says he's had a demon inside him for over a hundred years just waiting for a good fight.

We've heard before that when someone becomes a vampire, the demon takes over the person's body, but that person is gone. Angel, though, had his soul restored, so both apparently coexist within him.

So we have this idea that when Angel says the demon inside him has been wanting a fight, the implication is maybe it has been fighting Angel. Or fighting Angel's soul, or that the soul is somehow suppressing it. It's just been wanting to get out and fight, so he figured throw the demon, Eyghon, in there. And Angel's demon would be able to prevail over it.

Ethan Disappears

Ethan has managed to disappear again. We talked before about how he is the trickster. He creates chaos. And here he did not intentionally create this chaos, at least not now. There isn't any suggestion that Ethan did something to set this off. He seemed as worried and taken aback as Giles, although he is willing to sacrifice other people to save himself.

But being the trickster, it fits that he gets away. This is so Ethan's character. He didn't hang around to see what happened, he got out.

At school the next day Buffy tells Willow how she was saving money for some very important shoes and now she has to spend it on tattoo removal. Xander tells Willow she was brilliant.

Jenny's Actions Show Her Distancing From Giles

Jenny and Giles are inside the school, talking near the stairs. He asks if she's okay. Says he tried to call her. But she tells him she left the phone off the hook. She needs a lot of sleep lately. Though she reassures him she's fine, she sounds muted. And she says, "Not running with the wind in your hair, the hills are alive with the sound of music fine" but okay.

Giles wants to help. He suggests they get together sometime. She says yes, sometime, and steps up the stairs away from him as she says it.

This is a nice moment where the character's actions and her tone show what Jenny really means when she says okay, sometime. That she needs space from him.

It's also almost the same conversation Jenny and Giles had at the end of **Some Assembly Required**. Giles had said he would understand if she didn't want to be around him anymore. Then, she reassured Giles. Now she is distancing herself.

Buffy And Giles Bond

Buffy sees her walk away and asks Giles how Jenny is. And Giles says the hills are not alive. Buffy says, "I'm sorry to hear that." I think he says that maybe Jenny shouldn't forgive him, but Buffy tells him he should forgive himself.

She admits it was scary seeing him that way. She's so used to him being the grown-up, "and then I find out you're a person. Who knew?" Buffy also tells him that it was a little scary learning that he made mistakes and used bad judgment too. But they have that in common, and she feels all right about learning that.

Then she says they should be training. Giles says yes, and she tells him she has the perfect music. And we have this really nice exchange:

Buffy: Go ahead, say it. You know you want to.

Giles: It's not music. It's just meaningless sound.

Buffy: Feel better?

Giles: Yes, thank you.

And that is how the episode closes.

I have not yet commented on the title of the episode. I like it so much because it has more than one level. It seems like a reference to the Dark Ages in human history. In fact, I kept thinking it was called **The Dark Ages**, not **The Dark Age**.

It also can refer to Giles' age at the time that he and his friends summoned Eyghon.

Which is a nice segue to: Is this episode a coming-of-age story?

What Is A Coming-Of-Age Story?

Basically, a coming-of-age story chronicles the emotional or mental leap from childhood to adulthood. It is usually

186 L. M. LILLY

emotion-based and not action-based. So I would say yes and no as to this episode.

We have Buffy learning that Giles is, in her words, a person. So not just a grown up. Not just an authority figure. Or more to the point, learning that authority figures and parents (as Giles has a very parent-like role in her life) are also people. They are human beings. So you could see that as a mental or emotional leap to adulthood.

But Buffy has already for the most part made that leap. She's been pushed into adulthood and responsibility throughout the series to date. Also, this idea of the parent or authority figure as a person – I don't know if that always happens. Many people struggle to grasp that about their parents well into their own adulthood. And some people never reach that point.

So while certainly that can be part of a coming-of-age story, I don't know if that's really what we're saying about Buffy here.

Finally, a coming-of-age story usually is emotion-based. It's about the character evolution, and it's not action-based.

Here, as is almost always the case in **Buffy**, the main plot is action-based. It often is a metaphor for telling an emotional story, for some kind of character arc or theme, but the plot is about the action with only one exception that I can think of.

So given all that, I see this story as overlapping with coming-of-age stories and overlapping that genre, but I do not see it as primarily a coming-of-age story. However, it is about Buffy protecting Giles. And learning that Giles is a person, and he has a past where he was not always perfect.

And that informs the question of who the protagonist is.

Who Is The Protagonist?

Unlike in Season One where I felt confused about who the protagonist was supposed to be in Teacher's Pet (the praying mantis episode), here it's clear Buffy is the protagonist.

And this is a great example of how you can still have a significant storyline for another character, and see parts of the story through that character's eyes, yet that person is not the protagonist.

Our protagonist should have a strong goal that the protagonist actively pursues, and the protagonist should be the viewpoint character and have the most at stake.

The Viewpoint Characters

So let's look at how that fits here, The viewpoint character is mainly Buffy. We do get a lot of Giles, but primarily we see him through Buffy's eyes. Through her concerns – and sometimes her jokes about Giles. At the beginning, she sees him as someone who was always the way he is now. Very stable and very focused. Never daydreaming, or letting his mind wander, or not wanting to be in math class.

Then the story shifts to her fears about Giles and the need to protect him.

So while we do get other scenes from Giles' point of view – his visions, him identifying the body, his time with Jenny – primarily we are seeing this episode from Buffy's view.

Goals – Active Or Reactive?

Buffy's goal here is to, first, find out what's wrong with Giles. Then that evolves into protecting Giles. This is the main goal that we follow through the story.

Giles, too, is trying to figure out what's going on. But he is also dealing with his own distress. He is less active in pursuing the goal than Buffy is.

Buffy is asking questions. She's pushing him for answers. She's doing research and assigning the team to research tasks. And she is actively fighting.

Giles is more in reaction mode throughout. Yes, he's

making phone calls to get information. But we also see him drinking and passing out. We see him troubled by these dreams. Afraid. He doesn't know how to help Jenny.

Normally he'd be right in the library directing everyone. But he has withdrawn. Partly because he feels so terrible about endangering those around them. And I think that he feels ashamed and embarrassed for his past actions.

Those can all be feelings a protagonist can have. Here, though, it keeps Giles from actively pursuing his goal.

High Stakes

Who has the most at stake?

This is a really interesting question for this episode because Giles is the one with the risk, at least through most of the story, of being taken over by Eyghon. Once Ethan transfers that mark to Buffy, certainly she now has her life at stake as well. But Giles is at risk through the entire episode.

So in some ways he has the most at stake.

This is where I go back to what is the story about? The story is about Buffy switching roles with Giles. Being the one to be concerned for him, to figure things out for him, to protect him instead of how it is often the other way around.

So in that sense, Buffy has the most at stake. Because she is in danger of losing that one person that she can always count on. That she relies on and trusts. Her trust in Giles is undermined. At least her trust that he will always be there and will always be the one in the position to protect her.

In that sense, in a way Buffy loses a lot in this episode. She loses that view from back when you're a kid, if you're fortunate enough to have parents who did what they should and took care of you, that view of your parent as all-powerful. As being able to take care of anything and fix anything. And it is such a difficult thing when kids realize that is not true.

Also so very hard for parents as well when there's something that they cannot fix for their child.

And so here, in a way, Buffy has lost that. She has lost this sense of Giles as having all the answers. But she has gained something more important, which is a greater understanding of who Giles is. A feeling that he is not perfect, and that perhaps she can understand him better. And she can grasp that maybe he does understand her more than she thinks. Because he has struggled with some of the same things that she does and has made bad choices and used poor judgment.

In some ways this is reassuring. And it opens and further develops their relationship into that partnership that I talked about in **Reptile Boy**, where more and more they are working together. As opposed to Giles being the one who knows everything and tells her what to do.

Spoilers And Foreshadowing

ROMANCE

One bit of foreshadowing I never noticed before – Xander and Cordelia bickering. That is, I noticed the bickering, but I know I did not pick up the first time around on the chemistry between them as they are yelling at each other. They are stepping closer and closer together until they are face-to-face. Perhaps inches apart.

This is so similar to the scene we will get in What's My Line when they have the same type of argument, and they finally kiss. So this foreshadows that.

The reason I'm sure that I didn't pick up on it on first watch is that I remember being completely taken by surprise when that happened in What's My Line. (My defense is I was not watching the Season Two episodes back to back. I don't remember how long it was between the airtime from this episode to What's My Line.)

Themes

Also, this whole episode really foreshadows the themes in What's My Line. When Buffy will see her friends taking part in this Career Fair, taking these assessments, to see what kind of work they might be good at. And for her it all feels moot because she has this destiny as the Slayer.

And she really struggles with that having been imposed on her. Giles tries to help her deal with it. As I remember it, he doesn't do a terrific job. He really tries, but it is a real challenge for her.

The Dark Age foreshadows this in that we find out how Giles struggled with that and the terrible consequences. Maybe in some ways knowing this about Giles (though I don't believe it's ever explicit in the text, we'll find out in the next chapter) helps Buffy in some way. Helps her avoid going down quite as dark a path as Giles did. Because she sees how the consequences of that were still happening so many years later.

Questions For Your Writing

- **Consider your key characters. Was one of them once very different from the way others perceive the character to be now?**
- **If your protagonist suffers a significant reversal at the Midpoint, can that**

prompt a commitment? If not, how
else does it change the story?

- Have you used elements from a
coming-of-age theme? Might you in the
future?
- How does your main conflict affect
characters in addition to the
protagonist?

Next: What's My Line Part One

NEXT WE'LL TALK ABOUT **WHAT'S MY LINE PART ONE**,
including using characters' body language to convey emotion
and vulnerability and their actions to escalate tension.

CHAPTER 9

WHAT'S MY LINE PART ONE
(S2 E9)

THIS CHAPTER TALKS about **What's My Line Part One**, Season Two Episode Nine, written by Howard Gordon and Marti Noxon and directed by David Solomon.

In particular, we'll look at:

- **bringing exposition out through conflict**
- **using body language to show emotion and vulnerability**
- **showing the threat level through a change in our core characters' behavior**
- **replacing an answered story question with another question**

Okay, let's dive into the Hellmouth.

Opening Conflict

We start with some Opening Conflict over the Career Fair. We know it's happening because we see a giant Career

Fair banner at the high school. Xander and Buffy sit at a table near it.

Xander: Are you a people person or do you prefer keeping your own company? Well, what if I'm a people person who keeps his own company by default?

In the DVD commentary, Marti Noxon commented on all the spaces at school where the characters sit around and talk. She said that's because while we see them talking about school a lot, and at school a lot, they don't actually go to classes often. So they needed all these different areas for Buffy and her friends to hang out.

Buffy tells Xander to choose None Of The Above. But there's no box for that on the quiz or test they're filling out with their Number 2 pencils. Willow joins them. Not surprisingly, she is curious and excited to find out what she might do for a career.

Buffy: Do I like shrubs?

Xander: That's between you and your God.

Buffy, though, is not in much of a mood for jokes. She says it's all Mootsville for her. She's only doing this because it's Snyder's latest hoop for her to jump through.

Willow asks isn't Buffy curious about what she might do if she weren't the Slayer? And Buffy says why go there? Her future is a non-issue.

Exposition Through Conflict

At 2 minutes 22 seconds in we switch to Drusilla and Spike and more conflict. Dru is drawing tarot cards. It is a custom deck that's very striking.

Spike tells a vampire with glasses, Dalton, to read a passage again from an old manuscript. It's in Latin. When Dalton translates, it makes no sense. Spike punches him and yells and rants. Drusilla, though, wants to dance, and Spike snaps at her. Then he apologizes and says this manuscript is supposed to hold her cure. But even Dalton, the big brain, can't make heads or tails out of it. So Spike is very frustrated.

This is the first great example of getting exposition in through conflict. Something we have seen done over and over in the show. This scene tells us about what Spike and Dru are trying to do and a little about Dalton, who seems so nervous around Spike. Which makes Dalton seem very human.

The Story Spark

Drusilla holds Spike back from threatening Dalton further. She tells Spike the reason that Dalton can't do anything with the book is it's written in code, and there's a key. And she turns over another tarot card that shows a mausoleum on it and tells him that's where the key is. They are both very happy. So now they will dance.

This is at 4 minutes 42 seconds in, and it is our Story Spark or Inciting Incident. It sets off the main plot of the story and it comes about 10% into this specific episode. And we go to the credits.

In the DVD commentary, we also get from Marti Noxon some thoughts about Drusilla's illness. It's there to give Spike major motivation because the two have such a strong relationship. The goal of reversing the illness is the MacGuffin.

A MacGuffin is a plot device writers use that seems important and it moves the story along. But it is a device as opposed to an end in itself.

Noxon also said Dalton is a character who was an ongoing surprise. She says he was probably meant, as far she can remember, to be a one-off character. But they really liked either the actor or the character, so they kept bringing him back.

Dalton Steals And Angel Visits Mr. Gordo

Back from the credits, Buffy walks in the cemetery alone and hears sounds coming from a mausoleum. She peeks in through the slightly open door and sees Dalton chipping away at something.

She waits outside for him to leave, planning to confront him. But another vampire sneaks up behind her. Or tries to. She hears him, turns around, and dusts him. Though she won that fight, Dalton is gone.

At 7 minutes 41 seconds in, Buffy is about to come in through her open bedroom window. She sees Angel in the bedroom pacing. His back is to her. Having a little fun, she tosses her bag through the window and onto the floor. The thump that it makes startles Angel. He spins around. He's holding her stuffed pig.

Buffy: Just dropping by for some quality time with Mr. Gordo?

Angel seems nervous. She tells him he doesn't need to whisper, her mom is away for the week. He asks why she came through the window, and she says, "Habit."

Do You Have To Kill Your Darlings?

This moment, and the commentary about it on the DVD, makes me think of the rule in writing that you should kill your darlings. That's the idea that if you have a line or a joke, something you just really love, but it doesn't need to be there for the story, you must cut it. Because sometimes as writers we get so enamored of a particular moment, or some little side thing, but the reader doesn't need it.

In fact, it can be distracting. Because to the reader it will stand out as this thing that doesn't belong.

Marti Noxon said that at the last minute on set they realized this moment where Buffy tosses the bag through the window didn't make sense. Because her mom is out of town. So why wouldn't she just come through the door?

But they didn't want to lose this joke with Buffy surprising Angel. He is always the one who sneaks up on other people. The writers really liked flipping that. Plus the chance to have some humor with Angel, who was up to that point usually so deadly serious.

So they added the question about why did Buffy come through the window, and she says, "Habit."

Marti commented that was a long way to go to preserve a joke.

I, though, love the thing about her coming through the window out of habit even more than the startling of Angel. It says so much about Buffy's life and what's normal for her.

So in this case I think it's great that they didn't follow that rule to kill your darlings. It's a great example of there being exceptions to any rule. Times that breaking it works regardless of what the conventional wisdom says.

This Can Never Work

In that same scene we also see Buffy and Angel reflected in the mirror, except we don't see Angel because he can't cast a reflection. Marti commented that in that scene, the missing reflection is meant to further show Buffy's isolation. Often, though, she said they will show the lack of reflection to emphasize not so much isolation, but the fact that this relationship can't ever work because of this fundamental difference.

As they're talking, Buffy snaps at Angel over something. Then she apologizes, saying that it's about Career Week.

Buffy: It's a whole week of What's My Line only I don't get to play.

She goes on to say she really wants a normal life. Angel looks depressed and says a normal life with a normal boyfriend, not someone like him. But she says he's the only part of her life that's good and makes sense.

He notices a photo of her ice skating when she was little. And she says she loved ice-skating as a kid. Her parents were fighting a lot, and it was her escape. He tells her he knows about a rink that is closed on Tuesdays, which is tomorrow. She's very happy about that.

Careers For Characters

At school the next day Cordelia finds out she could be a personal shopper or motivational speaker. Which really seems to fit. And she laughs at Xander because the printout says he has a future as a prison guard. There's nothing on there for Willow. Which really upsets Willow. She was so looking forward to finding out, and she's puzzled why she wasn't included.

Buffy is assigned to a Law Enforcement Professionals seminar.

In the library, Buffy helps Giles steady a huge stack of books that's about to fall over. Giles tells Buffy he has been cataloging the Watchers Diaries.

Giles: You'd be amazed how numbingly pompous and long-winded some of these Watchers were.

Buffy: Color me stunned.

Then Buffy tells him she saw the vampire stealing.

Buffy: Giles, you're in pace mode. What gives?

He's upset that she didn't try to figure out what was stolen. She figures it was just the usual vamp hijinks. But Giles says what if it was important?

Buffy gets irritated with him and says if he doesn't like the way she does her job he should give it to someone else. Oh, wait, he can't. She's the only one. She didn't pick this job. It chose her.

Bringing In The Big Guns

We switch to Spike and Dru. They're studying a large ornate cross that Spike is holding with a cloth so that it doesn't burn him. Dalton tells how the Slayer almost ruined it. Spike raves and kicks things. He's afraid that they'll never find a complete cure for Dru. But then he has an idea. He needs to bring in the big guns. The Order of Turaka. Drusilla says they'll be at her party, and she shows three tarot cards.

Dalton gets very nervous, which helps get in some more exposition. Because he is commenting about the Order of Turaka and how frightening they are. And he says isn't that overkill?

Spike: No, I think it's just enough kill.

We are at 15 minutes 56 seconds in, but remember, this is a two-episode arc. So we haven't yet reached the one-quarter point of the double-episode story. So while Spike getting this idea is something of a turn in the story, we'll look for the major plot turn for the first major double episode at about 22 minutes into this episode.

Willow And Oz Meet At Last

Back at the Career Fair, Principal Snyder is looking for Buffy. She just went somewhere with Giles. Willow tries to cover for her, but Snyder remains suspicious.

A man in a business suit touches Willow's arm and asks her to come with him. He sounds very serious. He takes her behind a set of curtains to a closed off area where classical music is playing. Someone offers her a tray of canapés.

The man is a recruiter for the world's largest software concern. They've been watching Willow, which makes total sense given how much hacking we have seen her do so far. The recruiter also tells her they are very selective. Only one other student met their criteria.

The camera pans and we see it's Oz. So they are finally going to meet. He is clearly happy to see Willow. And he offers her the tray of appetizers and says, "Canapé?"

Giles And Buffy Talk Careers And Religion

At the cemetery, Giles is breathing hard, trying to keep up with Buffy, who is walking fast on purpose. He tells her she's being immature. And he tries to reassure her about Career Week. He says she can find some other employment just the way he did. He's a Watcher and a librarian.

She points out that it's different. Those two things go together. No one is going to find it strange that he spends a lot of time with a bunch of dusty old books. And then he says, "What about law enforcement?" She glares at him.

At the mausoleum, they find a reliquary. Giles explains that's the word for this small vault that houses relics. Like a Saint's finger or other body parts.

Buffy: Note to self: Religion, freaky.

At 21 minutes 9 seconds in, Giles says something is coming, and he can guarantee it's not good.

The One-Quarter Twist

At 21 minutes 21 seconds in we get what I see as our One-Quarter Twist. This is the plot turn that spins the story in an entirely new direction, but comes from outside the protagonist. It also usually raises the stakes.

Here, it is the arrival of the assassins from the Order of Turaka.

Before this point, the story is about the Career Fair and Buffy trying to find out what Dalton was up to. Now it will be about Buffy and her friends trying to deal with this new and very serious threat.

We see a bus pull into the Sunnydale bus terminal.

A large white man with a scar and long hair gets out. He is wearing boots, and he just looks ominous and frightening. Then on Buffy's street we see a different man, also white. He's not ominous in any way. He's carrying a briefcase. And he's wearing a trench coat. He looks very unassuming. He has receding curly hair, wears glasses and is middle-aged.

The man rings the doorbell at the house next to Buffy's and says he is Norman Pfister of Blush Beautiful. He tells the woman who answers that he's not selling anything. But he's offering some free samples.

The neighbor says "Free?" and lets him in. The door closes. About 22.5 minutes in we hear a scream.

That scream fades into a screeching sound as we see in the next scene an airplane landing. In the cargo hold is a young pretty Black woman. She kicks and knocks out a uniformed airline employee and climbs out of the cargo hold.

Compelling Exposition About The Du Lac Cross

At the library. Giles tells Willow, Xander, and Buffy that du Lac, the monk whose mausoleum they were in, invented the Du Lac Cross. He previously told Buffy that the Vatican excommunicated du Lac partly because he wrote a book of spells that were dangerous. And that is the exact book the vampire stole from Giles' library in **Lie To Me**.

Giles explains that the cross was created to read the book. Buffy calls it a basic decoder ring. Xander jokes about the actual name of it, which is the Du Lac Cross. And he says why would you invent something really cool and give it such a boring name. Giles snaps at Xander and Buffy for joking around.

This dialogue shows another way to keep the exposition interesting.

In the commentary, Marti Noxon noted that she always felt bad for Anthony Stuart Head (who plays Giles) because he had to deliver so much exposition. For that reason, the writers called the library the death set – because it was so easy for it to become boring with people just sitting around and talking. Also, the set itself remains pretty much the same from episode to episode.

So they did things to try to keep it visually interesting. For instance, that earlier scene where Buffy helps Giles steady the stack of books that is about to fall over. And there are similar stacks all over the table in that scene.

Here, they are sitting and talking, but they use humor and joking around to break up the exposition.

Marti also said that Anthony Stuart Head has such an air of authority that it helps sell the exposition. And the last thing she said is that they also got away with a lot of exposition by calling it out at times and making fun of it.

Now Giles says that du Lac destroyed all the crosses he made, except the one buried with him. The group speculates that maybe it's because du Lac realized how dangerous the book was.

Giles says they need to work late figuring out what that book contained and why the vampires are so interested in it. Willow's excited and says, "Research party!" Xander tells her she needs a life in the worst way. Another good example of a joke breaking up the exposition.

Buffy leaves, promising to come back tomorrow. She claims she's not good with book research anyway. And she needs to get some rest, and she has somewhere to be.

The Skating Rink Attack

Next, we see Buffy skating. She looks very serene as she skates and does some turns and spins. When she's ready to stop, she slides. And falls a little bit, landing with her back against the side of the rink.

The big guy we saw getting off the bus attacks her from behind. They fight. Things do not look good for Buffy. But Angel comes in. He's in vamp face. He starts fighting, and then the guy gets Angel against the wall. But Buffy fights him off. She kills the assassin by kicking and slicing his neck with her skate blade.

The scene changes, and Drusilla turns over the card that looks something like that assassin. There are two cards left.

But Spike says he's not worried. All they needed was to buy some time, and they just need a little more of it. They're close to decoding the book.

So we know that of course Spike wants to kill Buffy, but even if he doesn't succeed at killing her with these assassins, he will still achieve his main goal. Which is to get that book decoded.

Back at the ice rink, Angel sees the guy's ring. He tells Buffy to go home. That they need to get her somewhere safe.

Angel Afraid And Angry

Angel gets angry when Buffy jokes about it. She thinks he is partly upset because his face got cut. He jerks back when she touches it. But that's not the issue. He says she shouldn't have to touch him when he's like this, meaning when he is in vamp face.

I have a little bit of a question about this because later we will see that vampires can pretty much go in and out of vamp face whenever they want. In fact, I think that we already have seen that. And here it seems like Angel is not able to change back to his human face.

But I'm willing to go with that inconsistency because it gives us this really nice moment where Buffy says she didn't even notice. And she kisses him.

The young woman from the cargo hold watches from a distance.

Marti Noxon commented that this scene showed that Buffy had finally really accepted Angel's vampire side. She's not afraid of him anymore. And we saw in the season pilot, **When She Was Bad**, that she did feel wary of him. And had concerns because of his vampire side.

Also, Marti commented that this was a scene they needed for the plot. Because they needed the young woman, Kendra, from the plane to see Buffy kissing a vampire. But there was no way that Kendra could know from a distance that Angel was a vampire unless he was in vamp face.

So the scene came about due to a very practical need in the story. And it led to this wonderful emotional moment for Buffy and Angel.

The Order Scares Giles

At the library, Buffy shows Giles the ring and he tells her about the Order of Turaka. That they are deadly assassins and bounty hunters. He tells her their credo is to sew discord and kill the unwary.

Giles yells at Xander when he jokes around about it. Much the way Angel snapped at Buffy. Giles tells Buffy they need to find a secure location for her while they figure out what to do.

Behavior Changes Show The Stakes

This really scares Buffy. Because now both Angel and Giles have said she needs to run and hide.

This is a great example of how to convey not just to Buffy but to the audience how serious this threat is. We have two characters we trust who always feel great confidence in Buffy. And they both tell her to run and hide. Neither has ever suggested this before.

They also both snap at her, which is unlike them.

Yes, Giles gets irritated sometimes when Buffy jokes around. But he rarely shows genuine anger at Buffy. Same thing for Angel. Having them both change their behavior this way and suggest she hide, which is also so counter to what the Slayer is supposed to do, is so much stronger than if they simply described the Order of Turaka as dangerous.

It's a great example of showing your reader or audience something rather than merely telling them.

Notice, though, that we do also have Giles tell Buffy information after the tension escalates. Giles says of the

Order that they are a breed apart. Unlike vampires, they have no earthly desire other than to collect their bounty.

I think that's such an interesting distinction from what we see from Spike and Dru, who exhibit the very humanlike emotions of love and jealousy.

Giles sees that difference as making these assassins more dangerous. Probably because there's no way to trip them up. No way to appeal to them. He also says where there is one, there's another. They find a target, and their only goal is to eliminate it. They won't stop until the job is done. Some are human and some aren't. So Buffy won't know who they are until they attack.

The Worm Man

We switch to the neighbor's house. There are worms everywhere and they are gradually forming back into Norman Pfister, who is drinking a cup of tea.

So that illustrates what Giles pointed out – that there's no way to know the assassins until they attack.

(Marti Noxon also referred to this character as The Bug Man. And the worms do look a little bit like elongated bugs.)

Buffy Feels Vulnerable

We next see Buffy walking in the hall at school. We can tell from her body language how vulnerable she feels. She keeps one arm over her stomach. She startles at every loud noise. And she's peering this way and that whenever anyone makes any sort of move or so much as looks at her.

We see a woman police officer look over at Buffy, and Buffy kind of jerks away. She hones in on a man who pulls out a comb. Discordant music plays in the background. Buffy is walking very slowly, which is unlike her. It's such a contrast with how she walked so fast in the cemetery that Giles couldn't keep up.

Oz walks up behind Buffy and almost overtakes her. She spins, grabs him by the throat, pins him against the wall.

Buffy: Try it.

Oz: Try what?

Buffy apologizes.

Oz says: I'm still not clear what I'm supposed to try.

Buffy apologizes again and she runs off.

Oz: Intense person.

We cut to Buffy walking alone on the street in the dark. She pauses across from her house and looks at it. It's dark, and she leaves.

In the library, Giles is worried about Buffy because she just took off. Xander says there's no answer at her house. Giles says maybe she unplugged the phone, but Xander tells him no. It's a statistical impossibility for a sixteen-year-old girl to unplug her phone. Willow nods.

Giles says maybe he scared Buffy with his intense warnings.

Xander: You think?

Willow reassures Giles that it's good that Buffy took him seriously. Buffy in the meantime has gone to Angel's underground apartment. He's not there, creating more isolation for Buffy. She looks around his place.

Angel's Apartment Tells Us About Angel

I love the way Angel's living space is decorated. It is mostly underground. It's dark. The lighting is indirect. We see these beautiful sculptures. One is in a glass case. And there are paintings arranged very artfully on the wall.

Marti Noxon in the DVD said they really thought about Angel's home, and the fact that he lived hundreds of years. So they figured he would have accumulated a lot of artwork from different time periods.

This is a great example of showing something about the

character and reminding the audience of his background by carefully choosing his surroundings and where he lives.

Buffy is wearing a flannel shirt over a tank top. She sits on the bed, sighs, and lies down curled up on her side. Almost in the fetal position. More body language showing how vulnerable she feels.

Angel is at a dive bar. He walks in, and the proprietor, Willie, says, "Hi Angel." So we know that they already know each other. Willie seems a little nervous. And we find out why, because Angel immediately starts threatening him.

He wants to know who called out the Order of Turaka. Willie claims that he turned over a new leaf. He's not trading on information anymore. But Angel doesn't buy it. He gets Willie in a choke hold. Willie spills out that Spike will draw and quarter him if Willie tells Angel what's going on.

Of course, he has already told him that Spike is behind it. But Angel wants more, and he continues to threaten Willie.

Kendra knocks him with a board from behind. The two fight. She's a great fighter, and she kicks him into a cage and locks him in. She asks him about his girlfriend, but he won't say anything. She points out that the sun will rise in a few hours when he threatens her. And she says she won't have to kill him, the sun will do it.

Willow's Frog Fear

In the library, Willow has fallen asleep hunched over the books. Giles wakes her and she says something about "don't warn the tadpoles." She's very confused. And she says, "Giles, what are you doing here?"

He tells her she fell asleep and asks about the tadpoles. Willow says she has frog fear.

Giles found something. He calls Xander, who has gone home, and tells him to go to Buffy's house to check on her.

Xander must've said something about not having a way to get there because Giles says to get Cordelia to drive him.

Giles tells Willow that he learned that the book includes a ritual to restore a sick vampire to full health. They realize what Spike is up to.

More Story Questions

Then we see Spike reading a page from the book. He says they've got it, the missing link. And Drusilla says it was right in front of them the whole time.

This is a great story question. Before we were in suspense to see if Spike would succeed in getting this translation. Now we raise another question: What is the missing link? What do they still need to make this work? And how is it that it was right in front of them?

That is a great example of questions to keep the reader coming back to Part Two.

Cordelia and Xander bicker as they walk toward Buffy's house. Cordelia is complaining that she isn't there just to give Xander rides. He tells her if she wants to be in the Scooby gang she has to be willing to be inconvenienced.

I'm pretty sure this is the first reference to Scooby Doo and the Scooby gang that we get in the series.

Cordelia responds by saying something like, yes, she lies awake "hoping that you losers will include me in your group."

No one answers the door at Buffy's. Xander pretty easily gets in through the front window and lets Cordelia in. He goes upstairs to look for Buffy.

Cordelia is on the first floor when there's a knock on the door. It's Norman Pfister offering her free samples. She lets him in. This too is a great story question because we aren't going to see what happens to Cordelia during this episode.

Starting A Midpoint Reversal

I feel like Cordelia letting Pfister in starts the Midpoint

Reversal. Normally we will see the protagonist suffer a major reversal or make a major commitment at the Midpoint. Which here is going to be the end of the episode.

There are a couple things that happen here that are a significant reversal for Buffy and her core team. This first is Cordelia letting one of the assassins into Buffy's house, especially given that she and Xander are there alone.

Next, we see Angel in the cage.

He's cowering against the back wall as the sun rises and shines over most of the cage. The danger to him is undercut a bit because we see that the lock on the cage is a really small padlock. And Marti Noxon commented on the DVD about how disappointed they were when they did the filming and saw that it was this tiny lock.

She said it's very inconsistent how strong Angel is. Sometimes he can move mountains, other times a bicycle lock stops him. This is an example of one of those things where (I assume) they needed to film a certain amount that day, so there wasn't time to get a different lock, one that would look serious enough to keep Angel in.

Ending With A Hook

We switch from that scene with Angel at the point of death to Buffy waking up. She's still in Angel's bed. The sunlight shines in her eyes. She opens them just as Kendra attacks her.

Buffy: You must be Number Two.

She's referring to the assassins because she doesn't know about Pfister, so she's aware only of that first guy she fought in the ice rink.

Kendra and Buffy fight in the middle of Angel's place. They have a similar fighting style. Sometimes one gets the better of the other, then it switches. Finally, they reach a point where they are facing each other almost in the same fighting position.

Kendra: Who are you?

Buffy: Who am I? You attacked me. Who the hell are you?

Kendra: I'm Kendra. The Vampire Slayer.

And we cut.

What a great hook. This is such a major story question. Is Kendra really a Vampire Slayer? She says it with such conviction. She clearly believes she is, so how can there be another Vampire Slayer and what does it mean? Wonderful end to the episode.

Spoilers And Foreshadowing

RETURNING AND REPLACEMENT CHARACTERS

The other character that Marti Noxon mentioned that the writers thought would be a one-episode character is Anya. And I find that so striking.

Season Three's **The Wish**, where we first see Anya, is one of my favorite **Buffy** episodes ever. That is where Cordelia wishes that Buffy had never come to Sunnydale. Anya, who has been posing as a teenaged girl new to the school, turns out to be a vengeance demon. She comes back in Dopplegangland (also in Season Three). (I assume that at least that was planned.)

The fact that the writers didn't know Anya would be a series regular doesn't entirely surprise me. Because I don't think early on they knew that Angel would become a spinoff show. So most likely they figured if they continued, Cordelia would stay on Buffy.

Cordelia eventually leaves to be part of **Angel**, the show. And Anya in some ways steps into Cordelia's role. She is a different type of character. But there are similarities in that she is a truth teller – someone who bluntly says whatever comes into her mind and doesn't worry about social niceties.

Also, Anya and Xander will get into a relationship. So in that sense, too, she sort of replaces Cordelia. I can't wait to talk more about that, because Anya is a very different type of character.

So much in the way that Principal Snyder comes in and replaces Principal Flutie in terms of the role of principal, but is nonetheless a very different person, we will see that with Anya. She takes on a Cordelia-like role in certain ways, but she is definitely her own person and not just someone who slid into that open slot.

Spike And Drusilla

On to Spike and Drusilla. I loved this quick reference by Giles to contrasting the assassins, who have no earthly desires, to vampires. In a few episodes we will see the character of The Judge who comes to rid the world of the scourge of humanity. And he finds that Spike and Drusilla are somewhat human. More so than he thinks is appropriate.

You get the sense that he could burn and destroy them because they are more human than the other vampires. I think that also applies to Dalton, a character The Judge does burn.

Paranoia And Frogs

I also love that we get this glimpse of this woman cop Buffy jerks away from in the hallway. I am sure that's something I didn't notice before other than it shows Buffy's paranoia. But then we see her again on Career Day, and it turns out she is one of the assassins.

I just love how well that fits because, yes, Buffy was being paranoid. She was wrong about the guy with the comb. She was wrong about Oz. But she was right about that cop.

And a quick, fun foreshadowing: Willow says she has frog fear. Later in the season in Killed By Death, Buffy is in the hospital with a really bad flu. And Willow will distract the orderlies by pretending that frogs are crawling all over her. Basically pretending to have kind of a psychotic break or episode so that they think she is the escaped patient, not Buffy.

Xander And Cordelia

And of course we have Cordelia and Xander bickering more.

Marti Noxon commented on the DVD how much she enjoyed getting to write Xander and Cordelia and gradually build their relationship to this point where they kiss. And she says she doesn't think the audience saw what was coming.

As I mentioned before, I didn't. Maybe other people did. She and the other writers were trying to weave this in and yet not make it obvious. I think they did a great job at that.

Number Two

I also love Buffy's line to Kendra: "You must be Number Two." At that moment she says it, we think she's talking about the second assassin. The first time I watched, I was fooled. I thought Kendra was one of the other assassins. And the writers do some things to suggest that. I don't think I mentioned that at one point Drusilla points to another tarot card right before we see Kendra, implying that she is one of the other assassins.

Also, this line is such a quick hint that in fact Kendra is a second Slayer.

Throughout Part Two of What's My Line we're going to explore that Kendra was called when Buffy died. I think

Buffy says something like "it was only for a minute." And how Buffy feels about this.

She has been complaining this whole episode about her destiny. I shouldn't say complaining because that makes it sound kind of petty. She's been struggling with this idea that she was chosen. That she is the only one who can do this, and she really feels the weight of that.

But now, in Part Two, she will deal with how it feels when there is someone else. There is a Number Two. A second Slayer.

I also love that Kendra likewise is very different from Buffy. So again we will see the writers not just bringing in a Buffy clone but someone who has a totally different background, a different take on slaying. A different approach.

Kendra also will bring out the difference between seeing slaying as a job or something imposed on you versus it being part of your identity.

And Kendra is so full of confidence when she says that she is Kendra the Vampire Slayer. Not just confidence but pride. I feel like it echoes what we saw from Buffy in the pilot episode. Right at that Midpoint where she said, "Don't you know who I am?" And really embraced being the Slayer.

Here we see that that is how Kendra feels. Buffy I think underneath does still feel that to some extent. But she also is struggling with this being imposed on her. So it's wonderful that Kendra's intonation, the way she feels, also signals what Buffy is going to grapple with in the next episode.

Questions For Your Writing

- **Is there exposition at the start of your**

story? Does it come out through conflict? If not, could it?

- Choose a character and imagine that person's body language. What gestures does the character make that convey emotion? How does the character stand or sit?
- If your characters are in danger, do their actions show that?
- Once you've answered a story question, can you add a new one to keep your readers engaged? More than one?

Next: What's My Line Part Two

NEXT WE'LL TALK ABOUT **WHAT'S MY LINE PART TWO**, including how the Midpoint Reversal spins the story in a new direction and changes Buffy's mindset about slaying and why readers and audience members don't always believe something even if it's authentic.

CHAPTER 10

WHAT'S MY LINE PART TWO (S2 E10)

THIS CHAPTER TALKS about **What's My Line Part Two**, Season Two Episode Ten, written by Marti Noxon and directed by David Semel.

In particular, we'll look at:

- **why readers and audience members don't always believe something that's authentic or really happened**
- **quickly reminding your audience of past events without slowing down your story or losing their interest**
- **saving your darlings for a new story**
- **writing yourself out of a corner**

Okay, let's dive into the Hellmouth.

Opening Conflict For Part Two

We still start with an initial conflict even though we are picking up from the last episode at the story Midpoint.

Kendra and Buffy are facing off against each other after fighting. Buffy says something like, "Once more. Who are you again?" Kendra says she is the Vampire Slayer, which is how we ended the last episode. But notice how we pick up again with this repetition. And it fits because Buffy of course does not believe Kendra and is still processing what Kendra said.

Buffy: Nice cover story. Try it on someone who's not the real Slayer.

Kendra: Nonsense. There is but one Slayer and I am she.

Buffy proposes they back off and go see her Watcher and Kendra agrees. We are 1 minute 44 seconds in, and we switch to more Opening Conflict.

Remember How Angel's In Trouble?

Angel is breathing hard in the corner of the cage. There is sunlight all around him. So again we're getting a very quick flash of what happened last time. Even if you had not watched the prior episode, you would already know that we apparently have a new Slayer who was fighting Buffy. And that Angel was overpowered and knocked into this cage and is about to die.

We switch to the credits.

That's where we really pick up the story and it moves forward.

Buffy's Sarcasm

We start in the library. Giles says he spoke to Kendra's watcher, Mr. Zabuto, whom Giles knows. Buffy remains skeptical of Kendra. She's sarcastic when talking to her, including making fun when Kendra says she has no last name. And Buffy says something like, "Stuck in the eighties much?" She also sometimes mocks Kendra's accent. Later when they're friendlier she will jokingly mimic it.

From today's perspective, that seems a bit insensitive and

something we wouldn't want to see our hero do now. At the time I don't think there was as much awareness.

Real Doesn't Mean Believable

In the commentary, Marti Noxon said they got a lot of flak about Kendra's accent. (I remember that on the Bronze, which was a message board about Buffy at the time. People argued that Kendra's accent was generic and seemed to belong to nowhere in particular.)

The irony is Marti said they worked really hard with a dialect coach. He narrowed the accent down to this very specific part of Jamaica. I believe she said a particular town because they wanted to have this real sense of Kendra having come from a specific place with specific traditions.

But in that effort to be so specific, it did not match up with what audience members perhaps expected or thought. It didn't quite sound like a Jamaican accent to them, and it didn't sound like anything else they were familiar with.

This is a good example of a couple things. One is that sometimes despite your best efforts as a writer you may find that you're not able to convey to readers what is clear behind the scenes. You can do a ton of research and something can be absolutely correct, and somebody will say, "Oh, this author should've done some research on this. They just made it up and it's really dumb."

A scenic designer I knew had a reviewer critique one of her sets, saying it wasn't authentic to Egypt during the time period of the play. It was, but it wasn't what that reviewer had in her mind about Egyptian pyramids. If reality is different from what's in the general consciousness, or even what a particular reader or viewer knows about a topic, the audience member often reacts badly. It can be tricky as an author to walk that line of potentially being too authentic, and people will think it is not correct because it doesn't fit with what they "know."

In short, because something is authentic, or because it truly happened, does not mean the reader will believe it.

It has to be believable within the world of the story. Sometimes that means you will need to have a flavor of authenticity but include enough that's familiar to readers and audience members that they will get it without a lot of explanation.

I said this critique of the accent was an example of two things. The second is you are never going to please everybody. So you do your best to tell your story the way you see it and just accept that there are going to be criticisms.

Two Slayers

Willow comes into the library. Kendra is shocked to learn that Buffy has friends. And surprised that Giles allows it.

Giles is more amazed by the idea of two Slayers. He says that has never happened before. A new Slayer's only called if the previous one died. And then he puts it together.

Giles: Good Lord. You were dead, Buffy.

Buffy: I was only gone for a minute.

Giles says it must not matter. Her death, no matter how brief, caused the activation of the new Slayer.

Kendra: She died?

Buffy: Just a little.

In the commentary, Marti Noxon said it was Joss Whedon's idea to bring in this new Slayer because Buffy died. She wasn't sure if he planned that from back in Season One, or if he only realized later that since Buffy died, the next Slayer should be called.

Giles says it's unprecedented. He's flummoxed, having two Slayers. And Buffy says, "What's the flum?" She's not dead, so they can send Kendra home. It was a mistake and it creeps her out to have Kendra there. But Kendra says she can't go home. Her Watcher told her a very dark power is about to rise in Sunnydale.

Buffy is definitely not happy about this. And we are starting to see the effect of this Midpoint Reversal with a new Slayer fighting Buffy.

In the last episode, Buffy was really struggling with not being able to have a future like everyone else, not taking part in Career Week in any real way. Feeling saddled with this destiny. But now we are seeing that despite all of that, she does feel pretty strongly about her place as the Slayer. This is important to her, and the idea of someone else in that role as well is an adjustment she will continue to struggle with in this episode.

Buffy also sarcastically says to Kendra how is she going to help – by randomly attacking people? And Kendra explains that she thought Buffy was a vampire because Buffy was kissing a vampire. We get some of the best Willow lines in this episode.

Willow: Buffy would never do that. Oh. (looks at Buffy) Except sometimes you do that. But only with Angel, right?

And Buffy says right, and she explains that Angel is good. Giles confirms it. But Kendra says she's read about Angelus. She calls him a monster and says he looked like a monster when she.... And she trails off.

Willie Gets Angel Out Of The Cage

We cut to Willie. He has gotten Angel out of the cage. Angel is very weak. So Willie is able to drag him across the floor and drop him down a trap door into a tunnel under Sunnydale. There is water running all over. (At some point I think we're told that these tunnels are sewer tunnels. It's pretty clean for a sewer, if very damp. Definitely full of water. I just try not to think too much about whether there's sewage or not.)

Spike meets Willie and gives Willie money for turning over Angel. Willie asks what he's going to do with Angel.

Spike: I'm thinking maybe dinner and a movie. I don't want to rush into anything. I've been hurt you know.

Cordelia And The Worm Attack

At Buffy's house. Cordelia is asking Norman Pfister, who is the assassin who can turn into a mass of worms and back again, about colors from his cosmetic case. Because remember, he's posing as this cosmetic salesman door-to-door.

He asks Cordelia if she's the only lady in the house and she says yes. Xander comes back downstairs just as Cordelia starts to get nervous about the robotic way Pfister is answering her questions about the cosmetics.

Pfister begins to disassemble into worms. Cordelia and Xander run for the basement and slam the door. The worms are crawling under the door. Xander and Cordelia use duct tape to seal up the opening and stamp on worms that have gotten through.

Kendra And Buffy Question Willie

At Willie's place, the cage is empty and Kendra says there are no ashes, so she didn't kill Angel. Buffy says that's a good thing because now she doesn't have to kill Kendra.

They threaten Willie, but he claims he saved Angel. That Angel is fine. And Kendra says okay, that's it. Angel's fine, so they need to go back to the Watcher for orders.

Buffy: I don't take orders. I do things my way.

Kendra: No wonder you died.

One-Quarter Through What's My Line Part Two

At 11 minutes, 8 seconds in, Spike brings Angel to

Drusilla. He says all they need now is the full moon. Angel will die and she'll be restored.

This is one quarter of the way through the episode. Despite that we have a two-episode story arc here, so we're already well past the major One-Quarter Twist for the overall story, I found it interesting that I still saw some pretty significant turns at the episode quarter, halfway, and three-quarter marks.

That's part of what keeps this episode moving along so well.

Drusilla asks Spike to let her have Angel to play with. He says okay, but Angel can't die until the ritual.

Back at school, Giles is walking with Buffy and Kendra in an outdoor walkway. Willow is also there, and Giles says he and Mr. Zabuto conferred and decided the two Slayers should work together. Buffy is definitely not thrilled about that.

Giles informs them that Spike is trying to revive Drusilla and tells Kendra Spike sent the Order of Turaka after Buffy. Kendra knows right away who that is. She has read all six volumes of some very dense text about Slayer history. Giles is really impressed.

Buffy asks why Kendra knows that and has all this time to study. And Kendra says the Slayer Handbook requires that.

Marti Noxon said in the commentary on the DVD that she made up the handbook because she thought it was a funny way to show that there were a bunch of things that Giles bypassed because Buffy's not really a rule follower. She also noted the writers wanted Kendra to be from a very different world from Buffy to raise the conflict between the two.

So Kendra is more book smart. She really has more in

common with Giles than Buffy does. Buffy acts more on instinct.

We get another nice quote from Willow, who expresses surprise about the handbook.

Willow: Is there a T-shirt too? Because that would be cool.

Buffy asks why she doesn't have a handbook. And Giles says after meeting her he realized in her case the handbook would be of no use. Buffy is kind of taken aback and says something like, "In my case? What's wrong with my case?"

She feels worse when Kendra and Giles joke about all the footnotes in that volume that Kendra read.

Buffy (to Willow): Get a load of the she-Giles.

Willow reassures Buffy that she'll always be first with Giles. She's the real Slayer. But Buffy says maybe it wouldn't be so bad to be replaced. After this crisis is over maybe Kendra can take over and Buffy will go to Disneyland. And then later have a normal life. Do Career Day stuff.

Back In The Basement

We switch to Cordelia and Xander. Cordelia is pacing in the basement, driving Xander crazy. He tells her to stop. She tells him they should be coming up with a plan.

Xander: I have a plan. We wait. Buffy saves us.

Cordelia: How will she even know where to find us?

Xander: Cordelia, this is Buffy's house. Odds are she'll find us.

Cordelia wants to go upstairs and check to see if the worm man is gone. Xander yells at her for letting the guy in to begin with just because he offered her some free samples. They argue. He says he's not stopping her from leaving.

Cordelia: I bet you would. I bet you'd let a girl go to her doom all by herself.

Xander: Not just any girl. You're special.

They continue to yell at each other, stepping closer and closer until they are less than an inch apart. And they kiss. Romantic music crescendos.

They break apart.

Xander: We so need to get out of here.

Cordelia agrees, and they run for the stairs.

They don't see any worms, so they go out the basement door into the hallway. As they are running for the front door, worms gathered on the ceiling fall down on Cordelia. She runs out to the front yard and screams at Xander to get them off of her. He sprays her over and over with a garden hose and they run for her car. It squeals away. (And we see her license plate, Queen C.)

Quick Reminders Through Dialogue And Conflict

We're now at 17 minutes 42 seconds in. And we are at Career Day in the school. Buffy and Willow are heading towards the law enforcement area. Buffy tells Willow there's a cute guy checking her out. Willow glances over and says that it's Oz. He's just expressing computer nerd solidarity.

But Buffy says then why is he walking over here? And he does come over to Willow.

Oz's hair is a different shade than when we last saw him.

Willow: Your hair. Is brown.

Oz: Yes, sometimes.

Notice in these last couple scenes how many quick reminders we get of what happened last week. They are worked in so fast and as part of conflict, so it doesn't feel like these lines of dialogue are there just to catch us up.

There's Cordelia with Norman Pfister asking about these free cosmetic samples. The conflict between her and Xander where he's yelling at her for letting the guy in. And in that dialogue it's clear that they are in Buffy's house.

All of that gives the audience information, or reminds us of it, but it works because Cordelia and Xander are so angry at each other. So they aren't just saying to each other things the other one knows solely to inform the audience. They're saying it as ammunition against one another.

Likewise, we get Buffy's wish for a normal life and the Career Day background, which all comes out in the context of how she feels about Kendra being there. And we see Buffy processing all of it. First, she was very upset that there was a second Slayer. Then she was a little jealous of Kendra and Giles. But now she is taking all that in and thinking, hey, there might be a good side to this. Maybe I can have a normal life.

I love that moment from Buffy. It's such a realization on her part. And I like that while we see throughout the series Buffy acting on gut instinct and emotion, she is also thoughtful about the issue she confronts. Here, she's able to take a step back and kind of look at all sides of this. And think about what Kendra's existence means for her.

A long way of saying that all of that is really key for Buffy and the story, but it also gets across this information that a new viewer would need. Or that any viewer might want if they saw Part One a week ago.

Similarly, with Oz and Willow, the fact that Buffy points out Oz, thinking he is a stranger, and Willow tells her a little about who Oz is reminds the audience of a lot of things. Including that Willow and Oz have computer skills in common. And we will get a little bit more in dialogue now between Oz and Willow that also feels very organic.

It all comes based on who these characters are, and it's funny or comes from conflict or both. So it keeps us engaged.

These are good things to keep in mind when you are writing either in installments or in one novel and you've shifted away from a plotline or set of characters for a while. When you come back, it's a good idea to remind readers very quickly what's going on or who the characters are.

You don't want to overdo it, though. People read at different paces. So one reader might spend three weeks or a month reading your novel and might really need that reminder. Someone else might read it in two days. So you want to use a light touch.

And I feel like it is so perfectly done in this episode.

Oz asks Willow if she will be becoming a corporate computer person and wearing a suit.

Willow: I think I'm going to finish high school first.

She asks about him. And he says he's not really a computer guy, he just tests well. Which is bad because it tends to lead to work.

So she asks what interests or ambitions he has. And he starts telling her about his guitar playing and joking about it.

An Assassin Strikes

The law enforcement seminar starts. The woman cop that we saw so quickly in the last episode tells the students to raise their hands when she calls their names. She calls Buffy first. When Buffy raises her hand, the cop pulls a gun on her.

Buffy disarms the cop. But there are shots fired because the cop has a second gun.

Oz pushes Willow out of the way and he gets shot in the arm.

Kendra appears, She kicks the second gun from the cop's hand. The cop pulls a knife and grabs ahold of poor Jonathan.

Buffy and Kendra stand together in the fighting stance, facing the cop. And this is nice. It's the first shot where we see them ready to fight together.

The cop throws Jonathan aside and runs out. Kendra follows, but she is not able to catch her.

Willow goes to Oz and asks if he's okay.

Oz: Yeah, I'm shot. You know, wow. It's odd. And painful.

Jonathan asks if it was a demonstration.

Gathering In the Library

In the library. Buffy tells Giles about what happened. Willow says the paramedics said it was only a scrape and Oz will be okay.

Xander and Cordelia come in and fill everyone in on Norman Pfister. Giles explains to them that Kendra is also a Slayer.

Xander: A Slayer. Ha. I knew this "I'm the only one, I'm the only one" was just an attention-getter.

Kendra stutters and stumbles and looks down when Xander talks. And she calls him Sir. We find out later that she is not allowed to talk to boys at all. Cordelia finds another worm and runs out to take another shower.

Buffy says that these assassins are definitely serious, "but fortunately for me, so is Kendra."

The Three-Quarter Turn In What's My Line

At 22 minutes in, Giles says he found the remaining keys to the spell to revive Drusilla. They need the presence of her sire and his blood, a new moon, and a church. Buffy reveals that Angel is Dru's sire.

All of this is happening halfway through the episode and it makes it a good Three-Quarter Turn in the double-episode arc.

So remember our Three-Quarter Turn, like the One-Quarter Twist, spins the story in a new direction. But unlike that first major plot turn, which generally comes from outside the protagonist, the one at the three-quarter mark usually arises from the protagonist's actions at the Midpoint. Or from that reversal at the Midpoint.

I see the Three-Quarter Turn here as Buffy and Kendra

uniting. Which will happen in a moment, and that really does grow from that Midpoint Reversal of Buffy confronting this new Slayer.

Willow tells Buffy not to worry. They'll save Angel.

And Kendra questions that, saying the priority is stopping Drusilla, not saving Angel. Buffy and Giles try to assure her that Angel is really good now and they should save him.

Xander: Angel's our friend. Except I don't like him.

Buffy tells Kendra that right now their priorities mesh, so let's work together. And Kendra finally says okay.

I see this is that turn where, despite Kendra's reluctance and Buffy's continued feelings about Kendra, they decide to work together.

Buffy says she's had it. Spike is going down. He can throw whatever he wants at her, "but nobody messes with my boyfriend."

This is also a nice Midpoint Commitment for the episode for Buffy.

Now we see that the entire story shifts. Because it is not just about stopping Spike and Drusilla from reviving Dru or restoring Dru to her full power. It is about saving Angel.

Drusilla is torturing Angel with holy water as she talks about things that her mother loved. And what her family liked to do and eat.

Marti Noxon commented that Drusilla is really Angelus' work of art. It represents the worst – or in Angelus' mind the best – of what he did as a vampire. The way that he tortured Drusilla and drove her mad before turning her into a vampire.

Angel now feels guilty about this, seeing the effect on Dru. He tries to apologize for torturing and killing her family. But she won't let him. She says they used to eat cake and eggs and honey. "Until you came and ripped their throats out."

Angel screams as she tortures him.

Dialogue Fills In The Back Story

This is another example of quick dialogue that fills us in on the past. And gives us a little bit of exposition, yet it all fits in the current scene and moves the story. Because we believe Drusilla would say these things to Angel as she is torturing him.

It also reveals complexity to Drusilla. She is angry at Angel over this still – and I don't mean still, because a human, of course, would still be angry. She is angry despite being a vampire. Despite that we know Spike has done terrible things, killed people. She probably has as well.

And her vampire self no doubt admires Angel for what he did to her and her family. We will see she is very enamored of him and attracted to him. But at the same time, I feel there is a bit of her human self still there which is why she is still angry at him.

Buffy And Kendra Spar

We switch to Buffy whittling stakes in Giles' office with Kendra. Kendra's holding the crossbow. And she criticizes Buffy for all the people who know that she's the Slayer.

Kendra: Did no one explain secret identity to you?

Buffy: It must've been in the Slayer Handbook. After the chapter on personality removal.

So there is still a fair amount of tension here. Buffy tells Kendra to be careful with the crossbow. And Kendra says don't worry, she is an expert in all types of weapons. But the crossbow goes off and we hear a crash. Giles calls in to find out if they're all right.

Buffy: Yeah, it's okay. Kendra killed the bad lamp.

Kendra apologizes to Giles. She tells Buffy the trigger is different than the one she's used to. But then she kind of softens and says maybe when this is over Buffy can show her more about this one. It's a nice moment between them where Kendra recognizes Buffy's expertise and lets down her guard a little bit.

She then says that Buffy's life is different from hers. Kendra was taught that things like friends, school, and family distract from the calling. Her parents gave her to her Watcher when she was so little that she doesn't even remember her parents. That's how seriously her people take the calling.

This all is so different from Buffy's experience. Buffy didn't know she was the Slayer until – and this happened in the movie – the previous Slayer died and she was called. She had no idea. But we see in other parts of the world there is this tradition where a girl might know she's a potential Slayer. And her family would know, and she would start preparing.

Kendra sees Buffy looking a little sad and says, "Don't feel sorry for me."

Emotions As Power

Kendra doesn't feel sorry for herself, and she tells Buffy that she shouldn't entertain emotions. That it's weakness.

But Buffy argues her emotions give her power. Kendra says she prefers to keep an even mind. And Buffy says something like, "That explains a lot." She says Kendra's technique is better than her own. To which Kendra says, "I know." But Buffy says she would've won the fight between the two of them in the end because Kendra lacks imagination.

She goes on and on in this vein, goading Kendra until Kendra gets mad.

And Buffy says, "That's anger you're feeling," and asks her doesn't she feel the power? Anger "gives you fire and the Slayer needs that."

As they're talking. Buffy gets an idea about Willie and how he might be able to help them.

Angel Taunts Spike (And We Get More Exposition)

We switch to Spike. He tells Drusilla it's time to go to the church. Dru seems disappointed because she's not done torturing Angel. Spike says Angel will die soon enough.

Spike: I've never been much for the preshow.

Angel: Too bad. That's what Drusilla likes best as I recall.

Spike: What's that supposed to mean?

Angel goes on in that vein, taunting Spike and suggesting he (Angel) knows better what Drusilla likes. Drusilla seems to agree, and Angel tells her that she should let him give Spike some pointers. He tells Spike that he can tell Drusilla is not satisfied.

Angel: Or maybe you two just don't have the fire we had.

Spike is angry. He's about to kill Angel. Drusilla stops him because Angel is her cure.

Spike: Oh, right you almost got me. Aren't you the throw-himself-to-the-lions sort of sap these days?

He goes on to say that if he kills Angel now, Drusilla won't have a chance. And Buffy and all her friends will be spared Dru's coming out party. Spike is not falling for it. Angel has to die slowly during the ritual.

Willie Comes Through

At Willie's place, Willie claims he doesn't know where Angel is. Kendra tells Buffy to just hit him. Finally, Willie says he'll have to take Buffy there himself.

Kendra argues with Buffy, saying they must return to Giles for instructions, it's procedure. Buffy says she if she doesn't go with Willie now Angel could die.

Kendra: He's a vampire. He should die.

She leaves and Buffy goes off with Willie. As we'll see later, although they do continue to disagree, Kendra and Buffy are fighting to fake Willie out.

At 31 minutes 58 seconds in Willie brings Buffy to the church.

Willie (to Buffy) There you go. Don't ever say your good friend Willie don't come through in a pinch.

A moment later, they turn the corner and there are two of the assassins and a couple vampires.

Willie (to Spike's crew): There you go. Don't ever say your good friend Willie don't come through in a pinch.

Inside the chapel, Spike is reciting the spell as he waves around this large metal container on a chain. (Which is called a thurible.) Incense burns inside it. When he swings the chain, smoke disperses through the air. Spike also waves a cross.

Dru and Angel are standing near the altar bound together. Angel, still looking very weakened, is unconscious. And Spike says, "From the blood of the sire she is risen." There is a huge flash of light. Spike says now that they've come to a boil, he just needs to let them simmer over a low flame.

Episode Three-Quarter Turn

Willie walks in right at that moment with Buffy.

Willie (to Spike): I got your Slayer.

This is a nice Three-Quarter Turn (maybe a little bit late) for this episode because it spins it in yet another new direction. Now Buffy is right where she wants to be. In this church. And Spike has got to deal with the Slayer. It all came out of his own actions.

Spike is not pleased. He can't believe Willie brought the Slayer here. But Willie says he heard there was a bounty for Buffy, dead or alive. And he wants the bounty.

Buffy sees Angel and Drusilla and realizes the ritual is done. She whispers, "Angel." Spike tells her not to worry,

Angel will be dead in five minutes and out of his suffering. And that's five minutes more than Buffy has.

But Kendra enters doing flips and knocking out one of the vampires.

Catchy Lines Spark A Story

Then we get the classic lines from this episode.

Spike: Who the hell is this?

Buffy: It's your lucky day, Spike.

Kendra: Two Slayers.

Buffy: No waiting.

Marti said that in some ways the whole episode grew from Joss thinking of the two Slayers, no waiting line. Then she said that's a little bit of an exaggeration, but there are episodes that grow out of one great line.

I think that's so interesting because I talked before about that writing rule that you should kill your darlings. Often the darling is a line or joke or moment you just love that doesn't really belong in the story. But maybe it's not surprising that it's Joss Whedon's show and the writers he works with would subvert that too. Because Marti is saying, hey, okay, instead of killing your darlings you might just create a whole story around them.

Which might be the answer. If you have something that you love so much in a story – that line, whatever it is – but you realize it doesn't fit, it could still be a great line. A great joke. So try pulling it out and creating something new around it. There are worse ways to come up with a story idea.

The Climax Of What's My Line Part Two

So we are now at the Climax of this two-part episode. Everybody is here because Giles, Xander, Willow, and Cordelia came in with Kendra. Fighting breaks out all over the place.

Xander taunts "Larva Boy" and draws Pfister (the worm

man) into a separate room. He and Cordelia already smeared a very thick paste on the floor. They slam the door. When the worms ooze under the door, they stick in the paste. And Xander and Cordelia stamp on them.

There is a really nice moment where Cordelia keeps stamping after all these worms are clearly dead, and Xander stops her. It's very quick, but I feel like he is very kind about that. And I like that moment of them working together. Also of him understanding why Cordelia is so intent on killing every last worm.

Buffy and Kendra are fighting separately. Buffy says, "Switch." One somersaults over the other and they are facing different opponents. Buffy is now facing Spike.

Spike: I'd rather be fighting you anyway.

Buffy: Mutual.

This is more of that worthy adversary concept I talked about in **School Hard**, the episode that introduced Spike. Both of them prefer to fight someone they regard as an equal in strength and skill. But Buffy knocks Spike away for the moment and runs to save Angel and kill Drusilla. But Spike manages to intervene.

Willow and Giles, working together, slay a vampire.

The cop assassin is fighting Kendra. The cop rips Kendra's shirt. Kendra gets very angry. She says something like, "You ripped my favorite shirt. You ripped my only shirt!" And her anger does give her more power, and she prevails.

Spike flings a lit torch. Part of the church goes up in flames. He retrieves Drusilla and tries to carry her away. Buffy, while staying near Angel, grabs that thurible and swings it in circles over her head to get momentum. She flings it at Spike. It hits him and knocks him down into a giant pipe organ.

The pipe organ breaks and splinters and cascades down

on Drusilla and Spike, burying them.

Falling Action In What's My Line Part Two

We are now to the Falling Action. Buffy cradles Angel after getting him out of his bonds. She's touching his face. There's soft music.

Kendra comes over to them and says, "Let's get him out of here." They all leave as flames engulf the church.

The next day Oz is getting animal crackers out of the vending machine at school. His arm is in a sling. Willow asks how the arm is. Oz smiles and says, "Suddenly painless."

Willow asks if he can still play the guitar okay. And Oz says, "Well, not well. But not worse."

Willow tries to thank him for saving her life but he says she'll embarrass him and starts talking instead about the animal crackers. He's joking about why is it that the monkey is the only one who gets to wear clothes? And how the monkey must mock the other animals. In the middle he tells Willow she has the sweetest smile. Then goes right on talking about the animal crackers.

He does a French accent for the monkey.

Willow: The monkey is French?

Oz: All monkeys are French. You didn't know that?

Cordelia And Xander

Cordelia avoids Xander in the hall. But he follows her and says they need to talk. They go into an empty classroom. He tells her there's no reason they should avoid each other. She agrees, but the two argue about who kissed who first. They bicker some more. They finally agree it won't happen again, and neither one of them will say anything to anyone else. But they get closer and closer and kiss again. And we have more romantic music.

Kendra And Buffy Give Each Other Advice

Buffy and Kendra walk out of the school towards a taxi.

Buffy tells Kendra to get on the plane with her ticket and not to ride in the cargo hold. Kendra agrees but still protests that doing it that way is not traveling incognito. But Buffy tells her she earned the plane ride. She also advises her to watch the movie unless it's about a dog or Chevy Chase.

Buffy thanks Kendra for helping her save Angel. Kendra says it's too strange – a Slayer in love with a vampire. She won't be telling her Watcher about it. Still, Angel is "pretty cute."

Buffy: Well, maybe they won't fire me for dating him.

Kendra: You always do that.

When Buffy asks what, Kendra says Buffy talks about slaying as if it's a job. And she then says it's not. "It's who you are."

Buffy asks where Kendra got that – was it from the handbook? Kendra gives a little smile and says, "From you." They part on a friendly note as Kendra gets into the taxi.

That would seem like the end of the Falling Action. We have wrapped up the main plot and all the subplots. But now we get one more scene, and it's a game changer.

The Game Changer

A cliffhanger is where you don't wrap up the main plot. Usually you leave your protagonist in great peril and the reader or the audience member has to come back for the next installment to find out what happens. To resolve that main plot.

In contrast, with the game changer we have resolved the main plot. So you have presumably satisfied your reader, satisfied your audience. But something happens that changes the field of play. Changes the world going forward.

And here we have perhaps the best one in **Buffy**. I feel like I can't say that for sure, though, as there's so much good in **Buffy**. But this one is really amazing.

Spike is lying under the boards in the burnt-out church. And we see Drusilla. She is in vamp face. She is standing, and she lifts Spike with one hand until his feet are off the ground. Then she swings him up into her arms and tells him not to worry. "I'll see that you get strong again. Like me."

What a great ending. I am pretty sure when I first saw this, I thought Spike and Drusilla were done. Because we saw them under the pipe organ. We saw the church burning. Our main characters leave. Then we find out not only have both survived, but the ritual was complete. Drusilla is revived, even though Angel did not die.

So I can't wait to talk about what happens after that.

Why A Two-Part Episode

This comment is from the DVD, and it's about writing. Marti Noxon talked about why they did a two-part episode. She said at first they weren't planning that. But there was so much lore to put in about Slayers and about how Kendra could be there at all, and about her background, that they needed more space. And she said that sometimes with two-part stories there really is only enough story for about an episode and a half.

But Buffy was on network TV. The episodes had to be a certain length. And Marti said you can end up with filler, but she felt really happy with this one. She felt like the two-part story really worked, and there wasn't any filler.

I agree with that. Also, I thought that structure worked really well in our two-part pilot. But in the Spoilers I will talk about a time where (before I ever heard this commentary) I did feel like there was filler. And I did feel like there was only about an episode and a half of plot, not two whole episodes.

Spoilers And Foreshadowing

ACTIVATING SLAYERS

When Giles says that Buffy's death must've activated a new Slayer, I was so struck by that word. Because when I saw Season Seven – both the first time and on other re-watches – I was certain that "activating" a Slayer was new language.

I don't know why, but I just never liked that term. And I thought it was something that got created because the writers decided to do this storyline with all these potential Slayers.

So it opened my eyes and gave me more faith in the long-term planning here. Or maybe not planning but in the continuity when I heard that Giles actually said a new Slayer was "activated."

Kendra having been given to her Watcher early, I feel like that foreshadows some of Season Seven as well. There we will see that some of the potential Slayers (at least one I remember) had a Watcher. And that one says something about she saw a photo of a vampire, though she never fought one.

But other girls, like Buffy, had no idea they were potential Slayers.

So this contrast between Buffy and Kendra does foreshadow all these young girls coming from different circumstances, with different amounts of what they know or don't know about the Slayer lore, before they are brought together in Season Seven.

Ripping Throats Out

Drusilla – that dialogue where she talks about Angel ripping her family members' throats out. Those words and all the Angel-Drusilla dialogue foreshadow all the ways Angel will torment Buffy. All of this really raises the audience's fears when that starts happening.

And what I love is the way it so works in this episode. I had no idea when I watched this the first time that part of purpose was foreshadowing. Yet now, looking at it, I'm sure that it is.

Two-Episode Stories

Going back to the comment about two parters and how sometimes there's only enough story for one and a half episodes. That's how I feel about the Season Six opener. Where Buffy comes back from the dead after dying not just for a minute (as in the end of Season One), but where she's been dead for quite some time.

When we came back at the beginning of Season Six, I was so looking forward to the episode. And I seem to remember they played both parts in one night. So I was excited about that as well, that we would get to see that whole story arc. Then I saw it. And it felt like there wasn't enough story for two episodes.

In particular, the extended scenes of demon motorcycle gangs riding dragged. I felt frustrated because I wanted so much to love this season premiere. And there were amazing things in it. When I look back, there is just so much that is good. But I kind of wish they could've cut a bit of it.

So I found it fascinating that Marti said sometimes they had to put in things that even the writers felt were filler.

Kendra And Buffy

Marti noted that with Kendra and Buffy we see this hint that they could have become friends though they would always have conflict because of their differences. So when Drusilla kills Kendra in the finale it hits Buffy so hard. Both because of that hint of friendship and because she couldn't stop it.

Oz And Test Scores

On a lighter note, Oz commenting that he tests well and

unfortunately that leads to work foreshadows the beginning of Season Three. He was a year ahead of the rest of the gang but is still in school with them when Season Three starts. And he says to Willow remember how he didn't graduate? It's because he didn't do all the coursework, and she says that's what summer school was for. And he says remember how he didn't go?

Which is why he repeats his senior year. The first time I saw it, I thought that was just because Oz really developed into a great character, and they were able to get the actor for another year and so needed to explain why he is still in high school with them.

So I find it interesting that here he makes that comment, and he says right out, he doesn't want to do the work. Which means I'm going to reassess and say maybe they always had this plan for Oz. They knew that he was going to hang around another year. Or maybe they just took advantage of something that was built up so well in his character and used it to work in a plot development that they needed.

Writing Yourself Into A Corner Isn't All Bad

This is a great way in your own stories, if you have to deal with something unexpected or when you've written yourself into a corner. Look back at what you have set up for those characters. There might very well be something there that will save you. Or that will take your story in an exciting direction you haven't thought about before.

Questions For Your Writing

- **Have you ever had a reader comment that something in your story "couldn't** happen that way" even though it's a true moment? Is there a detail you can add or change that might make it ring true for the reader?

- Find a section where you provide exposition within the narration. Can it come out through conflict between characters instead? Is there a character who doesn't know this exposition, to whom it makes sense for another character to share it?

- Find a favorite line or character moment that nags at you because it doesn't quite fit the story, but you don't want to lose it. Copy it into a new document. Is there a new idea or story you can build around it?

- Is there a place in your plot where you feel stuck? Can you use it as a springboard for a plot twist – one that perhaps you didn't plan before but that makes sense? Or adds excitement?

Next: Ted

NEXT WE'LL TALK ABOUT TED. IT'S A ONE-OFF EPISODE that all the same foreshadows many future plot developments and expresses a key theme for the series about Slayers killing humans.

CHAPTER 11
TED (S2 E11)

THIS CHAPTER TALKS ABOUT **TED**, Season Two Episode Eleven, written by David Greenwalt and Joss Whedon and directed by Bruce Seth Green.

In particular, we'll look at:

- **how this one-off episode foreshadows key developments for much of the run of Buffy**
- **the way the show defines the limits on Buffy's actions regarding humans**
- **metaphors that might or might not mix very well and sometimes undercut the message**
- **dialogue that shows growth in the Buffy and Angel relationship**

Okay, let's dive into the Hellmouth.

Opening Lack Of Conflict Leads To Conflict

I'm excited to talk to you about **Ted**. It generally isn't a fan favorite, but as I re-watched for the Buffy and the Art of Story podcast I was struck by how well written so much of the episode is.

We start with, in a way, some non-conflict. Or, maybe more accurately, some extremely mild conflict in a joking way.

Buffy, Willow, and Xander are walking down the sidewalk at night and arguing about who had the real power. The Captain or Tennille. (For those of you who don't remember, that was a singing duo.) Buffy has no idea who they are, but she's enjoying the quiet in Sunnydale.

As the characters talk, we get a little quick background on recent non-events. Spike and Drusilla are presumed dead. The Order of Turaka has been called off. Essentially, we're told that all's right in Sunnydale, at least temporarily.

But then we do very quickly get conflict at Buffy's house.

The front door is ajar. Buffy tells Willow and Xander to wait and goes in alone. There's a crash from the kitchen, and Joyce says, "No!"

Buffy runs into the kitchen. Joyce is kissing a man Buffy has never met. The actor is John Ritter, and he plays Ted. The two break apart, and Joyce says she's sorry for scaring Buffy. She just broke a wine glass.

I'm not sure that timing works given how fast Buffy could get into the kitchen. But I'll go with it.

Ted is very cheery, and he says, "Hi." We're two minutes in, and Buffy says, "Hi."

And she is so suspicious. I love her expression. She's kind of looking at him sideways. And we cut to the credits at 2 minutes 58 seconds.

After the credits, Ted is putting something in the oven.

Willow and Xander are helping a little bit in the background. And Buffy and Joyce are talking.

Joyce says that isn't the way she wanted to introduce Buffy. She met Ted at the gallery. He came in to sell her software. She's been seeing him and looking for the right moment to introduce him to Buffy.

In the background Willow squeals in delight when Ted says he'll give her a software upgrade for free. Xander raves about the mini pizzas Ted has made. Buffy says no thanks to the mini pizzas.

The Story Spark In Ted

Joyce: I really want you to be okay with this.

At 4 minutes 37 seconds in, Ted intervenes.

Ted: Beg to differ. *We* really want you to be okay with this.

Buffy says she's okay but clearly she is not. I see that as our Story Spark. Usually that Spark or Inciting Incident comes about 10% into a story. And this episode is right about 44 minutes, so this is very soon after 10%.

As to Ted's use of "*we* want you to be okay" and Buffy's reaction – Buffy just met this guy. And already he is talking about himself and Joyce as a couple and almost as a parenting unit. I feel like that does set off the conflict between him and Buffy and the particular way that it plays out.

We get this confirmed pretty much in the next scene.

Vampires Stand In For Ted

Buffy is with Giles in the park. He's sitting on a bench while Buffy fights a vampire. She is beating it up pretty badly. Giles keeps trying to say, "Buffy, I think it's time – you can stake him now – "

And she just keeps beating on him and finally kills him. Giles has already sat down and I think just started reading a book. So he asks her if everything's okay.

And she says yes. But she goes on this wonderful rant about vampires and says everything's fine and then they come and kill people.

Buffy: And they take over your house and they start making these stupid little mini pizzas and everyone's like all look, a mini pizza!

Giles cuts her off.

Giles: I believe the subtext here is rapidly becoming text.

That may be yet another of my favorite all-time Giles quotes. Buffy, though still doesn't tell him what's wrong.

Ted At School

At school, Xander argues with Buffy. He says Ted's a Master chef and everything about him is great. And he teases Buffy about having parental issues. She insists it's more than that. She is going on about him when he appears behind her. He's at the school updating the guidance software. He invites the three friends to play mini golf on Saturday with him and Joyce.

Buffy says they can't. They have this thing to do, and Willow backs her up.

Willow: Thing. Oh, right, that thing.

But Xander says they can do that thing anytime. They're in.

Giles Goes To See Jenny

We switch to Giles. He has gone to Jenny's classroom with a flimsy excuse about some textbooks. Really to ask again how she is. You get the sense he's been doing this a lot.

She says she's doing better, but she's still not sleeping well. And she knows he means well by asking.

Giles: You need time.

Jenny: Or possibly space....You make me feel bad that I don't feel better. I don't want that responsibility.

I really empathize with both of them here. I feel bad for

Giles. He so much wants to make up to her what happened. He feels deep guilt that due to his actions she became possessed with this demon. At the same time, I really feel for Jenny. I think this is a very common thing when someone is grieving. And she is in a sense grieving over what happened to her and trying to deal with this.

I remember after my parents were killed (by an intoxicated driver) it was an extremely difficult time. On the one hand, people were wonderful. I was so struck by how caring and kind the people around me, and the village authorities and police, were.

At the same time, as time passed, I felt this pressure that people needed me to feel better so that they didn't feel bad. One of my nieces and I talked about this a few times. That feeling that there's not much room in our culture for grief. For the idea that when something traumatic happened that maybe it's not even healthy to just try to rush past it and feel all happy again or be yourself again.

Maybe the self you have is going to be different. You're not going to go back to being that same person. And it often makes the people around us uncomfortable.

I feel like that's what Jenny is saying. Something like, look, I don't feel better yet, and it's not my responsibility to feel better so that you can stop feeling bad.

On a less personal note, this is a great example of two characters where we really see both their points of view. There isn't at that moment a real way for them to come together. And you can see that after Giles leaves, Jenny feels bad about pushing him away.

Angel Helps Buffy Sort Through Her Feelings

Now we switch to another relationship – Angel and Buffy. And I really love the scene between the two of them because we finally see them interacting.

I think we got a little of this in the end of **Halloween**. We saw them having a good relationship where Buffy is able to share her feelings. And Angel is able to be supportive and also help her get a different perspective.

Here, she's going on and on about Ted. How her mother says this about Ted, and that about Ted, and does every conversation have to be about Ted?

Angel, in kind of a low-key joking way, says, "So are we gonna talk about anything other than Ted?"

Buffy says, "Okay I get it." She kind of smiles and says she doesn't need another man in her life or a new man in her life. And Angel says, well, maybe her mom does. And he talks about loneliness. Buffy half smiles and says she gets it, but does it have to be Ted?

Angel asks her is there someone else, a guy out there that she thinks would be better. And she kind of sheepishly says, "My dad."

Angel just looks at her and listens. And she says, "I know that's not going to happen."

You see this sense of relief for Buffy. She's a little more able to live with the idea that yeah, her dad's not coming back. And maybe her mom does want to have someone else in her life.

I love that Angel was both sympathetic and helped her sort through her feelings. But he didn't ever say to her "you're having parental issues" the way that Xander did.

Time For Mini Golf

About 11 minutes in, everyone is at mini golf. Ted says something about Buffy's grades being low. Buffy is upset that her mom told him about it. Joyce says it's because Ted cares. He wants to know all about Buffy.

Buffy swings too hard at the golf ball. It flies off the course. Joyce is all "we won't count it, it's just mini golf," but

Ted says "the rules are the rules." And "what we teach her is what she takes out in the world."

Which if I were Buffy that would get me pretty mad, too. She's irked but she says fine, she'll go hit from the rough. And she walks around the back. No one can see from that side of the hole. She picks up the ball and just kind of taps it in.

Buffy: I got a Hole in Two.

She didn't see Ted, who has come around behind her.

Ted: Beg to differ.

Buffy shrugs and says fine, just add it on her score. It's just a game. And he says, "I'm not wired that way" and goes on and on about the rules and doing things right. And he's slapping his golf club against his leg as he's talking, punctuating his words.

Ted: I don't stand for that malarkey in my house.

Ted Threatens Buffy At The One-Quarter Twist

Here I think we get to the One-Quarter Twist, that first major plot turn that spins the story in a new direction and comes from outside the protagonist. It's a little bit beyond the one-quarter point timing-wise in the episode. It's about 13 minutes 20 seconds in. But it definitely spins the story.

Buffy says well, it's a good thing they're not in his house.

Ted: Do you want me to slap that smartass mouth of yours? (spins around toward the others) Who's up for dessert?

That quick flip from menace to cheerfulness – I think John Ritter does it so very well. And it's unnerving. We know he was serious, and Buffy knows he was serious.

So this is a turn, because it's the first time we see that it's not just Buffy having parental issues. It's not just the sort of less-than-ideal way that she met Ted.

The others crowd around him and his picnic basket

exclaiming over his cookies, and Buffy stands apart in the kitchen.

The next morning Joyce offers Buffy a sticky bun that Ted made. And Buffy says can they have something Ted didn't make?

Joyce: I don't expect you to love him like I do.

But she does expect Buffy to treat him civilly.

Buffy: You love him?

Joyce says that just slipped out, and then goes on to say men don't exactly beat down the door of a single parent. Which is kind of interesting because she seems so excited about Ted, and yet in the next breath it's almost like she said, well, I don't have a lot of choices. So he is the best out there out of that lack of choices.

Buffy echoes that single parent line, finishes it with Joyce. So we know this is something Joyce says a lot.

Joyce's Mom Skills

I have talked about the great things I love about Joyce. But these kinds of scenes are where I understand when people feel Joyce fails as a parent. Because I understand her saying that men aren't running to go out with a single woman with a teenaged daughter.

If you want to say that to your friends, that's one thing. But to say it to your daughter is really saying, hey, it's your fault, it's all because of you.

Then it gets worse. Buffy tells Joyce that Ted threatened to slap her.

Joyce: He did no such thing.

She doesn't even consider what Buffy says. And though we find out there are reasons for that, it's still really hard to watch.

Joyce: Ted told me what happened. He caught you cheating, didn't he? .... But he didn't say anything to anyone else, did he? And I thought that was pretty decent of him.

Buffy kind of stutters, and when Joyce says that about how he didn't tell anyone else Buffy is saying she doesn't think that's the point. Which of course it's not. The fact that he didn't tell the others doesn't erase threatening to slap her.

But this shows Ted is this master of manipulation. He knew Buffy would tell Joyce. So he got out ahead of it. He told the story and framed it in a way to set Joyce up not to believe Buffy.

Which is no excuse for Joyce had there not been other forces at work here. The way she just rejects what Buffy says is really awful.

But Joyce is surprisingly cheery and she says Ted told her Buffy just needs time to come around. And she's having him over for dinner that night, so Buffy needs to be home on time.

Buffy, looking really discouraged, leaves. Joyce finishes the sticky bun, saying to herself, "This is so delicious."

Hints Throughout

These hints about food are woven in. And I feel like it's fairly subtle. I do not think that I saw this the first time through. The excitement. Willow squealing in delight after she ate the mini pizzas. And then at the golf course they're also all excited about the cookies.

And Joyce – even if she didn't believe Buffy, which obviously she didn't, let's say this was a real situation. There's no other influence. She doesn't believe Buffy. But she would have to be troubled about this conversation. And instead she's just saying, "Great sticky buns."

So I do think that is there but not overplayed. It was subtle.

The In Love Metaphor

It also goes to one of the metaphors I see here, which is

the idea of being in love as this feeling of ecstasy that colors everything you say and do. Because we'll find out later that these things Ted is making have something in them that both tranquilizes people and that Willow says has something in common with the drug ecstasy.

So it seems, in part, this metaphor is to Joyce (or anyone) in love. Swept up in this wave of passion so she doesn't even hear what Buffy says. Which makes me more troubled about Joyce. Because is this suggesting that this is how Joyce would be if she were truly, deeply swept away? If she were for real attracted to and feeling in love with this guy?

Or is it saying that's what happens to anyone in love?

Researching Ted

Back at school, Buffy enlists Willow's help to research Ted.

And I love Willow. She is such a great friend. Her dialogue and her expression tell us that she sort of agrees with Xander. She thinks that maybe Buffy is having issues just because Ted's dating her mom. And I can't remember – I don't know if it's clear that Buffy tells Willow that Ted threatened her.

But regardless, Willow may think that it is just the issues Buffy's having. Yet she is right there to help her friend.

So 17 minutes in Willow has found out where Ted works. And Buffy is in this cubicle farm. Ted is on the phone selling software. He has his back to her. She's kind of hiding, and he is on the phone.

Ted's not overly pushy. He points out the benefits of the software. He turns the weaknesses, how expensive the software is, into a strength. After he makes another sale, he marks it on the board and goes to lunch.

Another guy comes up and Buffy pretends to be a temp there for the day. The guy's grumbling about Ted, who has always been top salesperson. And he says, "Nobody beats the machine." Also something about at least Ted is taking some time off for the wedding. Which he tells Buffy is in two months.

Buffy checks out Ted's desk, sees a photo of Joyce there. When she takes it out of the frame, it is a photo of Buffy and Joyce, but the photo has been folded in the back so Buffy is hidden.

Dinner With Ted

At 19 minutes in we are at dinner. Ted says a very passive-aggressive grace about how hopefully God will help the people in this house to be more hard-working and more honest.

Buffy won't eat. So again we get these food hints woven throughout. Earlier, Buffy not eating Ted's cookies and mini pizzas because she doesn't like Ted. And here because she's upset, so she's just sitting there not eating.

Buffy: Are you engaged?

Joyce says No right away. Not as if she would never consider it, but just surprised, like where would Buffy get that idea. But Ted says he hopes someday soon if things go well. And how would Buffy feel about that?

He encourages her to share her feelings.

Buffy: I'd feel like killing myself.

And we get more really bad Joyce. Because rather than listening to these feelings or being concerned that her daughter said this, she gets mad at Buffy. And sees it as Buffy just trying to make trouble.

Ted says no, "we asked her to share her feelings."

When Buffy asks to be excused, Joyce tells her she can go to her room.

After she's gone, Ted says he didn't get to be top salesman by giving up.

We next see Buffy in the park in the dark. She's swinging on the swings with her stake, saying, "Here, vampires." But there aren't any. She comes home, climbing in through her window.

The Midpoint Of Ted

Now we get to the Midpoint of the episode. We're about 21 minutes 37 seconds in. This is all slightly before the Midpoint, but we have two things here that happen that spread across those few minutes in the middle of the episode.

First, we get a major reversal. Which is one thing we see in a well-structured story, this major reversal for the protagonist. And after that we get a commitment, which is the other thing that drives a strong story forward.

Here, as in some stories, we get both. In this episode it's really interesting because that commitment also triggers another reversal.

So instead of talking in the abstract, let me go into it.

Midpoint Reversal 1: Ted Threatens To Expose Buffy's "Delusions"

When Buffy gets into her room, Ted is waiting for her. And he has read her diary. She says, "How dare you?" But he asks how different is it than snooping in his workplace.

Ted: What exactly is a Vampire Slayer?

She tells him to get out. And he says, "Or what? You'll slay me?" Ted goes on to say, psychiatrists have a word for what Buffy is – delusional. And from now on, she'll do what he says because otherwise he'll tell Joyce and show Joyce the diary.

And Buffy will spend her best dating years in a mental institution.

This is a little bit of another metaphor here. This idea that young women get put into psych wards or mental institutions at times because they are not complying with what society expects of them.

Buffy Commits

Buffy tries to stop Ted from leaving her room and taking the diary. He punches her really hard, knocking her down. She recovers, says, "I was so hoping you'd do that," and punches back.

I see this as Buffy's Midpoint Commitment. Which is where the protagonist commits to the quest and goes all in. Because she does. They fight on. The momentum takes them into the hall.

Ted again hits her hard enough that she is on the floor. And he then grabs her and lifts her up to hit her again. Of course, Joyce comes out just as Buffy has managed to hit Ted back and get the upper hand. Buffy then kicks Ted. His momentum is pushing him down the hall and toward the stairs.

Joyce is yelling at Buffy to stop. Buffy kicks one last time.

This is 23 minutes in and Ted goes tumbling down the stairs and is motionless at the bottom.

Midpoint Reversal 2

Joyce runs down, checks Ted's pulse, and says, "You killed him."

So we see Buffy's commitment led to an even more major reversal because no matter how awful Ted was, to kill him is a huge thing. And also that her mom did not see what began that fight. So it's completely out of context for Joyce.

We cut to the commercial. Talk about a hook.

When we come back, the police are taking Ted away. Detective Stein asks what happened. Joyce says Ted fell, and the detective asks how.

Buffy: I hit him. I hit him.

She sounds really dazed.

I like that Joyce was not going to say that. So at least now she is trying to protect her daughter. And that Buffy tells the truth. She's not going to sit there and have her mom lie.

At the station, the detective interviews Buffy alone. We can tell she's somewhat disoriented. He's asking questions.

It's a wonderful scene. If you haven't watched the episode lately, I would at least go back and watch that. Because the detective's being kind of low-key in his questions. But he's trying to get the story. And the way he does it, Buffy ends up a little more confused about when Ted threatened her. She says he hit her. The detective asks where, and she shows him her cheek.

And he says something like, "Well, it couldn't have been too hard. There's no mark." It doesn't seem accusatory. It's more like a comment. And Buffy says, "I don't bruise easily."

So he says, "You've been hit before." And she says yes. And he says, "But not by Ted?" She says no. And she starts getting upset and is saying she didn't mean to do it. I think she starts to cry.

And the detective says that Ted's a big guy, and he believes her.

Outside the office he tells Joyce basically the same thing. That Buffy says that Ted hit her. If that's true, everything will be okay. But he says, "We're not bringing any charges right now." So there's just enough – he's not threatening, but there's just enough to leave both Joyce and Buffy uneasy. And to have this hanging over Buffy because the detective does say they need to look into it further.

Buffy's Feelings Of Guilt Through Appearance And Action

At school the next day, Buffy is in baggy overalls, a big contrast to how we normally see her dressed at school. Usually she wears clothes that are very fashionable and cute, and that make her look great. Now she's in these big overalls. Not that Sarah Michelle Gellar ever looks bad, but it is not at all Buffy's style.

And she's kind of slouching. She says she had to come to school. Her mom won't look at her.

Xander asks what was he, what kind of monster, assuming that Buffy must have killed Ted because he was a monster. And Buffy says no, he was human. Willow says she's sure it wasn't Buffy's fault, Ted started it.

Buffy: That defense only works in six-year-old court, Will.

Willow and Xander are both shocked about the mention of court. Buffy also says she's the Slayer she had no right to hit Ted like that.

I feel like in some ways her feelings of guilt are clouding her memory of what happened. Because Ted hit her really hard twice. Enough to knock her down. So she was defending herself. Yet at the same time, she's not wrong in the sense of she did say, "I was hoping you'd do that." She wanted a reason to fight Ted.

And now she's saying basically, "Look, I knew I had the superstrength. I was not right to do that."

So I think she's drawing a line between she could defend herself, but she went beyond what she needed for self-defense.

Different Rules For Buffy?

Xander tries to reassure her and says he knows her. She'd never intentionally hurt anyone unless – and Buffy says unless he was dating her mom? She's upset. She heads for the library, but there she finds out that the cops talked to Giles to ask about her behavior. They are now talking to someone else at the school.

Giles is at a loss, and Buffy leaves.

Xander, Willow, and Cordelia gather in the library with Giles. Xander is saying how awful Ted must have been for Buffy to kill him.

Cordelia: I thought you liked him.

Xander (looking right at Cordelia): I sometimes like things that are not good for me.

Willow is researching. She's frustrated and finding nothing.

Cordelia: It's not fair, Buffy's like a Superman or something. Shouldn't there be different rules for her?

Willow: Sure, in a fascist society.

Cordelia: Right. Why can't we have one of those?

I love that Cordelia's sticking up for Buffy, even if she might not quite grasp the philosophical or ethical implications of that. (More on that in the Spoilers.)

A Major Turn

Giles says that Buffy killed a human, and the guilt will be overwhelming for her.

Cordelia: I guess you should know since you helped raise that demon that killed that guy that time.

Giles: Yes, let's do bring that up as often as possible.

Giles is putting together weapons. He says he'll patrol that night as there's no Slayer until Buffy is herself again.

Willow is still frustrated and trying to find answers. Xander, who is eating a cookie he found (I think in Willow's backpack), says don't worry, it'll all be fine. They'll work it out. Suddenly cheerful.

This seems a bit like our Three-Quarter Turn. We are 30 minutes in, and Willow grabs that cookie. We can see by her expression that she knows there's something wrong with it. So it's the first time our friends find a solid clue that there is really something wrong with Ted.

Willow puts together in her mind all this good cheer and the food.

I also thought at first that this moment was the Three-Quarter Turn because, as it should, it spins the story in a new direction. Now our friends focus on the food. They have a solid clue, and they are jumping on it to help Buffy.

Also, it does come out of the reversal that put Buffy and Ted directly in opposition. And from Buffy's commitment and killing Ted, which means our friends have to find answers.

Before Buffy killed Ted, Willow in particular wanted to help Buffy because Buffy was upset. But her friends didn't have a driving reason to help. Now that Buffy might be faced with a court trial and murder charges, they are driven to do these things.

All of that made it look like that major plot turn that comes out of that Midpoint and turns the story yet again.

Joyce And Buffy, Jenny And Giles

At home, Joyce is cleaning out cabinets. Buffy tries to say she didn't mean it and apologize. But Joyce says she can't talk now, and more or less tells Buffy to go to her room.

In the graveyard, Giles is patrolling. Jenny startles him. She saw his car and she wants to apologize to him. He's very uneasy and tries to stop her. And she says let her talk. She feels bad about how they left it, and she knows how bad he feels about putting her in danger before.

Giles: Imagine how I must feel now.

A vampire is behind them.

Back to Buffy, we're about 33 minutes in. She's in her room, and she seems restless and sad. She goes to the window to climb out. It's nailed shut. She's talking to herself under her breath. She thinks her mom nailed it shut.

Buffy: This day can't get any worse.

A Surprise Three-Quarter Turn In Ted

From behind her, Ted says, "Beg to differ."

This I think is the real Three-Quarter Turn. It's a bit of a surprise, which is nice. We thought we had a turn. And now there is the real plot turn that truly shifts the story. Because Ted is back and there's something about him clearly not human.

So previously we thought, okay, he's drugging everyone. There is probably something else going on. But now he *is* something else.

And he asks Buffy is she sorry about killing him.

Buffy: What are you?

He says he's a salesman. No matter how you put him down, a good salesman bounces back.

Many Metaphors

Part of me wonders if this continued salesman theme is part of what doesn't quite come together in this episode. At first, I was thinking it doesn't work at all. Because we've got here so far not just a metaphor for feeling "in love," but for an abusive relationship. The way Ted is charming on the surface, and everybody loves him. And then behind the scenes he's threatening Buffy. He's punishing Buffy. Her mom isn't listening. We will find out he is controlling. There are a lot of abuse metaphors here.

But then we get this salesman metaphor. And it seems weirdly comic. I was thinking it didn't really fit. Later on, we'll see that maybe it does.

But it still may be one too many metaphors here. Or more than one too many. I'll get to that.

Jenny Shoots Giles

We switch back to Giles and Jenny. The vampire attacks. Jenny is struggling with the crossbow.

Giles is telling her to shoot. But I don't think she's used

one before. And even if she had, Giles and the vamp are a moving target. She finally takes a shot. And of course it's right at that moment the vamp spun around so Giles' back is to Jenny. The arrow goes into his back.

Giles, though, is so cool. He yanks out the arrow and stakes the vamp with it.

So we get a little bit of comic relief there. And a little bit of movement in our ongoing Jenny and Giles subplot.

More About Ted

Back with Buffy and Ted. They're fighting. He says he had to shut down for a while to get her off his back. Now he chokes Buffy. Buffy grabs this little nail file and stabs him. Sparks fly. There are flashes. And we see his skin has come off and there are wires and machinery underneath.

It's unclear if Buffy quite gets that because he kicks her and knocks her out.

Xander, Willow, and Cordelia break into Ted's home. They went the old school way and got paper records from somewhere in the village. Those include four marriage certificates, one from over fifty years ago.

They don't see anything in the house at first. Until Cordelia spots a rug that doesn't fit the décor. There's a trap door underneath it.

Joyce, in the meantime, is in her kitchen. She hears something and thinks it's Buffy and starts to apologize for not talking to Buffy earlier.

But it's Ted. Joyce is shocked. Ted claims that he was dead for six seconds and then unconscious for a day. That the medical people told him it was a miracle. She hugs him and says, "Oh my God, Buffy."

And he tells her not to worry.

I'm happy to see that, while she's glad Ted is back, Joyce's first thought really is that they have to tell Buffy. Because Buffy is feeling so horrible about this.

At Ted's, our friends have gone down through this trap door. The lower level is all fifties décor. There's an old record player. There are bars on the window.

Xander opens the closet. We don't see what's inside. But he says, "Let's go." And the others are saying but they need evidence.

Xander: We got it. His first four wives are in there.

It builds more danger for Joyce. We already know that Ted is dangerous, particularly to Buffy. But until now it's been unclear whether he's a threat to Joyce. Perhaps he doesn't intend to harm her.

It's still a problem, obviously, that he is homicidal towards Buffy. But as an audience we feel pretty confident Buffy will recover and can take care of herself. Now he's a more direct threat to Joyce.

Ted tells Joyce what brought him back was her. The thought of her. And she says she should talk to Buffy first. And I have to say, "Yay Joyce." Maybe it was the cookies after all.

And Ted says something like, "Do we have to talk about Buffy? What about Teddy? I'm the one who died."

Joyce: Sorry, I don't know what to do.

Ted: Don't I always tell you what to do?

Metaphors On The Mark

This is also where I think the abuse metaphor just starts getting so direct and so right on the mark that it loses some power. Joyce is looking troubled already.

Then Ted turns his head to the side and says something about gravy. I think I forgot to mention that when he was fighting Buffy, he did that when she stabbed him. He started saying all these random different things. And his head would go to the side when he did it.

Joyce tells him he needs to rest for a while.

Ted: I think you might want to stop telling me what to do. I don't take orders from women. I'm not wired that way.

It's such an obvious statement and metaphor. I might have liked the story as a whole better if it were a little bit more subtle.

Here is where I started to think, though, that maybe the salesman metaphor in a way should've worked. Because throughout Ted is saying, "I didn't get to be salesman of the year by giving up."

Also, "I don't take no for an answer" is his mantra as a salesman. I can see a little more how that fits with this idea of the abuser. "I don't take no for an answer." "I always tell you what to do."

And maybe it would've worked better if they stuck with the salesman thing and didn't have him saying more on the nose things like "I don't take orders from women."

Building Toward The Climax

Back to Jenny and Giles. He is claiming he's okay. She says that she'll get him to a hospital, and then laughs and says something like, "Some night. You really know how to woo a girl back."

Giles laughs. And then says, "Ow." And Jenny says, "Hospital."

So more comic relief there.

Our main plot is building towards the Climax.

Buffy wakes up in her room. We're 40 minutes 25 seconds in.

Downstairs Joyce is trying different ways to distance herself from Ted. She says she wants a drink. He says they need to hit the road. And he does a little turning of his head to the side, saying weird things again.

Joyce says she better pack and tries to go around him. He grabs her arm and says he already has her clothes and they're your size.

Ted: They're always your size.

And he says she left him before but he kept bringing her back.

The Climax

Now we are at the Climax.

Joyce tries to pull away. He shoves her into wall and she's knocked out. Ted thinks he hears Buffy. He walks around downstairs calling to her to come out. He doesn't stand for malarkey in his house.

Buffy surprises him. She underhands him hard with a giant frying pan.

Buffy: This house is mine.

The frying pan is a really interesting choice. On the one hand, it's kind of cartoony. But on the other, it fits that abuse metaphor. It is Buffy taking something in the house and using it to fight back as she says, "This house is mine."

Ted goes down. More of his skin comes off, this time on his face.

So we see half of the human face and half that looks like a robot. Which makes it pretty scary. Buffy strikes again. This time he's really out. And she looks very sad.

Falling Action

We move to the Falling Action. Joyce and Buffy are sitting on the front porch, eating chips.

Joyce: You want to rent a movie tonight? But not horror, romance, or men.

And Buffy says she guesses they're Thelma and Louising it again.

If you don't remember, Thelma and Louise was a movie out maybe a few years before Buffy started. It's two women who are taking a road trip. It turns into a flight from the law after Louise kills a man who tries to rape Thelma outside a bar.

Ted On The Scrap Heap

Joyce says she still thinks Ted will jump out at her, especially after what police found in his house. That's the first time I realize that apparently Buffy didn't tell Joyce that Ted was a robot. And didn't tell the police.

Buffy: Trust me. He's on the scrap heap. (Joyce looks at her.) Of life.

I'm not that clear why the police couldn't know that Ted was a robot. Unless our friends were concerned (maybe rightly) that the authorities in Sunnydale would use Ted in a bad way.

At school, Willow says the sad thing is the real Ted must have been a genius.

Buffy: Tell me you didn't keep any parts.

Willow: Not any big ones.

Buffy tells her she's supposed to use her powers for good.

Willow: I just want to learn stuff.

Cordelia: Like how to build your own serial killer?

Xander says let's just drop the whole topic. Buffy is happy to forget all about it.

Except that when they get to the library she looks in and through the little round windows in the doors.

Buffy: That's it. I give up. Do I have to sound an air horn every time I walk into a room? What is it with grown-ups today?

And we see that Jenny and Giles are kissing.

That is one of the things I enjoyed in this episode. This very gradual bringing of Jenny and Giles back together.

Buffy And Philosophy: Humans Have Special Status On Buffy

There's no DVD commentary for this episode. Instead I looked at my favorite book discussing Buffy. **Buffy The Vampire Slayer And Philosophy: Fear And Trembling In Sunnydale**, edited by James B. South. There're a number of great essays in it.

This is from **Morality On Television: The Case Of Buffy The Vampire Slayer** by Richard Greene and Wayne Yuen. The authors talk about Ted and how Buffy killed him believing he was human because he poses a direct threat to her mother and herself.

They explore a bit the philosophical implications of that. First, I think that is part of the issue for Buffy. As I mentioned, I feel like later she reframes it in her mind that she killed Ted solely because she couldn't deal with him in her mother's life. But when you look at those scenes before she kicked him down the stairs, he was definitely a threat to her.

Later he knocks her out completely. She didn't know he was capable of doing that, but she certainly knew he hit her hard enough to knock her down on the floor. But her guilt is so overwhelming that it clouds her judgment.

I also believe that on some level she did know that he was something other than human. But maybe not.

The authors go on to say that Ted poses a threat that's equal in severity to the threat vampires pose. And yet Buffy is despondent when she thinks that she killed him because he was human. So later she's relieved to discover that Ted is not human but an android robot.

So they say that humans, therefore, have a special status in Buffy's moral system. This special status makes them exempt from being seriously harmed by her, even if they do harm to others.

We will see that play out throughout the series.

Not Who I Thought You Were

The other essay here that talks about **Ted** briefly is **High School Is Hell: Metaphor Made Literal In Buffy The Vampire Slayer** by Tracy Little.

Little comments that Season Two includes a constant theme: You are not the person I thought you were.

I hadn't thought about this. But it's a really good point. We've already seen it in **Inca Mummy Girl**. Ampata is not at all who Xander or anyone thinks. In **Reptile Boy**, the frat boys are not who Cordelia or Buffy think they are. In **Lie To Me**, Buffy's old friend Ford is not who she thought.

And here, Ted clearly is not who either Joyce or Buffy – well, Buffy obviously had her suspicions from the start – but he's definitely not who Joyce thought.

And in **The Dark Age**, Buffy feels like she doesn't recognize Giles. And when he says he's sorry she's saying, "Don't be sorry, be Giles."

It's really interesting that **Ted** is part of this theme for the season. And I'll talk a little more in Spoilers about that.

In the end, the thematic elements are what I love about **Ted**. I love this beginning exploration of what does it mean if Buffy kills a human, even sort of accidentally. I do not believe she ever meant to kill Ted when she thought he was human, but she did let herself use that strength. So what does that mean?

***

Spoilers And Foreshadowing

THEME: NOT WHO I THOUGHT

From the **High School Is Hell** essay by Tracy Little – the theme of "You are not the person I thought you were" is the theme of the major story arc for this season.

When Angel turns evil again it is all about that. And then it is echoed by Giles and Buffy finding out that Jenny was sent there to keep an eye on, or track, Angel.

Also Spike's sense of betrayal and anger at Dru when she is so enamored of Angel. Angel is in a way taking Drusilla away from Spike. And then Drusilla's sense of betrayal when Spike allies himself with Buffy in order to defeat Angel. Spike's also not who she thought he was.

So we have this theme on so many levels.

The Ethics Of Killing Humans

More from the essay **Morality On Television: The Case Of Buffy The Vampire Slayer**, where the authors comment on the ethics of killing a human. And I had been thinking while watching **Ted** that we really see that issue addressed in the Faith storyline.

After Faith accidentally kills a human in **Bad Girls**, Buffy in the next episode tries to get Faith to fess up and deal with it. Instead, Faith goes down this very dark path. And there we really dig into what it means when a Slayer kills a human being.

Giles tells us that it does happen, and that there are procedures for dealing with it. But by that time his faith in the counsel has shattered, as has Buffy's. So they're not willing to go to the Council. And Faith is completely in denial.

We see the issue again when Buffy thinks she has killed a human in Season Six. She is ready to go to jail for it. It's a very complex set up. Buffy is already going through a very dark time. Her feelings over thinking that she killed someone take her to an even worse place. Her friends, and particularly her sister, do not understand why she would turn herself in.

Or, I take it back, I don't think her friends ever find out what she plans to do. But her sister – another big spoiler here, that she'll have a sister – feels so abandoned. Dawn feels that Buffy is turning herself in just to get away. But even very early on in the show we see how seriously Buffy takes killing a human being.

The authors of **Morality On Television: The Case Of Buffy The Vampire Slayer** also talk about another part of Season Six, where the reasoning for the humans' special status in **Buffy** is explained more. When the friends talk about a revenge killing – Willow killing Warren after Warren commits murder – Buffy says Willow doesn't have the right to do that. And Xander and I believe Dawn are saying Warren was horrible and he deserved it. And how is it different from demons?

But Buffy says that for human evils there is a human justice system. She is not there to be the one who punishes people. She will stop them. But she's not going to kill them. Unlike with demons and vampires.

It's going to be so interesting to talk about it at that time. Why those distinctions are there. I do like Buffy's point that there is a system to deal with that. It might not be perfect, but there is this process. Where for demons and vampires there is not. She is it.

The Diary And The Detective

Ted reading Buffy's diary and threatening her with a mental institution foreshadows **Normal Again**. There, Buffy comes to believe that she is in a psychiatric institution.

That her parents sent her to a psych ward when she started talking about vampires. I so would love to know if the writers planned that from the beginning of the show. Or at least had that idea in their minds.

Or did it just evolve organically from Ted making this threat and later they picked up on that?

In Season Six. Detective Stein will be back. (That's the reason I mentioned his name. I hadn't realized before that we ever got his name.) I'm pretty sure he interviews Joyce in the Season Two finale.

And he comes back in Season Three when Faith kills someone. He is again the detective. And we may see him more than that, I'm not sure. (I'm excited about looking for future Detective Stein spottings.)

I really like the detective's low-key style. He seems so reasonable and so suspicious at the same time, and it's always fun. I think when you see an actor like that coming back to reprise a role we get a sense of continuity in Sunnydale.

Willow

Willow's story arc is also foreshadowed when we have Buffy telling her to use her powers for good. And Willow says she just wants to learn.

We will see as the series progresses that Willow's learning is such a strength for her. This desire for knowledge and to keep growing. Yet it becomes dangerous to the people around her and out of control.

If you watch **Agents Of Shield**, which Joss Whedon also produces, there are a lot of things about that theme. The responsibility of people who build and create things, who are super smart and able to invent things. But then those things are used in a dangerous way.

While Willow doesn't invent things, there is that same

idea. Intellect and power and knowledge. What responsibility comes with that.

Robots

And, of course, we have the foreshadowing of robots in the Buffyverse. I feel like there is always a mix among fans over whether we should have robots. Robots are more science-fiction, and Buffy is more fantasy. And every time we get robots there is a sense that partly they can be so real and lifelike, and so much further advanced than the technology is, because Sunnydale is on the Hellmouth.

I don't mind mixing the two. But I understand people who are more purists about science fiction versus fantasy, maybe for them that mix doesn't work.

I particularly like the Buffybot that we get in Season Five. (And even April, the robot we see before that.) The Buffybot works far better than Ted.

Ted is sort of this early version. It feels like the writers are exploring, saying, okay, what do we do with this robot character? Later, with the Buffybot, we explore so many more issues of identity and character and personality. Of what from Buffy goes into that Buffybot.

Buffy's Clothes Show Her Feelings

One more thing – the overalls. We will see Buffy in baggy overalls again at the end of Season Two.

There is a sense that this is what Buffy wears when she maybe feels not herself. Feels defeated. Feels depressed or sad and like there is nothing she can do.

Questions For Your Writing

- **Do you foreshadow later developments in the beginning of your novel (or in**

Book 1 of your series)? How subtle or obvious is the foreshadowing?

- **Are there philosophical questions your story explores?**
- **If you use a metaphor in your story, does it make sense when you follow it throughout your plot?**
- **If there is more than one metaphor, do they undercut one another in any way? How well do they fit together?**
- **Look at a section of dialogue between two characters. Does it convey their relationship to one another?**

Next: Bad Eggs

The next Season Two episode is **Bad Eggs**, which I'll start out with in **Buffy and the Art of Story Season Two Part 2**.

Can't wait that long? Check out the podcast edition of Buffy and the Art of Story at LisaLilly.com.

Visit LisaLilly.com/contact to receive bonus materials and be notified of the author's new releases and sales.

ABOUT THE AUTHOR

An author, lawyer, and adjunct professor of law, L. M. Lilly's non-fiction includes **Happiness, Anxiety, and Writing: Using Your Creativity To Live A Calmer, Happier Life**; **Super Simple Story Structure: A Quick Guide to Plotting & Writing Your Novel**; **Buffy And The Art Of Story Season One: Writing Better Fiction By Watching Buffy**; and Creating Compelling Characters From The Inside Out.

Writing as Lisa M. Lilly, she is the author of the best selling **Awakening supernatural thriller series** about Tara Spencer, a young woman who becomes the focus of a powerful religious cult when she inexplicably finds herself pregnant, and of the **Q.C. Davis mystery series**. She is currently working on the latest book in that series.

A member of the Horror Writers Association, Lilly also is the author of **When Darkness Falls**, a gothic horror novel set in Chicago's South Loop, and the short-story collection **The Tower Formerly Known as Sears and Two Other Tales of Urban Horror**, the title story of which was made into the short film Willis Tower.

Lilly is a resident of Chicago and a member and past officer of the Alliance Against Intoxicated Motorists. She joined AAIM after an intoxicated driver caused the deaths of her parents in 2007. Her book of essays, **Standing in Traffic**, is available on AAIM's website.

ALSO BY L. M. LILLY

Happiness, Anxiety, and Writing: Using Your Creativity To Live
A Calmer, Happier Life

Super Simple Story Structure: A Quick Guide to Plotting and
Writing Your Novel

Creating Compelling Characters From The Inside Out

Buffy And The Art Of Story Season One: Writing Better Fiction
By Watching Buffy

Buffy And The Art Of Story Season Two Part 1: Threats, Lies,
and Surprises in Episodes 1-11

As Lisa M. Lilly:

The Awakening (Book 1 in The Awakening Series)

The Unbelievers (Book 2 in The Awakening Series)

The Conflagration (Book 3 in The Awakening Series)

The Illumination (Book 4 in The Awakening Series)

The Awakening Supernatural Thriller Series Complete
Omnibus/Box Set

When Darkness Falls (a standalone supernatural suspense novel)

The Tower Formerly Known As Sears And Two Other Tales Of
Urban Horror

The Worried Man (Q.C. Davis Mystery 1)

The Charming Man (Q.C. Davis Mystery 2)

The Fractured Man (Q.C. Davis Mystery 3)

The Troubled Man (Q.C. Davis Mystery 4)

Q.C. Davis Mysteries 1-3 (The Worried Man, The Charming
Man, and The Fractured Man) Box Set

Printed in Great Britain
by Amazon